Up in Smoke
A Hot in Chicago Rookies Novel

Kate Meader

This novel is a work of fiction. Any references to historical events, real people, or real places are used fictitiously. Other names, characters, places, and events are products of the author's imagination, and any resemblance to actual events or places or persons, living or dead, is entirely coincidental.

Copyright © 2022 by Kate Meader

Cover photo: Wander Aguilar

Cover design: Lori Jackson Design

Editing: Kristi Yanta

Copyediting: Kimberly Cannon

Proofreading: Julia Griffis

ISBN: 978-1-954107-12-0

All rights reserved.

No part of this book may be reproduced in any form or by any electronic or mechanical means, including information storage and retrieval systems, without written permission from the author, except for the use of brief quotations in a book review.

One

Abby

"Here's to fucking us!"

Sam looks at Jude who has just uttered that beyond classy toast and shakes his head. "Is that your sneaky way of suggesting a threesome?"

Jude grins, all blue-eyed devilish sparkle. "You really think I have the hots for you, Killian? After six months of watching your ass on every ladder at the academy—figuratively and literally—I can safely assure you I'm not interested. I'm done with falling for straights."

Laughing, I clink my glass against theirs, eager to get us back on track. "Here's to us and our hot graduate asses. We made it, guys! We fucking made it!"

Sam puts his arm around me. "Yeah, graduation's great and all, but why doesn't Jude want me, Abby? Am I not sexy enough?"

"Oh, you're plenty sexy." Sam is probably the hottest guy I've ever seen in real life. Think a more feral Tom Hardy. "But you're also, I'd say, a ..." I check in with Jude.

"Zero?" he offers with little conviction.

"Let's go with one on the Kinsey scale." I pat Sam's very muscled, very hot arm. "You probably get a little turned on by gay porn but only because you like the grunting. Otherwise, no interest in boys."

For the last year, I've become close enough to Jude Torres and Sam Killian—my best buddies in the academy—to be able to talk frankly about our sex lives. Though really, it's frankly about *their* sex lives which are varied and productive. As for mine, it's an arid desert with not a green shoot of sexual hope in sight.

Not a problem as I'm determined to focus on my career. Four years as a paramedic has led me to the Chicago Fire Department and its training academy. After six months in the program, I'm now a fully-fledged candidate, meaning I have another year to make my mark and earn my wings on the job.

I have things to prove and people to prove wrong. So that sounds like the start of some underdog sob story, but we all have obstacles to hurdle and the journey can be treacherous to your mental health. Just thinking of the "people" sends a corkscrew of discomfort rippling down my spine.

I take a sip of my rum and coke, determined to make it last. Knowing these two, a club is in my future and I want to keep my wits about me given that I'll be starting at legendary Chicago firehouse, Engine 6, the day after tomorrow. Sharp mind, keen focus, no traces of a hangover.

"I wish we were all at the same house." Both Jude and I were assigned to Engine 6 in Bucktown while Sam will be kicking things off at 70 in Uptown.

"We knew they'd never put three candidates on the same engine," Sam says with a shrug of one broad shoulder. Jude and I wouldn't even be on the same crew. He's starting tomorrow on the A platoon, a day ahead of me. "This might be it. We're never going to see each other again."

"Good, you can finally get over your obsession with me." Jude leans in to kiss Sam on the cheek. "And see if you can find someone else to crib notes from."

"Uh, never fucking happened." Sam points a finger at Jude. "I am going to miss you guys, but I'm guessing it'll make our get togethers all the more meaningful." He divides a heartfelt look between us. "Look after each other, okay? Even though you're not on the same shift, do what you can to have each other's backs."

He clears his throat, probably a little embarrassed at his moment of gravity. In all our time together, Sam's never taken anything seriously except scrambling up a ladder quicker than anyone else and making it out of the smoke box in sixty seconds flat. Of the three of us, he's the one most likely to capitalize on his hot firefighter status. I've witnessed him working his charms on any number of women in any number of bars, and even here in O'Neil's on Wells, the Killian force is strong.

Jude holds Sam's gaze squarely, not letting him off the hook, awkward emotions be damned. Never one to shy from the touchy-feely stuff, our Jude. "Wish you were with us, Sammy. Gonna miss you."

"Don't worry, I'll take care of him," I assure Sam with a side glance at my guardian angel-slash-precious charge. "Make sure he doesn't get into any trouble."

"Actually, I'm more worried about you, Ms. Thrillseeker."

I tap my collarbone and mouth "Moi?"

"Yeah, you. Have you ever met a dangerous situation you haven't wanted to cozy up to?"

Sure I like to get my kicks going toe to toe with the boys. All my life I've been forging ahead, anxious to prove I can meet anyone on the battlefield of life, regardless of gender. *I* was the one shoving frogs down little boys' pants and generally making their puny little lives a nightmare on the playground. Strike first, atone later.

To be honest, I'd rather hit a dirt bike track or a climbing wall than a club. But this is graduation night and I'm dressed to the nines. One look at the boys tells me we'll be hitting that club before the hour is through.

"Okay, I'm out."

Sam bestows on me a drunk-eyed squint. "You had one dance! With me! I thought you were here to celebrate."

"I am. I was." The night is already history. "You know I don't like this thump-thump music and how we can't hear each other speak and—"

"What?"

Jude has paired off with a metal-enhanced Cyborg hipster. Several women are giving Sam come-hither looks (or come-on-my-face looks as Jude calls them) and he's been kind enough to limit his usually meandering attention to me. I'm merely cramping the boys' style.

I thumb over my shoulder toward the exit. "I'll catch an Uber."

"I'll walk you out," Sam yells.

Two minutes later, I'm in a car, heading home. Strangely I'm not tired, but then the excitement of the next phase of my life is still thrumming through my veins. A new job, a new workplace, a new start.

Thinking on that new beginning sends me to the place I've been trying to avoid all night. All year, to be honest, since I told my father I wanted to join the Chicago Fire Department. When you're the daughter of a powerful man, a man who has some say over your career because he effectively controls the playing field, it's tough to maneuver. Fire Commissioner

Chuck Sullivan didn't want his only child to become a firefighter and the big man usually gets what he wants. Today's graduation ceremony was the first time I'd seen him in four months. As he pinned that badge to my uniform and congratulated me, he practically choked on the words.

I touch the Claddagh pendant around my neck, a precious memento from the late Joanne Sullivan. My mother would be on my side in this, even though her own dreams had crashed and burned long ago. At least she got a few good years in. Thinking about her life cut short would usually be enough to conjure empathy for my father, except the memory of the last time we spoke before the ceremony today ices it out.

You'll quit in the first month, Abigail. Tops.

I growl, causing the Uber driver to catch my eye with concern. Eager to not look like more of a weirdo than usual, I check my phone and see that Maria Fernandez from CFD Media Affairs has left me another message reminding me to route any media enquiries through them. I don't expect any, but the brass seem to think my candidacy has feel-good sap oozing from its pores.

Rookie Female Firefighter Follows in Trailblazer Mom's Footsteps.

That I might turn into a circus curiosity pisses me off to no end. My situation shouldn't be that newsworthy, but I understand why the human-interest stories grab attention in our shit-soaked world. People need heroes—and city governments need heroes in underrepresented groups. Maybe I've brought it on myself by requesting to be stationed where my mother served, but it means a lot to me to be assigned there.

At least I'll have someone in my corner, even if that someone is a ghost.

Sam has sent me a photo of Jude with his hand down Metal-Face's pants—in the middle of the club! The things these boys get away with. A message follows: ***text me when you get home.***

Only I'm not ready to go home yet. I want pie. A big slice of cherry pie—and I know just where to get it.

Made it, I text, so he won't be worried. Then I give the driver new directions.

Fern's Diner is quiet, not unexpected for a Tuesday night in early May and perfect for me to ease the bass thump of the club from my head. Fern is actually a grumpy Greek guy called Stavros, but he's not usually here at night. Instead my favorite server is on duty.

Tessa grins at me, then does a double-take. "You're wearing a dress!"

"Damn right I'm wearing a dress. It's graduation night, baby!"

"Hey, congrats. And you decided to spend it at the 24-hour diner like a loser?"

"I did a bar crawl."

"What constitutes a bar crawl in Abby's world?" Finger quotes for extra derision points.

"One drinking establishment. But then ..." I hold up a finger of my own to halt her colorful commentary. "I hit a club. For twenty minutes." So I pretty much failed as a club kid. "I can't keep up with the boys. They're too sexy for me."

"To have your problems."

Yet my measly problems are a thing of the past because it seems Tessa and I are telepathically linked. How else to explain what's waiting on the counter right in front of me? The perfect slice of cherry pie with a heaven-sent scoop of vanilla ice cream is haloed by the diner lamp above like an offering.

I throw my purse on a seat and clamber onto the one to the left of it, right in front of the pie. "How did you know?"

"How did I know what?"

I gesture to the pie. "That I would be stopping in at this very minute with pie-shaped intentions?"

"I'm good but not that good." Sadness drifts across her face. "That pie is not your pie."

"I beg to differ." I pick up the fork. "It's positioned right in front of me and I am seated right in front of it. This pie has my name on it. How is this not my pie again?"

"Because it's mine."

Alas, no, that is not one of my chatty voices asserting its right to pie. This is deep, external, and designed to send a sensuous shiver to every one of my nooks, crannies, and extremities. I swivel and yep, not a projection of my pie-hungry brain.

The guy claiming the pie is tall, dark, hazel-eyed, and steel-jawed. I've been working with buff firefighters for the last few months, but none of them hold a candle to what this guy is serving up. He's older than them, for a start. Maybe early-thirties with that confidence that comes from seeing shit and knowing how to deal with it. His square jaw is dusted with stubble that has the makings of a sexy beard. His untucked blue Oxford strains a little in the chest and shoulders area, and while there might be interesting things happening further down, I'm not the ogling type. Not in public, anyway.

"*Your* pie?"

"*My* pie." A diner-full of amusement is conveyed in those two syllables.

"Your seat, as well?" I sneak a glance at Tessa who is wiping a counter, resolutely neutral, the Switzerland of servers. There are ten empty seats at the counter and I have somehow landed on the one already occupied.

"Yep. I stepped away for a second. Didn't expect to have to fight anyone for it."

As I slip off the stool, the action moves my dress up a few inches. Not intentional, but the guy notices. And I notice him noticing.

That shiver from before graduates to a full-scale shimmy.

Leaving my purse, I aim for the seat on the other side of it which means I have to bypass Pie Guy who steps aside to let me, oh, about two seconds too late. Those two seconds have us standing there trying to decide if this is awkward or sexy. My fantasy says sexy. My history says exceptionally awkward.

"Sorry," I say because he didn't.

"No problem." He takes the seat I've just vacated.

While every booth is empty except for the one where diner regular Doris and her gentleman friend are kicking it old style with chicken noodle soup, that doesn't mean I could slip into one of the free ones. Stavros has a policy that singles eat at the counter, and even though he's not present, he would somehow know and give Tessa hell for it.

So I sit at the counter two seats over with my purse as a buffer between me and the pie thief, who has picked up a fork and is contemplating that slice of heaven. This gives me a moment to contemplate him in profile. Tiny lines feather out at the corner of the one eye I can see. Dark, thick, lustrous, and charmingly tousled hair tops his head—tousled, possibly because he's spent time scrubbing one of those big fork-holding hands through it. Who could be that frustrated with pie in play?

Now that the seating has been rearranged and pie ownership has been determined, Tessa saunters over to me. "What'll it be?"

"I'll have what he's having." Cute rom-com diner moment for those who know or care.

Tessa looks despondent, not the response I expected. "That was the last slice."

"It was?"

I direct my most forlorn glance toward the pie that should have been mine. My counter-mate has yet to make a dent. Fork in one hand, phone in the other, he's hovering in pre-pie-eating mode. Somehow this makes it worse.

Just eat the damn pie, idiot.

Tessa must have noticed my unattractive envy manifesting because she coughs to get my attention. Only it's more than a cough—she's trying to tell me something.

"What's that?"

Another cough, this time with the word "up" at the end of it.

"I have no idea what you're saying."

She winks, though it looks like winking is a brand-new activity for her. Punctuating the move is a weird chin swivel to my left.

"Are you having a stroke?"

"She's trying to tell you I've been stood up."

Okay, if the pie-that-should-have-been-mine didn't have my attention, that laconically delivered statement would do the trick. I snag gazes with Pie Guy—still with fork in hand and slice intact—and find him with a very expressive eyebrow in supreme arch.

"Sorry?"

"I think she's telling you this so you'll cut me some slack about having the pie you so clearly want."

"I don't—" I glare at Tessa who's giving me a look that says Pie Guy has read the room correctly. There's something different about his accent, too. It's rougher with an East Coast flattening of the vowels. "So I came in here with cherry pie in mind but I can just as easily go for ..."

"Apple or Boston cream?" Tessa offers.

I'm not a fan of apple and Boston cream isn't pie, it's cake, dammit.

"Coffee would be fine."

There then follows the most beautiful sound in the world: a plate sliding across the counter surface.

"Oh, no. I couldn't." I most certainly could. The pie has now taken on epic proportions in my night's narrative.

I raise my gaze from the pie to him. A river of sensual heat threatens to overwhelm me. I really love pie.

Just kidding! It's all him.

"You came in here expecting your favorite dessert." I hear it clearer now. New York, I suspect. "I haven't taken a bite yet."

Tessa pours my coffee and pushes it toward me with an eyebrow tilt of her own.

"I really couldn't." I look at my friend, who should be offering to officially split it with a knife and two separate plates, but strangely ... isn't.

Matchmaker instincts are overriding server ones, I assume.

I grab a Splenda packet from the caddy and use the adding and stirring time to contemplate my next move. Refusing to acknowledge his offer would be rude. This way, he can have it back with a bite taken out of it and we can return to our respective corners, pie enemies once more.

"How about I take a small bite?"

A fork appears—the ever so helpful Tessa again—and five seconds later my taste buds are dancing to the tune of tart fruit and buttery pie crust. I must have moaned on my way to Heaven because when I come back to earth, Pie Guy is staring at me.

"Well, that was worth it."

I push the pie back to him. "Your turn."

Two

Roman

I'd been stood up and was forced to share my pie. Yet somehow the night has improved.

Don't get me wrong, I'm still ticked off about my lack of a date. My co-worker and former friend, Luke, spent weeks that felt like years trying to talk me into meeting up with a friend of his wife's at the bar around the corner. Or maybe she was a friend of a friend of his wife's. Whatever she was, "present" wasn't another one of her attributes (hence the *former friend* label because Luke's going to fucking hear it when I see him next).

Between my job and my kid, I don't have time for dating. And I certainly don't have time for dates that are no-shows.

But I do have time for pie.

After waiting for a fruitless hour at the bar, I decided to walk around Andersonville on Chicago's Northside, a cute neighborhood of bars, at least three dog groomers, and one good-looking diner tucked off the main drag on a quiet side street. I'd passed it a few times when I varied up the route on my morning run. Not a great place for a business but I had to admit I'm glad it's low key.

I'm even more glad it no longer is. Because *she* walked into it.

The woman who lusted after my pie is tall, about five-ten in flat-heeled shoes, with pale skin, almost translucent except for the freckles dotting it like a map to destinations sexy. Auburn red waves fall in loose curls over her shoulders, which are bare except for the narrow straps of her green dress. I wouldn't call it overly sexy but she is hella sexy in it—it hugs her curves in a way I haven't noticed on any woman in years.

When Luke said it was time to get out of my rut, I resisted. Especially as (a) I'd known him for all of three months so where the hell did he get off? And (b) the fucker was right and that chapped my ass more than anything. I don't like to be pushed. My sister Chiara would say I'm stubborn to the point of it getting in the way of life. That would be the sister who got all the drama genes, so she's a fan of pointing out my flaws.

I'm trying to be less stubborn and more open-minded to new things. Which is why I'm sitting in a diner, sharing pie with a beautiful freckled stranger.

"Your turn." She pushes the pie back.

I really should let her have the whole thing. I mean, what are we going to do? Nibble on the sides of the slice until our forks meet in the middle like something out of Disney?

"You can finish it."

"Wouldn't dream of it." She smiles and I realize I should accept this for the gift it is.

It's more than pie. It's connection.

I fork a sliver off the slice, decide it isn't enough to get a decent taste, and carve out a bigger bite. Once in my mouth, I try not to get too excited about it but damn, that's mighty fine pie.

"Kind of wish I hadn't offered to share it now," I say once I finish chewing. "Second worst decision of my life."

"Oh, now I need to know." She sections off a small piece and holds it close to her mouth, waiting for me to fulfill the promise of that cryptic statement.

"Maybe after a few more bites. I hardly know you."

Another killer smile precedes the wrap of her lips around the fork. Her mouth looks as sweet as the treat in it, or maybe it's just too long since the last time I've gotten laid. The way this woman is eating the pie is about as close to sex as I've come in a while.

The fork tines slide from her mouth slowly as she makes sure she didn't miss a crumb. Maybe she's doing it to tease me. Intentional or not, it's working.

My turn.

"Stood up, huh?"

I nod. No idea what possessed me to share that with the server but she was kind of chatty when I arrived and I blurted it out, probably to justify why I was sitting single at a diner counter at 9:15 on a Tuesday night.

"Is that your worst decision? To go on a date with this rude, unfeeling individual?"

I shake my head. Take a bite. Finish chewing.

She watches my mouth. Nice to know I'm not the only one with the oral fixation.

"You're not getting my worst decision out of me that easily."

"Worth a shot. Did your date even text you?"

I check my phone. Just a flurry of messages from Chiara, each more dramatic and intrusive than the last.

How's it going?

Then thirty minutes later. ***Must be getting along if you're still out and not responding.***

Twenty minutes after that. ***Should I wait up? Not wait up?***

Ten minutes ago. ***Did you bring enough condoms?***

She will be so disappointed, though I'm not. Because if it had gone well, I wouldn't have stopped in here and had the perfect slice of pie.

"Nope." *Your turn.* I push the plate toward her.

"Chatty, aren't you?"

"Not as much as you." I don't mean it to sound like a dig. It's a reflex because in truth, I'm enjoying the conversation even if I'm not contributing to it much. "Tell me where you were before you got here."

"Where I was? Oh, that's a long story."

I want to hear it but it already sounds too invasive. "Out with friends?"

She assesses me, and I can't tell if she's glad I reeled in the conversation from an enquiry about her life to this point to the more manageable "why are you dressed up and looking so damn fine?"

"Yeah, a celebration. But my buddies wanted to club-hop and I'm feeling a bit old for that scene."

"There comes a time when we all feel we've aged out of the discotheques."

Her smile acknowledges that as cute. Never knew I had it in me, to be honest, given my rustiness. She takes another bite. "Anyway, I left the youngsters to it and came to get me some pie."

"And I almost ruined it."

"No, not ruined." A couple of spots of color flag her cheeks and make me warm inside. *Not ruined.* She's enjoying the conversation as much as me.

"What were you celebrating tonight?"

"A graduation from …" She hesitates, likely rethinking how she wants to phrase it. "College."

"College?" Christ, had I reached the point where everyone in college looks the same and I can't discern ages anymore?

"I'm kind of a late bloomer," she says, assuring me that she isn't jailbait. Still, I'm definitely older than her, maybe six or seven years. She can't be more than twenty-five.

I shouldn't be even thinking that. We're just chatting over pie.

Her phone pings and she looks down at it with a conflicted expression.

"Need to get that?"

"No, it's ... well, some guy on a dating app."

My heart does a backflip that lands inelegantly balls-first in the pool. "Some guy?"

"Yeah, we've been feeling each other out, trying to decide if it's worth the effort."

"Has he seen you?" I did not just say that.

She blinks, acknowledging that I did. *Pret-ty smooth, killer.*

"I've been holding off on sharing pics. He's sent me an abs pic, though." She scrolls through and shows me. The shot shows him standing in front of a mirror—aren't they all?—and has managed low-slung provocative while keeping it PG-13.

"Not sure how I'm supposed to react to that." I can't imagine doing that to anyone I was considering for my dating future.

"Give your opinion. Good abs or not?"

"Not sure that's the right question. I would be more inclined to ask 'douchebag or asshat?'"

"Because he's showing off his abs? That's what everyone does these days. It's like 'hi, how are ya? Here's my calling card.'"

"That's where I've been going wrong."

She pulls a finger trigger at me, which makes me smile.

"So what do women do in return?" The idea of her

sharing some intimate part of her body with some frat bro makes me itchy. Is that what I have to look forward to in a few years with my daughter?

Sure, you're worried about Lena, and not in any way jealous of this guy who already has abs in the mix.

"Oh, my abs would be better than his." She scrolls down the thread to the latest message. "He's wondering if I'm free tonight."

"You haven't met him yet?"

She shakes her head, takes another glance at the screen, weighing her options. I don't want to stand in her way yet ... okay, I completely want to stand in her way. I want to cock-block that abs-totin' dickhead and make a play myself.

"Got any spark with him?"

"Hard to tell with a text exchange. He's amusing and likes the movies of Kurosawa."

"Sounds like a winner. Vain *and* pretentious."

That makes her laugh, and boy do I like that sound. It's got a dirty, husky quality that shoots straight to my cock. I rub my jaw over the makings of a beard I'll have to shave before I go back to work. I'd taken a few days off to fix some stuff around the house and enjoyed not touching my razor.

"You asked," I comment, though she only asked my opinion on his abs. She's definitely feeling me out on the topic. Perhaps looking for a signal I would like her to throw over fuck boi, as my sister would call him.

She inhales deeply and that in-drawn breath drags my eyes to her cleavage. Her breasts are spectacular and if I had my way, she would not be snapping them to send off to D-Bag Abs. Those beauties would be all for me.

"Pretty pendant."

"My mom gave it to me." She touches the Claddagh symbol and for a moment, looks a little lost. My heart hitches at the pain I see clouding her lovely blue eyes.

Before I can enquire further, the server stops by. "More coffee?"

There were, by my calculations, three bites left to the pie. Once gone, the night would be over. I didn't have to work tomorrow and the only reason I needed more caffeine was so I could stay awake for the night ahead. If Cherry Pie wanted more ...

I raise my gaze to hers and she holds it captive for a charged second, the moment balanced exquisitely on the edge of a thundering heartbeat. Speaking might ruin it. Silence might screw it up spectacularly. I'm usually more decisive—my job demands it—but it's hard to translate that to your personal life, especially when your life lacks personality.

Slowly, she turns her phone over and it's all I can do not to stand and cheer. *Yes, fucking, yes.*

"Sure," she says to the server.

"Hit me." I nudge my cup a smidge before taking a slightly larger forkful of pie and pushing the rest to her. "All yours."

There's that subtle blush again. *All yours.* It certainly feels like I'd give her anything.

We've spent the last hour talking about pie, TV shows, my sister's desperation to get me "out there," my mother's favorite catchphrase, God rest her soul—"Copernicus called. You're not the center of the universe"—and now we're talking about free climbing because apparently she likes it. For fun.

"You go on vacations to climb?"

"It's the rush. I love it."

"So you have some sort of Tom Cruise in *Mission Impossible* death wish?"

She grasps my arm and my entire body goes on high alert, as if I haven't been touched by a woman in years. "I love that movie. Well, all the movies. But that one is awesome. Tom, just hanging there off a rock like the coolest guy on earth!"

Sure. I can't imagine enjoying that because I'm often forced to climb in my job. I certainly wouldn't be choosing to do it for fun.

But I could see how it might be fun if I was with this girl.

"We all have ways to get our kicks." She runs a finger over the edge of her coffee cup. "How about you? What gets you pumped?"

There's a silken tease to her voice, an invitation, for sure. I could step right in and take the baton, run with it and a whole flurry of innuendo, guide this night to where I'd like it to go.

What's stopping me? Performance jitters, maybe. Not my dick—that wouldn't be a problem around Cherry Pie. All that lush red hair and natural sweetness. But I might be too rough, too desperate after going so long without. I'm already imagining pushing that dainty strap off her shoulder and going to town on her neck, barely managing to hold myself back from the main event: those gorgeous, perfect, full breasts I need in my mouth soon followed by driving deep inside her to the hilt.

I would be a beast and then I'd feel like a jerk afterward.

"My kid."

"Your—oh, you have a kid?"

Not what she expected at all. Not even what I expected. But the truth is, my daughter fires me up and makes me think I can be a better person every day. She's the only person I can trust to love me unconditionally. Even my sister has her limits.

"Yeah, a daughter. She's eleven going on eighty." When she dips her gaze to my left hand, I murmur, "Divorced."

"How long?"

"Almost a year." And what a year it's been, with the move to Chicago and the wrench from my old New York life, like a limb from a socket. I'd tried to shove it, dislocated as it was, back into place but the clean break was necessary.

My revelation has shifted the energy between us. "Kind of ruined the moment there."

"Why would you think that?"

"You're talking about daredevil feats and what gets your adrenaline spiked. I call your hand with my kid. Real smooth."

Something sparks in her eyes. "Yeah, real smooth."

Am I trying to scare her off? Maybe. Or perhaps I'm trying to deflect from the lust that must be so obvious it's a wonder the diner hasn't incinerated by now.

"But kids are their own adrenaline rush, right?" she asks. "You'd do anything to protect her. That's kind of ... hot." She waves a casual hand. "If you like that sort of thing."

Her half-crooked, almost secretive smile says she might indeed like that sort of thing.

THREE

Abby

"You don't need to walk me home."

He stops and tilts his head. "Is that your way of saying you'd rather I didn't know where you lived?"

We left the diner together a couple of minutes ago to the soundtrack of Tessa snapping pics of us with her phone. *So they can track down your killer if necessary*, she added. Not the comfort she thinks it is.

Pie Guy is definitely giving off vibes of normal, but how can you tell these days? I'm sure plenty of women have gone on seemingly normal dates and regretted the reveal of a home address.

Not that this is a date.

Yet I'm thinking of the ways good dates end. The steamy ways.

"You said you were just a couple of blocks away ..." he prompts.

"Right, so too short for an Uber but now we're in this

problem gray area where I don't want you to know my exact address because, stalker. But you're probably a complete gentleman walking me home, which means you might get offended that I'd even think that."

He leans against the corner of the diner, a casual yet soothing pose. "You think my ego can't handle a woman being careful?"

"I don't know. Can it?"

"It can."

He has a straight-talking, laconic way about him that's incredibly sexy.

"Still doesn't solve our problem," he adds.

"Unless ..." I touch a finger to my lips. "You act as if you never met me and we haven't been talking for two hours."

"More like three."

Really? That's ... I don't even know what that is. "For all you know, I could be heading home right now, a total stranger, pie in my belly, keys at the ready, poised to jump into action if anyone tries anything." Little does he know I could probably kick the ass of any guy who crosses me. Some people don't think it very feminine and plenty of dates have upended on the reveal of my trainee firefighter status. "If you hadn't come in here tonight, you would never have been presented with this dilemma."

"Yet I did. And I was." His hazel eyes flash, and with the illumination of a nearby streetlamp, I spot a ring of green around them. Framed by those inky lashes, they're possibly the most beautiful eyes I've ever seen. "I enjoyed the pie," he adds.

It sounds like a non sequitur, except that pie is likely a catch-all for the whole experience. He's enjoyed the conversation, the pie, the sparks igniting between us.

"I enjoyed it, too."

We walk a few steps, comfortingly in sync.

"This is my street," I say as we arrive at the corner. It's not, but we're close enough. "I live about halfway down the block."

He puts his hands in his pockets. I hope it's because he's having a hard time stopping himself from touching me.

He says, "Do you think you might want to—"

"Yes." God, I'm embarrassing. "I mean—it depends on what you were going to ask."

"What question were you answering?"

"I'd like to get pie with you again sometime."

He smiles and Christ on a fire truck, I'm gone. For the last hour he's come close—a half grin here, a slight curve there—but this is the real deal. Mega wattage, governments falling, worlds destroyed and rising from the ashes through *Star Trek* terraforming.

"How about I give you my number?"

I hand off my phone. He enters his digits with his even better digits. When he hands it back, I check to make sure it isn't something fake with a triple five like the movies.

"Diner Dude?" That's what he entered in the name field, and it makes me laugh. He has a 212 number, so my hunch about his New York origins is correct. "We're not on real names?"

"Not sure I want to jinx it. Put your number in there."

I take his phone, enter my number, and hand it back.

"No self-selection of a cute nickname?"

"Curious to see how imaginative you can get."

His eyes haze over. "Where you're concerned, very." He taps on the screen.

"What did you call me?"

"Wouldn't you like to know."

"I would, actually."

He licks his lips. "Cherry Pie. Does that work?"

I don't want to say I love it because I might love it too much.

Instead I respond with, "So now, we have numbers."

"And the potential for more pie."

The night is over, or it should be, yet I'm not ready to leave. There's an energy in the air, a dance of molecules that prohibits me from stepping away. Neither does he look like he wants to go. If anything, he appears to have moved closer.

My pulse goes wild. I put my phone in my purse, then immediately regret it because now I have nothing to occupy my hands.

I have ideas, though. I want to squeeze those biceps, the ones straining the bounds of his button-down shirt. Suspecting he isn't a regular shirt guy, I wonder how he acquired all those muscles and how soon I can take advantage.

"You okay?" he asks, and now I know he's closer.

"Not sure. I feel like something else should happen here yet—"

"It's too soon?"

My heart kicks up, thrumming at his response. He feels it, too. "Yes. I really should go because if I don't ..."

I stay still, waiting impatiently, my breath on hold, my pulse drumming to an erratic beat. He reaches for me, and at the last moment, turns his hand so his knuckles brush my arm. My body goes haywire, electric sparks shiver-shocking across my skin.

"Do that again," I whisper. My voice sounds raw. Desperate.

He does, only this time he punctuates it with a curl of his hand around my hip and a step into my space. His chest brushes mine, tantalizing, sending my nipples into painful points. I'm tall, but he has four inches on me.

Then two.

Then one.

A heartbeat away from my lips, and his hand grips possessively and angles me closer. "Tell me to stop, Cherry Pie."

"Not a chance, Diner Dude."

Stopping is no longer an option. He stamps his mouth on mine, claiming it as his and ruining me for all others. That's what they say, right? I've never experienced it so it's always sounded like hyperbole. But now I understand. Oceans of newfound knowledge hit me.

Kisses aren't supposed to be the main event, but this kiss rages through me and sets every part of me ablaze. He still maintains a hand on my hip while the other cups my jaw and holds me in place for a thorough, professional invasion. The scrape of his facial hair adds a deliciously rough element to the kiss, sending my entire body into sensual oblivion.

After seconds, minutes, eons, he leaves my lips, and with them a shattered shell of the woman who existed before.

His voice is husky when he speaks. "You'd better go before I take you against this wall."

Wall? I look behind me and sure enough the building has a wall as buildings usually do. Bonus: I'm backed up against this wall, like an Abby Sandwich with Diner Dude on one side and the wall on the other. The weight of him feels so damn good and I have to rewind to what he said.

You'd better go.

But I don't want to. I want to drag him to my bedroom and fulfill the promise of that kiss.

"Maybe we could ..." I flick a glance down the block, which isn't even my block, hopefully leaving it obvious about where the *could* in that sentence might lead.

He leans his forehead against mine and closes his eyes. "Don't tempt me."

"Not good with temptation?"

"You've seen me with pie. What do you think?"

"I think maybe you should kiss me again and then say if you still want me to—"

His mouth is on mine before I can finish. Hot, wet, hungry. His hip hand slips so now it's a butt hand, meaning my butt, and the long, slow squeeze of my ass cheek is about the filthiest, sexiest thing I've ever experienced. I want that hand all over my body, between my thighs, rubbing and stroking me to a screaming, shaking mess.

He pulls away, blows out a breath, and brushes his lips softly over mine.

"I'd like to get to know you a little first."

My heart catches hard. He's turning down a sure thing and though it's enough to make me swoon, I wonder if this is the end of the road for us. If I've got it all wrong.

"Best be gone now," he whispers, as much to himself as to me.

It's hard to pull away but I manage. Just.

Yet in this strange, in-between moment, I feel I need to be as honest with him as he was with me. "So, this isn't actually my block. I'm a couple more away but I didn't want to offend you."

"Not offended. How about I wait here and you text me when you get home to say you made it okay?"

That seems like a reasonable compromise, considering I'm feeling anything but reasonable. My blood is humming, my body is alive with crazy, hot need.

But I rein in my worst impulses and nod my agreement to this plan. If I text, then it's like we're continuing our conversation. The night won't be over.

I walk away, and just before turning onto the street where I actually live, I look behind to see him still standing at the corner, hands in his pockets, the streetlight shining on his blue-black hair, making him look like a fallen angel.

I give a small wave.

He nods back.

And I know: this is only the beginning.

Four

Roman

I turn the key in the door quietly, conscious that it's later than my usual. Of course if the date had gone well, I would probably be on some slinky slither of shame right about now because there's no way I could get away with staying out all night, not as a responsible dad. But the date had not gone well.

It had gone spectacularly.

That's probably a strange reaction to getting stood up and not getting laid, but I can't help the vibrations rocking and rolling through my body. That kiss ... it's been a long time since anything excited me that much. Which says plenty about my sex life.

I might be divorced for all of eleven months, but my sex life had withered on the vine long before that. Sure, there'd been sporadic bursts of hate sex with Tori, my ex. No affection, little comfort, just release. After every encounter I'd wondered how I'd screwed up so much with my choices, how I had failed to see that this woman—the mom of my beautiful kid—wasn't cut out for that life. Stability, motherhood, wife.

Or wife to me.

She used to laugh at other married couples, saying how dumb they were, while we were married. Like the institution was a big joke and we were the butt of it. Never mind that a family life was everything I'd ever dreamed of, especially as I'd lost both my parents young.

Now I'm here in Chicago, trying to craft a different version of that life. Not with Cherry Pie—no, that's just physical, visceral, something that proves I'm still fucking alive. The life I'm rebuilding is for me and Lena.

"There he is!"

My tip toe move past the living room doesn't quite pan out. With the raise of the dimmer light, I find myself face to face with Chiara, sitting on the couch. Sure, who needs a mom when I've got a nosey sister?

"What are you still doing up?" I sound like a surly teen.

"It's only 12:30, old man." Chiara places her wine glass on the table and pats the seat beside her. "Let's chat."

I groan. "Listen, I'm kind of tired. Just tell me how Lena is and we can do the post-mortem of my night in the morning."

"Nope. I want all the details while they're fresh."

I know when I'm beat, so I take a seat and pick up her wine glass. More to stall, though I'm not sure I want to remove the taste of my sweet redhead so soon. I put it down without taking a sip.

"Date was a no show."

Her dark brows pull together. "What? Then where the hell have you been all night?"

"I went to get pie."

"Which is code for …"

"Pie. It's code for pie." But I would never think of pie

again without remembering the flood of sensation produced by that kiss.

Chiara is watching me closely so I need to be careful about showing my cards. She's my twin, five minutes older, but acts like it's ten years. It's always been that way. She's a caregiver to the core and when I told her Lena and I needed a fresh start, she moved heaven and earth to make it happen. I like to think she needed me as much as I needed her, given that she'd been going through a rough patch with her wife, Devi, who is working with a tech start-up in Europe. It's putting a significant strain on their relationship.

I thought it would be a pain living in the top floor apartment with my sister on the first floor, but it gives us both a chance to employ our hero complexes. Free child care, too, though I don't let Lena hear that. Eleven-year-olds balk at the child label.

"Yeah, but something happened," Chiara says thoughtfully. "You're ... wired."

I shake my head, trying to throw her off the scent, but realize I can't lie completely. "I got talking to someone at the diner, that's all."

"That's all? But you've been gone for hours! What did you talk about?"

"Nothing much. This and that. And I walked her home. Well, almost home."

My sister's eyes, hazel like mine, go wide. "Almost home? That's not how I raised you."

"You didn't raise me. She was leery—rightfully so—of me seeing where she lives. So I ... it doesn't matter. I know the street she lives on and I made sure she got home all right." I followed at a safe distance, then waited with a weird desperation for her confirming text. It came in within sixty seconds of her entering a three-flat brownstone, no more than four blocks from where I live.

Home safe and sound! I had fun :)

To which I'd replied, **Glad to hear it. Good night.** Not exactly the most sparkling of repartee, but an adequate answer for both statements. Glad she was safe and glad she had fun. Then I'd quit while I was ahead.

Chiara, detecting weakness as only a sibling can, leans in and sniffs. "Jesus Christmas, you kissed her!"

"You can't possibly tell, you witch."

"Sure I can. A faint hint of"—*sniff*—"gardenia and ..." —*sniff*—"essence of ..."—more sniffing that's starting to piss me off—"frustrated male."

"Shut up."

"I'm so proud of you. You didn't let this chick standing you up throw you off your stride. Back up on that horse!"

"Diner stool."

A movement catches the corner of my eye and I look up at the light of my world. "What are you doing up?" Really I'm thrilled to see her. I scoot on the sofa to make room and my daughter slots in between us. She's wearing PJ bottoms and a long sleeved tee that's two sizes too big for her. It says "Can't Hear You, I'm Gaming."

"I heard voices."

"From all the way up there?"

"Aunt Chiara has a high pitch."

"Sounds about right."

Lena curls her dark head into my shoulder. "So did you meet my new mommy tonight?"

If I'd been drinking, I would have done a spit take. My daughter peeks up at me, a mischievous grin on her face. She's taking this dating thing remarkably well. Most kids want their parents to reconcile, but not Lena. She knows that Tori and I don't work.

"No, I did not. I had a nice evening talking to ...

someone." Someone I'd like to have sex with at some point despite my hints that I was interested in more. Why had I said that? She clearly would have let me take things further tonight yet I'd shut it down.

Harder to get back on that diner stool than I thought.

"Aunt Chiara says you're lonely and that you need someone to listen to your emo grunting."

"Did she now." I make a face at my sister who sticks out her tongue. "How could I be lonely when I have you two occupying every minute of my precious free time? And are you saying you *don't* like listening to my emo grunting?" Not sure I even know what that means.

Lena giggles, liking being part of the grown-up talk. "I don't think you grunt in emo, Dad. That's what Chiara thinks."

"Oh, well, she'd know."

"I would." Chiara works with troubled LGBTQ+ teens, so she's well-equipped to recognize the symptoms of teen moodiness, even if they're manifested by a thirty-two-year-old man. "But we'll put up with your moods while we wait for this sainted woman to take you on."

She smiles at me over Lena's head, and I'm filled with a great fondness for her. I know I'm not the easiest person to live with, especially as I've gone sex-free for over a year now and apparently my emo grunting proves it.

"Okay, kiddo," she says, "you've got school tomorrow."

"But I haven't heard about Dad's date."

"She stood him up."

Lena goes "aww" but she doesn't look too cut up about it. She might be taking her parents' divorce remarkably well but neither is she ready for me to get serious with someone else. One of the reasons I've been reluctant to dive back into the dating pool is because my girl needs to know she's my number one. Dating has the potential to send mixed signals about her importance in my life.

She's at a tricky age and has a strained relationship with her mom, which is completely Tori's fault as she never fails to hide her disappointment that Lena isn't "feminine" enough. So she's a bit of a tomboy and doesn't really conform to the girly-girl blueprint. I don't care. She's the best thing that's ever happened to me and I will fuck over anyone who hurts her.

It's crucial I get this life right because there's no going back to my previous one. I've burned all my bridges in New York, become persona non grata, and now it's Chicago or bust. Which means that Lena comes first, followed by my job. Nothing can screw that up because this is the endgame.

I'm pretty sure I'm going to call Cherry Pie, though. Our chemistry is impossible to ignore and that doesn't happen often, at least not in my world. I can keep that on the down low—Lena doesn't need to know every detail of what her father gets up to.

"Okay, g'night!" She stands and kisses us both, then heads upstairs.

When she's out of earshot, I murmur, "Less of the detail about my dating failures, if you don't mind."

Chiara sighs. "She needs to know it's a jungle out there."

"Does she? Because I'd like to shelter her for as long as possible." That seems easier to do away from New York and all the drama with my ex.

Chiara covers my hand with hers. "You're doing the right thing, setting up here, putting down roots with us." She amends, "Me." She sounds so alone and I want to hug away her hurt, but she'll turn brittle if I get too mushy. "Forget everything that happened in New York and just enjoy your freedom and all the perks that come from being a hot, single dad."

That makes me think of Cherry Pie again, who seemed to

get a kick out of my single dad status. Most women her age wouldn't be interested in the reality of a guy with a kid, so I don't hold out much hope that the perks of single dad-dom when it comes to dating will last longer than it takes to eat a slice of pie.

FIVE

Abby

Holy shit, I'm nervous.

Sam and I met for breakfast this morning at Fern's before our first shifts at our respective firehouses to give each other a boost—and then I promptly threw up my scrambled eggs on toast in the bathroom. So not a great start to the day. Jude is already on shift at Engine 6, my new firehouse, and has been regaling us with texts for the last 24 hours, each more annoying than the last.

In no time at all, he's gone from wide-eyed wonder—"the kitchen fridge is huge!"—to a blasé "just got back from a three-alarm fire over on Western. News crews were there." Not even an exclamation point. Dick.

"Can't believe he's already been on a fire run," I mutter. Fire callouts aren't as frequent as the public would think, most of the runs being medical or road traffic accident-related. Jude had one on his first day.

"Asshole's probably lying." Sam's handsome features are

all concern, not because Jude is one-upping us in absentia but because I'm a mess. "You okay, Abby? You look pale."

"I feel pale." I shake my head. I don't even know what that means, only that I'm not feeling as good as I should. "Aren't you nervous?"

"Sure I am." The delay is almost imperceptible but I hear it. Meaning, not nervous at all. Sam is six feet two of ball-crushing confidence. If it was any way unjustified, I'd be all over it, but no. The man is just winning at life.

"You're gonna be fine," he adds.

"Except they'll probably know who I am. Maybe I shouldn't have asked to be stationed at Engine 6. Maybe it's tempting the failure gods."

"No, it's not. I suppose your dad could have done something to have you assigned somewhere else, but it sounds like he'd rather ignore you."

Yeah, no call from my dad this morning, not even a text to wish me well on my first day. It breaks my heart. We used to be so close. When I was a paramedic, we spent more time together—weekly dinners where he would cook up a big Irish stew—and we would catch up. Paramedics run into tricky and sometimes dangerous situations all the time, but not to the extent of firefighters. As soon as I told him I'd been accepted to the Academy, he froze me out.

"Jude will have your back." Sam's charming smile is quickly activated, which means ... "Hey, gorgeous, how's it going?"

That smile is not for me, but Tessa, who isn't buying it. She rolls her eyes and refills my coffee. "You okay, Abby?"

"Just first day jitters."

"Oh, I thought maybe it was post-date nerves. Did he call?"

I try to widen my eyes in warning but it's too late.

"Did who call? What date?" Sam ping-pongs between us.

Tessa grimaces, but she doesn't look too remorseful.

"You're fired as my friend," I mutter.

"What about coffee and pie?"

"I'll think about it."

She slinks away while I brace for the interrogation.

"What date?"

"I came in here the night of graduation for a slice of pie and met someone." I explain the rest, leaving out the kiss, not that it's too racy for my horny little friend. Sharing it at this point feels too fragile.

"He must have been impressed with the firefighter thing."

"As a date magnet, the firefighter thing isn't as useful for women as it is for men. Of course you and your muscles will draw them in like a bear to honey. Me and *my* muscles? Not quite as advantageous. Most guys are threatened by strong women."

"I'm not."

"Professions of the last five women you've slept with, please."

"Never asked."

"Asshole."

He laughs. "Okay, so you need to reel him in before you reveal you have a side gig as Lara Croft. Kind of ridiculous when all we men care about are great tits and a nice smile."

"If only I'd known! I'll add it to my Tinder bio."

"No need for the apps. You've got this pie-eating diner guy on your radar, even *after* he's spent hours in your presence and learned what a weirdo you are." He grins. "So when are you going to reach out?"

I haven't texted him beyond that initial "hi honey, I'm home" message because we're inside 48 hours, which is considered the golden period for crime-solving and date-dangling. I want to get through this first day before I even consider the possibilities. I have no idea if Diner Dude is into the idea of a date, though that kiss says he's into something.

Me, I hope.

Okay, that's a nice kick to my senses. I met someone. A gorgeous someone. I will have a fantastic first day on the job, and even if I screw up, I'll try to do it in such a way that ensures no one gets killed or maimed.

"I'll reach out to him tomorrow. One nerve-racking scenario at a time."

🔥

Thirty minutes later, I'm seated in my truck outside Engine 6 on the northwest side, where it all began and ended for my mom.

To my now familiar disappointment, my father still hasn't texted or called. I considered leaving him a message but decided it would only key me up further. My stomach hasn't settled and the last thing I need is another dance with the porcelain goddess.

My aunt Kathleen left me a nice message, though, wishing me luck and telling me to come over for dinner this weekend, which is awesome. Love that woman. My cousin Jackie also texted, ***Go kick some firefighter ass!*** accompanied by a pic of her husband's ass, which I recognize because it has a shamrock on the left buttock. (Usually said ass makes an annual appearance late on St. Patrick's Day, so it's weird to see it at any other time.) Johno's a firefighter at Engine 12 on the southside and Jackie's an ER nurse at Northwestern Memorial. Service runs in the family.

Straightening my spine, I walk into the firehouse bay where a few guys are seated at a table, playing cards. One of them raises his chin as I approach and is immediately recognizable as Luke Almeida of the legendary Dempseys. Five foster siblings, all in CFD.

"Hey, Lieutenant, I'm Abby Sullivan. Reporting for duty."

"Reporting for duty," someone at the table mimics.

Lieutenant Almeida shoots a shriveling look at the joker, who colors. The LT lays down his hand. "Full house, tens high."

Everyone throws in their hands with a mix of groans and whines.

"Luke Almeida." Standing, he holds out a hand and shakes mine. "Ignore these assholes. They're not on your shift so best not to give them any brain space. Come on, I'll take you to meet your lieutenant."

I've been half hoping Almeida would be my superior officer because I've heard he's rock solid and no one would make a better mentor, but that's okay. The rep of Engine 6 is such that only the best are sent here.

Why are you here, then?

No time for self-doubt! I follow Almeida through a couple of corridors, passing the Wall of the Fallen and there she is on the first row: Jo Sullivan in her dress uniform, her red hair tucked under her cap, her face unsmiling. She probably had to use that poker face so she wouldn't get assholes making fun of her for "reporting for duty." No problem, I don't need to be too friendly with any of them. They certainly aren't dating material. No firefighter is.

I know what it's like to lose someone in the service and before my dad moved into the upper ranks, I lived in nail-biting fear that I'd lose my remaining parent. So there's a certain irony—*Sing it loud, Alanis!*—that I've chosen such a dangerous profession yet won't consider a firefighter boyfriend. I figure there are plenty of safer options out there where I don't have to worry about whether someone I'm dating might not make it home after a twenty-four hour shift.

Speaking of not making it home …

Below my mom's picture is Sean Dempsey, Luke Almeida's adoptive father, who died fourteen years ago. He and his foster sibs at 6 had to pass these photos every day. Did they ever get used to it?

We arrive at a suite of offices a few corridors in. The name plate on the one Almeida knocks says 'Lt. Roman Rossi.' As far as I know, he's a relatively recent addition as a lieutenant but other than that I have no intel. He doesn't even have a photo on the CFD intranet.

"Roman, got your candidate here for you." Luke pushes the door open and I have a nanosecond to absorb broad shoulders, dark, lustrous hair, and a strong tanned neck just as the man inside turns.

This can't be right.

The look in this man's hazel-green eyes tells me it might not be right but it's happening anyway. Diner Dude is staring back at me.

At which point I throw up all over Luke Almeida's boots.

Six

Abby

I take another look in the mirror, pinch my cheeks, and try again.

Still as pale as the ghost of my dear departed mother.

I'd have thought I didn't have anything left to spew after I got sick once already but the stomach, it keeps on giving. How could I now be working with—for? under?—Diner Dude? I wouldn't have pegged him for CFD at all.

So he had a military air to him, but that didn't mean anything. Lots of guys have that ramrod straight bearing, the squinty stare, the hard-to-crack demeanor. But crack it I did. We had vibed, and it was weird to think that if I'd known he was a firefighter we would have had even more in common.

That's not the moral of the story, Abby.

The moral of the story is that this is really fucking bad. There are rules about fraternizing with your co-workers, and especially with your superior. Life and death decisions are being made on callouts and no one needs the distraction or the drama. Not that this was even an option, but I knew the shape and taste of his mouth.

We would have to report it to the higher-ups. My father would hear all about it and feel vindicated in trying to steer me away from the path my mom took. My shift hasn't even started and I'm already screwing up.

I open the door, expecting that Lieutenant Almeida will be waiting, but no. It's him. Diner Dude.

Lieutenant Roman Rossi.

Something sparks in those gorgeous—*nope, not gorgeous*—eyes on seeing me. Probably disgust. At least I'd missed *his* boots.

"You okay?"

I nod. Slowly shake my head.

"Not okay?"

"Physically, fine." I touch my forehead and offer a comical grimace. Diner Dude would have smiled, I'm sure of it. But that guy has left the building.

In his place is a hard ass with a CFD-issued tee and navy pants that should look like dog poop but don't. I didn't see his arms the other night, only felt them as I clung like a dinghy battered by a storm. They'd been strong, muscled, solid.

Now I'm seeing them, bare, tanned, and in the flesh, and I'm revising the Braille abilities of my hands. What I felt the other night had been wonderful, but these in-my-eyeballs beauties are absolutely breathtaking.

While I'm losing myself in the glory of his forearms, he's started to speak.

"...the last person I expected to show up in my firehouse this morning. I probably should have been a bit more nosey about your graduation." He's lowered his voice to an intimate volume, which sounds nice except that intimacy has nothing to do with it. Trying to ensure no one is clued in to our previous connection, no doubt.

"What happens now?"

He raises an eyebrow. Stories are told with that eyebrow but I'm suddenly illiterate.

"Is there some paperwork I need to fill out to, uh ..."

"To ..."

I wave between us, impatient now because he's either being deliberately obtuse or making fun of me. "Tell someone about this. What happened."

"We don't usually report when the probies vomit, even if it's on an LT's boots."

Now that has to be a joke. I cover my face with a hand, embarrassment overcoming me once more. With my pale Irish skin, I tend to flush more than the average human. "I can't believe I did that. I was so nervous this morning and I'd already puked at the diner and—"

"That was a repeat?" A strong grip curls around my shoulder and I'm led down the corridor to the office where we'd been ten minutes ago. Someone has cleaned up the vomit, though the tang of Pine Sol remains. I'm shoved gently into a chair. An uncapped bottle of water is thrust not so gently into my hand.

"Drink."

I down about a third of it. The coolness helps. Sort of.

"If you're that ill, you might be dehydrated. Either go home or lie in the bunk room for a while."

"I'm not going home." I look up at him. He's half sitting on his desk which showcases the man's thighs to perfection.

Have mercy, I'm still trying to recover from the arms!

He's also clean-shaven, that sexy beard no longer on display. It only highlights how strong and sensual his jaw and lips are, though, so I'm still in a state of inappropriate lust for the boss. Fantastic.

Determined to get ahold of myself, I grind out, "I get that I've screwed up here, but I'm not leaving."

Something in my tone must have resonated with him. There's the slightest kick to the corner of his mouth.

"How are you feeling?"

"Better. I'm sorry about getting sick."

"Not as sorry as Almeida."

Back with a hand over my reddening face. At least I'm no longer deathly pale, right?

"Hey, it's okay." He sounds concerned, maybe a little sorry for the teasing. Good. "He'll get over it."

I groan behind my palm. "I wish I could have seen his face. But I was too busy doubled over."

His lips twitch, and something in his expression softens. It makes him seem younger and quickly passes.

"We need to talk about the elephant in the room," he says soberly.

I nod, feeling nauseous again. "That's what I meant about paperwork. I figured we'd need to ... report it to ..." Not a jot of help from his quarter. I finish with, "Someone in authority?"

He crosses his arms. "Like Commissioner Sullivan?"

I supposed there was no keeping that a secret. After all, this engine must have hated hearing that Abby Sullivan, daughter of the Fire Commissioner, was posted here.

"That's not who I meant," I say. "But I suppose he'd eventually find out."

"Pretty by the book, are you?"

"I just want to get off on the right foot."

"And you think reporting the fact you were making out with your superior officer the night before reporting for duty—"

"Two nights," I whisper because I'm by the book.

"Is the way to start your career at CFD off right?"

I don't know anymore. Isn't it his job to figure out the plan? "I'll take my lead from you."

He blinks, like that statement clarifies something, though I don't know what. "I'm sorry, you're right. It's just ... a surprise to see you here. I don't want to ask you to lie. Of course you should report it if the idea of working here"—he pauses—"with me, makes you in any way uncomfortable."

That's more sensitive than I expected. Guess he couldn't keep up the nothing-to-see-here act forever. "What would happen if I did report it?"

He considers that for a beat. "Because it didn't go any further than ... it did ..." He seems to trip up on the rest and now we're both back to two nights ago, lost in that kiss, in the taste and feel and heat of each other. My color is rising, my body reacting and clenching. The regret waving over me that it didn't go further.

He coughs and goes on, his voice somewhat graveled. "Then you would likely be asked about whether you're okay with remaining on my crew or if you'd like to be transferred out. You could probably move to Almeida's crew, swap with the new guy over on A-shift, but why that has to happen will probably get out. There are very few secrets in the firehouse."

Something clouds over his expression, a memory that pains him.

"Do you think we should report it?"

He heaves a sigh. "Definitely less paperwork to not report it, but I'm fine with paperwork if you need off my crew. Trust and respect are key with any team. If you have a problem seeing me as your leader or are worried I'll treat you differently because of what happened, then those are reasons to consider reporting and making a move."

"Do you think you can treat me the same as anyone else?"

His stare is as intense as the kiss he laid on me when we last met. (I really need to stop thinking about that. Nothing good can come of it.) "I can be a professional, Sullivan. I will tell you that my crew is one of the best in CFD. You stick with me and you will learn what it takes to be a great firefighter."

That's what I want. That's the mentorship I crave. And with him calling me Sullivan, I feel as though he's drawn a line under the dangerously personal. Mixed cement into the quicksand. No more Cherry Pie or Diner Dude, that's for sure.

I could make a fuss, put an X on my back before I've even begun, suffer the whispers of the firehouse gossips, and the wrath of my father when he finds out. Or I could pull on my combat boots and figure this out.

"I want to stay on your crew, Lieutenant."

I'm not sure if he looks annoyed or relieved. I thought I could read him in the diner, but this version is a different species.

"You know what that means?"

I nod. "We're going to ignore it happened and ..."

"Never speak of it again."

Oh. Well, of course. I couldn't expect him to remember it with fondness. He's my CO and the man who can make or break my career in CFD. My life—in more ways than one—is in his hands. He also needs to be able to trust that I can do my job in a way that keeps him safe.

"Okay, that sounds like a good way forward."

"As far as anyone is concerned, you're the rookie who puked on Almeida's boots and I'm your commanding officer."

"Don't know you. Don't want to know you."

Something shifts in his gaze. I want to think he's closing the door on the past: the night, the pie, the kiss. Or rather, I don't want that at all, but it's better to think that's on his mind than the alternative.

He might wish for it to be different.

I don't need that kind of complication. I'm already under too much pressure to succeed and an inconvenient attraction to my lieutenant is a wrinkle I can't afford to iron out. Best to leave it twisted up in the bottom of my emotional laundry basket.

Besides, I don't date firefighters. Even if he wasn't my boss, this wouldn't be happening.

"What's next?"

He pauses a moment, and I get the impression that what comes out of his mouth is different than what he wants to really say.

"Breakfast is currently being served, then equipment checks. Here's your locker combo. Go stow your stuff and then head to the lounge." He hands off a slip of paper and I ignore the brush of his skin against mine.

I have to.

The locker room is empty and it takes me a second to find the one labeled "Sullivan." I rest my forehead against the cool of the steel door, trying to center myself for the day ahead, which has become crazily complicated.

"Hey, you okay?"

I glance over my shoulder at Jude, who's just walked into the locker room. Seeing him conjures up a weird mix of relief and embarrassment. My grand entrance must be the talk of the house.

"Yeah, just not a great start. That was probably the worst first impression to make. All the guys must think I'm a total snowflake, right?"

"No!" He bites his lip which is his tell. "They made more of the fact it was Luke's boots that got the benefit. People found that hilarious. And the fact that the FNG—fucking new guy, aka me—had to clean up vomit before my shift ended."

"Oh, God, I'm so sorry!"

"Yeah, well, it's all part of the job. We're going to see a lot worse."

He shoulders the locker next to mine and crosses his arms. "What did Rossi say to you?"

"When?"

"After you got sick. You were in his office for a while."

I swallow, not ready to tell all. Likely, I'll never be ready and it's probably best if I just pretend. I have a feeling I'll need to become very good at that for the next year.

"He was just concerned about whether I needed to rest or go home. I told him I was fine, just a spot of nerves." Eager to change the subject, I look at him squarely. "Everything go good on your shift?"

"Awesome! I'm only still here to check in with my bestie and get a little face time with Gage Simpson, seeing as he's the other gay guy."

"And married with kids, so off limits."

"I know that! He's pretty cool and I would never." Jude might be a man about town but he has scruples. He'd never hit on a co-worker, let alone one who's hitched and happy, so I don't know why I even pointed it out. Feeling testy, I suppose, because Jude clearly had a great first day and mine had such a rocky start.

He squeezes my shoulder. "How was it walking by the photo of your mom?"

"Weird, like it wasn't happening to me. I don't really remember her like that, with the stern come-at-me expression and the severe hair. It was like looking at someone you vaguely recognize. She was so different to that, but now I'm wondering if I ever saw the real her."

"You were six when she died, Abby. Our memories go through shifts, and she just showed her mom side to you. Still no word from Papa Sullivan?"

I shake my head. What did I expect? My father didn't want me to do this, and while I understand his concern, that disapproval weighs on my chest.

Jude thumbs over his shoulder. "Okay, I'm off home to shower and sleep. This will all look better after a few hours."

I hope he's right.

He kisses my forehead. "Gimme a call later and tell me how it's going, okay?"

"Okay."

Once he's gone, I key in the combination to my locker, bracing myself for some low-level prank or threat. It's not unheard of for female firefighters to suffer ketchup in their lockers or dead insects as a welcome.

All that greets me is an envelope with my name on it.

I look around. Still empty, and I'm keenly aware of the need to pull my shit together and make an appearance in the lounge.

But first the envelope.

I rip it open, surprised as all hell to find a handwritten note from Alexandra Dempsey-Cooper, the other female firefighter at Engine 6, and another member of the Dempsey clan.

Hi Abby,

I'm sorry I can't be there for your first day but I'm currently laid up at home with ice on my vagina, recovering from the birth of the largest child ever expelled from a human woman. Baby Sean emerged kicking and screaming at 10 lbs 9 oz and almost killed me in the process. (Definitely his father's son.) But all is well, just as all will be well for you now that you're on the best crew at the best engine in Chicago.

We've never met but I've no doubt you're a tough cookie. You've had to work twice as hard and repel ten times the shit because of your gender and maybe even because of the legacy you've inherited. Believe me, we understand that at Engine 6. The Dempseys get it and that makes you one of us. Your mom and my dad were heroes to so many of us, and sometimes that can be a hard act to follow.

But have no doubt: you're going to be fine.

Watch, listen, and learn. It'll get you far. Roman might seem like a hard-ass (okay, he is a total hard-ass), but he knows his shit even if he is from New Yawk. Not that we make fun of him and his weird accent. Oh no, not at all ;) Luke and Gage will also have your back. (Beck's in Fire Investigation now and Wyatt spends more time at the Academy, so you'll only run into them at the bar.)

If you need to talk to someone before I'm back on the job, then don't hesitate to reach out. All visits in person must include cupcakes, though. Just tell the people at Sweet Mandy B's that you're buying for me!

Your sister in fire,
Alex

Wow. I did not expect that and after the start I've had, I realize that I needed it big time. Roman—Lieutenant Rossi—said he ran the best crew, so it's good to hear it confirmed. And it's good to start thinking of him as the LT, and not the guy who was supposed to be a sexy reward for me getting through this first day unscathed.

I have no time for regrets. I stash my backpack in my locker, take a deep breath, and head for the lounge.

Seven

Roman

Candidate Sullivan—Abby—leaves my office, taking with her the dregs of my fast-disappearing composure.

I'd barely had a second to school my face to stone when she jackknifed in half and gave Almeida's boots the benefit of her stomach's insides. Not exactly how I expected to see her and all that lush red hair again.

And I'd been sure that would happen.

I had every intention of calling her today at lunchtime and asking her out for a date. A real one at a nice restaurant where I pull out her chair and act like a gentleman instead of the beast I devolved to the other night. That kiss, the pie, the whole evening, had given me hope.

One knock on the door was all it took to dash it.

Not only is she one of my crew, a candidate, and a direct report—a triple threat to everything I'm trying to rebuild—she's also Commissioner Chuck Sullivan's daughter. I'd been warned by my captain, Matt Ventimiglia, that she was to be assigned here. Rumor has it she and her old man aren't on the best terms. He doesn't approve of her joining the service, and who could blame him after what had happened to her mother almost twenty years ago?

But maybe they don't get along because he's an asshole. I have my own personal experience with him to confirm that much.

I'd been surprised to hear she was posted to Engine 6, her mom's old stomping ground but then it sounded like the kind of move some PR wonk in CFD Media Affairs thought would make a good story. Or maybe she asked to be posted here, because it has a special meaning for her, the place where her mom broke the glass ceiling with a Halligan and an axe.

Whatever the reason, I know this much: I do not fucking need it.

Relatively new to Chicago, I transferred in from New York only three months ago. I'm more than qualified—twelve years as a firefighter—and I had to go through a mini-academy to recertify for CFD but I did it all because New York is now scorched earth for me.

Because I didn't come up through the regular channels in CFD it took time to find my place and gain the trust of my crew. Complicating matters, there's some lingering resentment because I got the promotion one of the in-house firefighters felt he deserved. No one liked the blow-in.

As an outsider I need to keep my wits about me. Screwing around with the newbie is not the way to make friends and influence people, especially when that newbie is Chuck Sullivan's daughter.

Just when I thought I'd met someone nice.

Gorgeous.

Hot.

I wipe my brow, the heat of the forbidden creating a fire throughout my body. I could not be thinking those words about Candidate Sullivan. About any worker on my crew.

And especially not about the daughter of my boss, who already has me in his crosshairs.

Big boy pants, Rossi. It's time to face what I will have to deal with for at least a year—if the candidate doesn't quit first.

I'm scrolling through my collection of game faces when my phone rings. I don't really want to talk to my ex but I'm determined to start that mature attitude right now.

"Hey."

"Roman, I need a decision."

I close my eyes and pinch the bridge of my nose. "I'm fine, Tori, thanks for asking. So's your daughter."

"That's why I'm calling. I can't believe you'd refuse to give me this." She catches herself. "To give Lena this. She should be here at her mom's wedding."

I inhale a controlling breath. "Should she? I don't see why she has to be present. She won't want to wear a dress—"

"Of course she will! And please don't pretend that your reasons for preventing her from coming to my wedding are because of your concern about her body image. We both know that this is just you being petty and vengeful over what happened."

Maybe she's right.

Maybe I'm a bitter, twisted asshole.

Maybe I don't care.

But I also know that Lena would hate wearing some pink frou-frou number.

"Can you guarantee you'll let her choose her own outfit?"

Tori makes a sound of annoyance. "She can wear what the other bridesmaids are wearing. This is my day, Roman!"

And we're done here. "Sure, I've got to go. Work, y'know."

I can practically hear her eye roll. "Why does everything have to be on your terms?"

She slept with a colleague, made me a laughing stock at my

place of work, put in zero effort when it came to fighting for her daughter, and now wants everyone to dance to her tune. Sure sounds like "my terms."

"Because I'm a selfish prick, of course."

She sighs dramatically, knowing she won't get a rise out of me. I stopped playing her games years ago.

"Ask Lena if she wants to come to her mom's wedding. Her aunts and cousins all miss her."

"Gotta go." I click off before she can. Sure it's petty, but that's where we are in the trajectory of our relationship: hang-ups and holier-than-thous. While I might be using Lena's fragile relationship with her mom to justify her absence from the wedding, I'm self-aware enough to know this is mostly my problem.

I want to punish Tori for what she did, which probably makes me a terrible father. And while admitting you have a problem is supposed to be the first step in solving it, I'm not quite ready to make the leap to fixing anything, either.

No one's getting off that easy, not even me.

I head to the kitchen/lounge where the crew usually hang out, lingering over breakfast. Gage Simpson is rattling the pans today and can usually be relied on for something fancy for the shift before it officially starts.

"You made it, LT!" Not only is he a great cook, Simpson is a great firefighter and one of the Dempseys, the family of foster siblings who make up a significant compliment of the firehouse. Luckily they're spread out on different shifts because hell if I didn't need the added responsibility of all of them on my crew. Simpson and his sister, Alexandra Dempsey-Cooper, are on mine. She's currently on maternity leave, which means we have the one female crew member.

Abby Sullivan.

She's sitting at the table, the water bottle I'd given her still in hand, sipping and watching. I've already chatted with Jude Torres, the other candidate who was assigned to Almeida's crew, and got a good sense about him. Eager, bright, watchful.

I take a seat at the table. Now that the shift's commander has arrived, breakfast can officially begin. "What've we got, Chef?"

"Frittata with asparagus, mushrooms, and gruyere."

I take a bite. "Is that ... thyme?"

"Yes it is." Simpson looks pleased. Thyme isn't the hardest herb to spot but I know he likes when we make the effort. "Extra helping for you seeing as poor old Abby is worried she'll paint the floor with whatever she chokes down."

I flick a glance at "poor old Abby," glad to see she seems to be recovering. Also nothing poor or old about her; the woman is fine as hell. Her color is back and she no longer looks embarrassed. That's good because she's going to have to get over any ribbing that comes her way.

Dragging my gaze away, I ask, "Almeida still here?"

"No, he headed out. Has a baby to make."

"And he wants everyone to know that?"

Danny Acosta, one of my crew, laughs. "What he wants makes no difference."

Apparently Luke and his wife, Kinsey, have been trying for Baby No. 3 for a while, the details of which are common knowledge because everyone is all up in everyone's business at Engine 6. It bothered me at my old house in New York, especially as the whispers behind my back took an age to solidify into information I could act on. If I'd known sooner what was going on, maybe I would have handled it better.

Here in Chicago, I'm new and drama-free as far as these guys are concerned. But now that the rookie is on my crew, the rookie whose lips I've already tasted, I sure as shit need to lock down any gossip potential stat.

That means treating her like one of the guys. Being extra vigilant about keeping my eyes to myself but also not looking like I'm ignoring her. She's here to learn, I'm here to teach, and we'll be conducting business as usual. A delicate balancing act.

Looking around, I do a quick head count. "Where's Wozniak?"

Shrugs and murmurs of "haven't heard from him" float through the space. Paul Wozniak is one of the most senior firefighters on my crew but this has to be the third time he's late this month. He should be calling me if he's behind, but he's never felt the need to treat me like his lieutenant. I've let his insubordination slide because he's pissed about me taking the LT position he saw as his. Heavy is the head that wears the crown and all that, and it's never heavier than when I have to deal with crew members like Woz.

We're running a little late today, but the shift doesn't start right without a little vigorous debate. "Alright, whose turn is it for the question of the day? Brooks, I think you're up."

Tyler Brooks is a big bruiser redhead with an infectious grin. "Alright, alright, I've got a good one. Clean underwear but no showers for a week or daily showers but dirty briefs?"

Lots of *ews* and cries of "gross," but it doesn't take long for the crew to get over it and debate the merits in earnest. As the talk continues with Simpson trying to nail down a definition of "dirty" for the underwear part of the equation, I turn to Abby who has remained pretty quiet. When we'd first met she struck me as a bit of a smart ass, so this is definitely a different look on her. Maybe she's still recovering. Or maybe she's trying not to stand out because of who she is, those footsteps she's following, both her mom's and her dad's. Could even be that my presence is putting a damper on her spirits. If that's the case, I hope those spirits revive soon enough and any awkwardness passes.

"We figure that starting our days with the great moral conundrums gets us in the right frame of mind," I say to her.

She blinks, maybe surprised I'm talking to her. We can't ignore each other, and the way her mouth hooks in a soft grin, I wouldn't want to. I could live off that crumb of attention.

"Always good to get the neurons firing." She takes a slug of water. "Where do you land on this great debate?"

I don't have to think about it too hard. "Dirty body, clean clothes."

"Because?"

"Adding something clean to something not so clean can probably only help."

"But defiling the already clean with something dirty isn't an improvement at all? Hmm, maybe." The mention of "defiling" and "dirty" stirs my cock in a way that should not be happening during a morning jabber with my crew.

Tyler points at Abby. "But people wear the same unwashed clothes on daily showered bodies all the time, don't they?"

"But would you wear the same unwashed-for-a-week boxers on your clean ass? That is the question." Abby grins, getting into the spirit of the proceedings. Her color has returned and every freckle is glowing like a shower of stars.

I should not be noticing that.

"Are people wearing deodorant in this scenario?" Gage offers.

"Too many variables," Danny mutters. "Deodorant. Which clothes are we talking about, T-shirts or shorts? How bad is the underwear?"

And now we've reached the nitty-gritty. It sure didn't take long for the conversation to devolve to exactly where a conversation like this would be expected to go. I remain silent, letting the kids figure it out, and ponder how I'll be treating the new candidate on my crew from here on out.

What I know for sure is that I won't be digging below these surface interactions at the start of the shift. No cozy chats. No heartfelt discussions. Management-labor, a divide that will remain firmly in place if I have to slice a knife through my guts to do it.

Eight

Abby

"Equipment checks in five, people!"

Usually the daily equipment check would be the first thing done on a shift but apparently my morning upchuck has thrown the routine out of whack, so we're running late on it.

"Sullivan, you're with me," Lieutenant Rossi says. I follow him to the bay, trying gamely not to notice the play of his shoulder muscles as they fight for containment inside his CFD tee.

"Feeling better?"

"Yep. Fine." I nod too enthusiastically to distract from my ogling, which I'm sure he noticed. "Ready to get going."

He holds my gaze a beat too long and I return it with interest because now isn't the time to back down.

Manly sniff of disapproval. "What do you remember about the daily equipment check at the academy?"

"Well, there are three main areas. Personal gear, apparatus, and operational."

"Right. I'm going to take you through all of them while I do mine. You'll do yours, too. Let me know if you have any questions."

The next twenty minutes are spent checking my turnout gear, tools, battery for my radio, self-contained breathing apparatus condition and gauge, and every piece of equipment I would carry into the field. The LT is patient with my questions. Around me, I hear laughter, bro-banter, and the sound of chainsaws (we start them every shift to make sure they're ready for action).

About midway through, Roman looks up, his brow lined. "Wozniak, nice of you to join us."

A new guy has entered the bay, looking a bit flustered, probably because he's running late. He's midthirties, sandy-haired, and powerfully built.

"Car trouble."

"Okay, check your gear." Roman considers him, clearly wanting to say something else. Instead he shifts attention. "Simpson, how's that rig looking?"

Gage, youngest of the Dempsey clan, is busy checking the firefighter truck, which has an aerial rig.

"Someone left their coffee in here." He picks up a cup from the footwell and sniffs it. "Almond latte. Fucking Mackler."

Roman growls and I have to say, I don't *not* like it.

"Make a note. Take the rig outside and run the aerial check."

I pipe up. "Can I watch that?"

"Want to sit in the cab as well?"

He's teasing but I don't care. When my girlfriends were braiding Barbie's hair, I was all about my big red fire engine.

"You bet I do."

I can tell he's trying not to smile, sort of like the other

night. This is going to be a tough few days. "Go play with the fire truck, Sullivan."

I head out to the front yard and wave at Gage. "Permission to climb aboard."

"Permission granted! You hear that, assholes? That's exactly the kind of deference required next time one of you wants on my rig."

Gage runs through the checks, ensuring all the lights come on—I have to exit the cab to tell him—and then he extends the ladder while one of the other firefighters, a burly redhead named Tyler, runs up it in full gear and carrying a chainsaw. It's important to make sure every piece of equipment is working at all times, and the easiest way to do that is for each shift to take responsibility for their own.

"You on the mend, Abby?" Gage asks as we hop off the truck.

"I am, thanks. If you see your brother before I do, tell him I'm sorry."

His grin is puckish. He's awfully handsome with on-the-long-side blond hair, gorgeous blue eyes, and a grin that could power the city grid. "It could have been worse. You could have done it all over Luke's head while he was bent over tying his bootlaces. The stories I could tell." He pats my arm. "I kept some of the breakfast frittata back in the fridge if the mood takes you later."

"That's really sweet of you."

"You're part of the B-shift, which stands for badass. All my meals are badass fuel. Okay, looks like Roman's got ladder drills up next."

I aim for a casual tone as we walk toward the group gathering in the yard. "So what's he like as an LT?"

"Tough but fair. Doesn't suffer fools. Comes off as curt but that's his New York coming through. You're going to learn a lot, so just pay attention."

Most Chicago firefighters were born and raised in this town, often coming from a family legacy of first responder service. It's the kind of job that requires local knowledge and an appreciation of the town's history and ways. Not that a transplant couldn't make a go of it, but I had to wonder why he moved here.

He'd said he was divorced, so maybe his previous life in New York had left a bitter taste in his mouth.

Another reason to stay well away.

We're on ladder drills and I'm buddied up with Danny Acosta, who has three years' experience at this engine. Lieutenant Rossi is doing a great job of treating me like everyone else. Cool appraisal, nothing too friendly, unafraid to bawl me out when needed.

"Sullivan, you need to lock the butt with your heel!"

Exactly what a girl wants to hear from the guy who blew her mind with a kiss for the ages, then killed any chance she had of a normal dating life. Because let's face it, I'm never sharing pie with a man in a diner ever again. Burned doesn't begin to describe it.

I look down and sure enough, my foot isn't in the right position. Damn.

A quick adjustment gets me back on track. "Got it, Lieutenant!"

Danny grins at me from the other side of the ladder. "So you got a boyfriend, Sullivan?"

"What?" I grab the halyard, the rope used to pull the ladder extension up and start yanking.

"Smoother, Sullivan," Roman says. "Less jerk, more silk in that move."

Like your mouth.

I shake my head and try to focus on the drill. Ladder extension is a pretty basic skill, but it's good to practice with the people who would depend on me and I on them. The last thing I need is to be thinking of how Roman's mouth felt on mine.

"Now tie it off," Roman calls out. He's watching three different drills, and while it isn't a race to see who can throw the ladder against the wall first, it really is.

I start on mine, a standard clove hitch I can do in my sleep.

Danny smiles, a friendly shoot-the-shit grin that's very attractive. "You want to go for a drink after shift? I know a good place that's open early."

A drink at eight in the morning when we get off work? Is he hitting on me? "Um ..."

"Hey, loop it around," Danny says, and then for some reason I do exactly that, but the opposite way I should.

"Sullivan, who the hell taught you to tie a clove hitch?"

Roman's immediately at my side taking the rope and tying the knot exactly how it should be done. Somehow my brain has locked up because Danny was asking me out on a date—I think—and the guy I kissed is now my freaking boss.

"Sorry," I mumble.

He ignores my apology. "Show me how you do it."

Feeling foolish, I go through the motions of the knot as if I'd never done it before instead of the million times I'd practiced in my backyard, my kitchen, and at the academy. I could rope a steer with my skills, dammit!

"Now do it again."

I untie, then do it again.

Ten more times.

The other pairs have already thrown their ladders against the wall and are standing around, laughing and chatting. *Get your head in the game, Sullivan.*

The siren goes off with the mechanical voice calling out

the specifics: "Engine 6, Ambulance 59, RTA on Division and Cicero." Everyone goes on alert with Roman calling out instructions.

"All right, move it!" And then to me, "You stay here, Sullivan, and practice your clove hitch."

I open my mouth to respond but the crew is already bustling toward the equipment bay, except for Danny who quickly throws the ladder against the wall. Then he's on his way with a smile and a shrug. He seems like a nice guy, and while his gabbiness distracted me, that screw-up was totally my fault. I need to focus more and put thoughts of Diner Dude out of mind.

I follow the crew back into the bay. They're grabbing jackets and stepping into their boots, an efficient ballet of movement and coordination. My gear is ready—I checked it myself less than thirty minutes ago. "Lieutenant?"

Roman looks up, his foot halfway into his boot, those cool, hazel-green eyes assessing me.

"Yeah?"

"I—I want to go on this run. I shouldn't be stuck here where I can't learn anything."

It's completely the wrong thing to say. His expression turns stormy, those eyes dimming to a blackness I feel shriveling my internal organs.

But when he speaks, it's like I imagined that look.

"Yeah, but we're already heading out." His tone is patient, measured. "Listen, walk back to the admin office and ask for Billy. Tell her I sent you. We'll talk when I get back."

Okay, so that's not too bad. I'm not on the run but at least the LT isn't mad at me for speaking out of turn. I just want him to know I'm ready for this. Within sixty seconds, the crew is on the truck, heading out. Poetry in motion.

An eerie quiet descends on the station now that the crew has left. I head toward the administrative offices, stopping at the Wall of the Fallen on the way. There's another one at the Fire Academy, also known as the Quinn, honoring all the heroes lost in the line of duty since the founding of CFD, but this one at Engine 6 is more personal.

This was my mom's house—and now it's mine.

"Hey, Mom, I'm here," I whisper. "I wish you could see me, though maybe not today when I've not been at my best. But I promise to make you proud." I kiss my fingertips and transfer it to her photo. A whisper of cool air hits my neck—perhaps a door opening farther down the corridor—but ever the sentimentalist, I interpret it as a message from the beyond.

The administrative suite is around the corner from the lieutenants' offices. I poke my head past the door and spot a dark-haired Black woman about my age sitting behind a desk.

"Hey, I'm looking for Billy."

"That's me." She looks up and smiles a sun blast of a grin. "Billie with an e. You must be Candidate Sullivan."

"The very one."

"Heard you hurled this morning. How are you feeling?"

"Better, thanks. Anyway, the lieutenant said I should stop by."

She narrows her eyes, that bright smile a thing of the past. "What exactly did he say? Word for word."

Unfortunately the shape of his lips are embedded in my brain, so I remember it verbatim.

"'Ask for Billie. Tell her I sent you.'"

Her mouth twists in a grimace. "You must have really pissed him off."

"What? No, he was fine. Just told me to ... uh, talk to you."

She stands, smooths out her short skirt—a super cute tobacco-colored suede—and takes a deep let's-do-this breath. "Come with me."

Confused by her reaction, I trail her to a door further

down the corridor. She opens it to reveal a utility closet with a mop bucket and cleaning supplies.

"If you get started now, you might have it done by the time they get back from this run. The RTAs don't usually take as long as fire suppression calls."

A chill rolls through me. "Get started on what?"

"Latrine duty. You're it until the LT says you're not."

"But I didn't—wait, what?"

She smiles in pity. "I'm guessing you backtalked or disobeyed an order?" She doesn't even wait for confirmation. "If he tells you to come see me, that's what he means. You're it."

"You're sure?"

"Yep. See you on the other side."

Nine

Roman

"You going on another date, Daddy?"

I eye the reflection of the questioner in the mirror. The query might sound innocent enough but even an eleven-year-old knows how to yank my chain.

"Nope. Decided there's only one girl for me."

"Who? Aunt Chiara?"

I pull my daughter—the only girl for me—into a bear hug, which results in "No, Dad! Let me go!" and then a flurry of giggles. She's still my little girl even if she's growing like a weed before my eyes.

The last three months have been tough but she appears to be settling. Doing okay at school, making friends, finding her place. I've tried getting her to talk about her mom but she always changes the subject. That worries me but I don't want to force her into dad-daughter therapy sessions that would just upset the delicate balance we have right now. I know she has to be hurting. Her mother essentially gave up custody without a fight.

"Did your aunt put you up to this?" My sister's been angling for more information about the other night. *Had I called? When was the next official date?*

I'd kept it zipped. No more thinking about it, either, though it's easier said than done. As much as I try to expel Abby—Candidate Sullivan—from my mind, it's hard not to think about the first woman to light my fire in years. The bitch of a universe must have it in for me.

I hold on to Lena as we head down the stairs. She relaxes in my arms and I let myself absorb her soft body and sweet breath against my neck.

"You do your homework?"

A moment's hesitation I recognize all too well. "Yes."

"What do you have left to do?"

"Her math problems." Chiara appears at the bottom of the stairs.

"I won't be gone long, just a round or two." I place Lena down. "Math homework better be done by the time I come back. I'll check."

Chiara and Lena laugh evilly.

"I didn't say I'd know what I'm looking at but I'll know if you did it. I always do."

"Sure, Dad," Lena says as she heads to Chiara's kitchen. She likes to do her homework there while her aunt fusses about. "Good luck finding my new mommy."

"Cheeky." But she's already gone.

"Those firefighter bars are probably crawling with women," Chiara comments. "Hell, if I wasn't loved up, I'd be headed down there looking for a many-muscled queen for myself."

"I'm just headed out to relax with some co-workers." The Dempseys own a bar, still somehow managing to run it while they work at CFD. "No more dating for a while."

"You're going to let one bad experience—"

"I was stood up."

"—put you off? Have you called this other woman you met?"

"That's not going to work out."

"Gave you a fake number?"

"Something like that."

She folds her arms. "Chicago women are usually nicer than New York chicks. More friendly. In fact there's this really nice girl in my office—"

"Could we do this later? Or not at all?" I open the front door, then step back to kiss Chiara on the forehead. "I appreciate everything you do for me, sis. When I'm ready to get back out there I'll let you know."

She gives me that steely-sweet smile I know translates to "this isn't finished." "Enjoy the night and say hi to that hottie, Gage Simpson."

"Speaking of—"

"Hotties?"

I scowl. "Gay guys. We have a new one at the firehouse. Probie started a couple of days ago." Gage, who has all the gossip, mentioned that Abby and Torres were buddies.

"Well, if CFD isn't a hotbed of diversity and change. Be nice to him, okay?"

"I'm nice to everyone."

Dempseys' Bar in Wicker Park is probably the nicest firefighter-owned drinking establishment I've ever walked into. Most service-run bars are dives with little concession to the public outside of the primary audience: firefighters and cops. This one has a different feel to it, friendlier. The beers are more expensive, too, though still cheaper than New York prices.

Chiara claims that half the clientele, men, women, and non-binary, are here for Gage Simpson. The guy is happily married with a couple of kids but it doesn't stop him from flirting his ass off behind the bar. Tonight, though, no sign of my shift mate; instead I'm greeted with a different cock-eyed grin and a "Fuck, no!" when I push open the heavy oak door.

I take a seat at the bar and sniff my disapproval as the barman throws down a beer mat.

"Rossi, I can't believe my fuckin' eyes." My A-shift counterpart, Lieutenant Luke Almeida, starts the Sam Adams pour from the tap.

"Had to get away from the old ball and chain."

"Your sister's a saint and you know it."

"I do."

Luke puts down the full pint glass and an elbow on the counter. "Heard your date didn't pan out."

"Et tu, Almeida?" We didn't get a chance to talk it out at the firehouse after Abby's puke-a-thon sidetracked the shift change. "She's supposed to be a friend of your wife's. Any word?"

"Kinsey insists she's more a friend of a friend, and the latest is that she's back with her ex. You got caught in the crossfire of rekindled love, friend."

I shudder, and Luke laughs. "Dodged a bullet, then."

"Yes, you did. Don't worry, Kinsey's drawing up a list of alternates."

"Why does every woman hate to see a person alone?"

Luke grins. "They just want to put the world to rights, one heart at a time. How's your girl?"

"Lena is fine. An insolent monkey, but fine."

We chat some more about families. Luke has two kids, a boy and girl, and is trying for another, the outcome of which people are running a book on at the firehouse. Alongside that, the ever-expanding Dempsey clan gives him plenty of reasons to grumble and rejoice. He was the first person I clicked with at Engine 6 and was man enough to never feel threatened by the guy who got his wings in a different city. Firefighters are an insular bunch and it's hard to feel part of it if you come from outside.

Someone appears at my elbow, the new guy, Jude Torres. A premonition slithers across my skin, because if Torres is here ...

Don't look.

"Lieutenant," he says with a grin.

"Torres. Didn't take you long to find your way here."

He chuckles. "I was told it was a required stop on the journey."

"Yeah, gotta swear fealty to the kings." I raise an eyebrow at Luke, who tells me where I can stick my *kings* comment. Rude. The Dempseys are Chicago firefighting royalty, and I like to piss off Luke and his foster sibs about how all that kissing of the ring must get old.

"Can I buy you a drink, Lieutenant?"

"I'm good, but thanks for the offer."

Having paid sufficient obeisance to the firehouse leadership, Torres grins, grabs his beers—three of them—and heads off to wherever the fuck I am not looking. But then I make the cardinal mistake of checking out the reflection in the mirror behind Luke and lo and behold, there she is. No sexy as fuck dress this time, thank God, but her hair is down like that first night we met, a glorious auburn waterfall. I grip my glass so I have something cold and slippery to replace the hot and hard I know I shouldn't be feeling.

"What's up?" Luke frowns at me.

I sniff, take a drag of my beer, and shrug. Perfectly nonchalant. I'm pretty proud.

Luke isn't buying it. "You got something against my candidate?"

"Torres? Nah, he's fine. Another chatterbox like your little one." I mean Gage, the youngest Dempsey. "Fits right in."

"All the newbies are here tonight. Torres and some kid from over at 70 and Sullivan's girl. Wyatt said they were thick as thieves at the Quinn." Wyatt Fox is Luke's older brother, now a captain and an instructor at the academy. "What do you make of her?"

"Abby?" Fuck. All the new recruits go by their last name, so that sounds far too intimate. "Pretty nervous for her first day. She evened out, though."

I've never seen someone throw themselves into drills with such gusto. So she screwed up her knot because she was nervous. Still, I had to admire her gumption at trying to finagle her way back on the truck after I expressly told her to remain behind. She's probably cursing out the asshole LT to her friends this minute after spending the rest of the shift with a mop in her hand.

Better she thinks I'm a dick instead of about my dick.

"Heard her old man made waves at the academy," Luke says. "Tried to get her failed out."

I wonder if that's true. It sounds like the kind of shit-stirring people spread to make trouble. Maybe Abby Sullivan herself, to establish she's not a fox in the Engine 6 henhouse. The last thing I need is to get in between her and her father. It's bad enough her sweet mouth is paying rent in my head.

"Her old man is probably worried," I say. "I would be as well if it was my kid."

Luke nods. No one knows better than him the pain of losing a family member in the line of duty. Fourteen years ago, his father and foster brother died in a high-rise fire. Sean Dempsey was a legend and the loss was felt deeply throughout the department, the house, and the family. I know it, too, from my time in New York. I enlisted long after 9/11, but the cloud of emptiness still hovered for years, and we'd had our share of loss since.

"But we have to let the kids find their way," Luke says, all wise and shit. "Took me a while to get there. Hell, I didn't want Alex or Gage signing up, and they let me hear their thoughts, that's for sure. Gotta move with the times. So Old Man Sullivan can huff and puff all he wants. If his girl was good enough to get through the academy and she can put up with the shit thrown at her at the firehouse where her mother worked and died, then she deserves her place on our crew."

Luke's right. All the more reason to stay away because from the sound of it, Abby Sullivan is going nowhere.

Ten

Abby

I don't think I've ever been so shockingly aware of another human being—and he isn't even within ten feet of me.

Lieutenant Rossi is seated at the bar and hasn't glanced my way. Once. Perhaps he doesn't know I'm here. Jude spoke with him, offered a drink—or bribe, per Sam—and had been denied. No funny business with the LT.

I want some funny business. I want it bad.

I should be mad at him for slapping me with latrine duty all day yesterday, but apparently that's not enough to bank my lust. Probably because (a) I'm envious of his ability to separate the personal from the professional and (b) he was right. He's treating me exactly how he said he would—and that commitment to bias-free leadership, to doing his job and staying in charge of his emotions, is strangely attractive in its own right.

He's ignoring what happened between us and I'm weirdly turned on.

I'm such a loser.

Engaging with my superior officer is career suicide, and I've barely started my career. So, I'll be a good girl and squeeze my thighs together and try not to get all hot and bothered about the back of a guy's neck. How it's thick and tanned and positively lickable ...

"Earth to Abby?" My cousin Jackie waves in front of my face. After my mom died, I spent more time at my aunt and uncle's house than in my own because Dad worked 24 on/48 off like I do now. Jacks and I practically grew up together. "What is with you tonight?"

"Nothing!"

Jude's looking at me curiously. I'm pretty sure I've been keeping my eyes to myself, but maybe not.

"She's probably thinking about Diner Dude," Sam says slyly.

Jackie and Jude whip their heads my way and say in unison, "Who?"

I can feel heat rising to my face. "Just some guy I met the night of graduation at Fern's Diner."

"And you were going to text him? Did you?" Sam turns to the others. "She was pretty excited about it."

"It's not going to work out. He gave me a wrong number." Time for deflection. "So, Samuel, tell us about this latest woman of yours."

Sam squints. "You never want to hear about my adventures. You think everyone I date is ridiculous."

"More like gullible. I'm just glad I never have to date you." Not that I would even if Sam wasn't the wham-bam kind because firefighters are off the menu. Especially ones with dark, glossy hair and gorgeous, hazel-green eyes, who kiss like you're a source of oxygen ...

"Aw, but I wouldn't break your heart, Abby."

"That's a relief."

Sam grins. "Might break your bed, though. I'm that good."

Jackie bats her eyelashes in Sam's direction. "Oh, if I weren't married, Samuel ..."

Sam takes her hand and kisses her knuckles. "We can flirt, Jacks, but better not tell your bodybuilder husband. I like my pretty face."

"If I'm in the market for a good bout of bed-breaking sex," I say, "I'll keep you in mind." But Sam's attention has already latched onto the night's conquest.

This woman is sharp, with a Cleopatra bob and a royal attitude to match. She's just walked in with another woman, blond, also well-dressed. Two professional gals on the town. They head straight to the bar and Blondie taps Roman's shoulder.

He jumps up and hugs her.

Oh. I don't like that pinch of envy in my chest.

Two seconds later, introductions are being made. Blondie gestures to Cleo, and the LT offers his seat to her. That's nice of him. Maybe this is a continuation of that interrupted date from the other night. Maybe it's all resolved and ...

I don't need to see this. The little green monster is coating my insides and it's not pleasant. I refocus on the conversation at my table just as Jude drops this gem.

"So I heard something interesting about Rossi and your dad."

I jerk my attention to him. "What about them?"

Jude leans in. "Apparently a few months ago, they got into it at a callout. Rossi was reprimanded and there's been bad blood ever since."

"What happened?" I haven't been keeping up with my father's career though I imagine Chuck Sullivan angers scores of people on a daily basis.

"Not sure. Gage said it had to do with some sort of

territorial pissing contest. Not sure why your dad would even be there but maybe he turns up when the fires are big league. Makes it look like the brass are on the job 24/7."

That sounds like my father. Show up to grab the glory.

I line up another question, but Jude is no longer paying attention to me. He's watching the TV over the bar, not that it's possible to hear anything. From this angle, it looks like one of those sports shows where overprivileged frat bros shout at each other in two-minute increments. A photo of a bearded someone is on the screen and the talking heads are weighing in. Jude takes out his phone and taps the screen a few times.

I slide a glance to Sam who is still eyeing up the Queen of the Nile, not in this conversation at all.

"So glad I came out tonight. Love catching up with my boys."

Nothing. I share an amused glance with Jackie.

"I think maybe I'll get up on the bar and do a striptease."

Still no response. Sigh.

"I'm heading to the bathroom. You coming?" I ask my cousin.

"Hell, no. I'm going to chat up that hunk, Gage Simpson." Sure enough, Gage has just appeared at the end of the L-shaped bar, carrying a crate of bottles. She holds up a hand. "I don't care that he can never be interested. He fakes it better than these two."

Jude is still checking his phone and shooting glances at the TV, but gives me an absent nod. Sam doesn't hear me at all. He's monitoring the Rossi-Cleo situation, so I expect he'll give me a full report later, assuming he makes it back to the land of the living.

Five minutes later I come out of the bathroom and run smack bang into a wall of iron.

"Sorry—oh, hi." It's him, the lieutenant. He holds my arms to steady me.

Then he drops his hands like they've blistered and takes a step back.

"You okay?" he barks.

"Fine! Listen, I didn't come here thinking you'd be here. I didn't know you drank here."

"Well, it's the default watering hole for the engine, seeing as the Dempseys run it."

Put like that, it sounds like a criticism. Like I should have known he'd be here and should know better than to think I could avoid him. I suppose some small part of me realized it was a possibility. Wanted to see him outside the firehouse.

I'm not proud of it.

But his attitude gets my back up. The implication is not nice.

"I should get back to my friends." I go to skirt him, but he sidesteps and blocks my way.

"Abby," he murmurs, his voice a velvet rumble. "I didn't mean that to come out the way it did. Of course you're welcome to drink here. Anyone is, but especially crew members of Engine 6."

I cross my arms, feeling defensive. He's poked at something raw, and I don't like what it says about me more than what it says about him.

"Been practicing your clove hitch?"

I make my sourest face. "I can do that knot in my sleep. I don't know why I suddenly decided to make a mess of it."

"Different with an audience of your peers. You think I was too hard on you?"

"No, not at all. I've got to get it right. People depend on me getting it right."

His nod is approving and it makes me warm all over. I try to imagine not ever craving that and it gives me pause.

"And I realize I shouldn't have questioned your decision to take me off the run."

That surprises him. "Okay, glad you see it that way."

"And the silver lining is that now I know the inside of the bathrooms like the back of my hand. Have you heard that you can call someone nicknamed 'Baby Thor' for a good time and that Satin Rules?"

"Satin?"

"Satan's spelling-challenged cousin."

He wants to grin. The fight is playing out on his lips. "In the women's bathroom? Because I haven't seen those in the men's."

"Yeah, I soon learned that Baby Thor is Gage Simpson, so now I'm really confused. Maybe he wrote it himself."

"Right. Actually now I recall it's also in the men's bathroom because Baby Thor is nothing if not a shameless self-promoter."

I grin and it does the trick. His expression transforms from resting prick face to something I can work with.

Who am I kidding? I can work with the entire Rossi repertoire.

"If it makes you happy, you did a great job," he murmurs. "Could see my face in those toilet bowls."

I take a mock bow. "At your service, my liege."

That draws a low-graveled chuckle, my intention and hope. There I go again, craving his admiration.

His expression turns grave again. "Also, you didn't start your day well and if we're worrying about you being sick on a call, it distracts from business."

"Who would worry?" His grimace tells the story. "You don't need to worry about me."

"I worry about all the candidates but especially about ones who start their days puking their guts up and then forget how to tie a clove hitch. You'll get out there, but when I say you're ready."

Yet again, I'm aroused by his command of the situation.

He's the boss and that dynamic is doing strange things to my insides. I wonder what happened between him and my father—probably two bull-headed idiots locking horns—but I don't want to bring up Chuck Sullivan. Not now or ever.

I search for something else to say, anything to distract from the pleasurable tingle racing through my veins.

"Looks like your date showed up." That should do it.

He looks momentarily baffled. "Madison? That's no date."

"It's a space station?"

He appreciates the *Star Wars* reference. His eyes go all crinkly and my heart crinkles with it. Not good.

"She's a friend of Kinsey, Almeida's wife. I've never met her before and believe me when I say I am not in the market for dating right now."

"Giving up so soon, Lieutenant? Your sister won't like that."

"My sister will have to deal. Almeida and Kinsey, too." He leans against the wall, which in any other universe would look like he's settling in to chat. "It seems no one's happy until everyone's as miserable as they are."

That's a pretty cynical take. "Sounds like a tale."

"Not really. Just ..." He waves a hand to fill in the rest, and a touch of color spots his cheeks.

"It's okay, you don't have to tell me."

"Just left some baggage in New York. Or trying to."

The divorce. We all have pasts to forget, no reason to let it define us. Not that it makes a blind bit of difference here. The lieutenant and I would not be unpacking our luggage.

So I really shouldn't have asked, "Bad divorce?"

"You could say that."

"Sorry to be nosy." And then because I'm more curious than sorry, I add, "Your daughter lives with you?"

"She does."

His face goes all soft at the mention of her, and then I go all soft. Which is bad news for me because I need to harden every part of my being around this man.

He's here in a bar, out on a school night. *Carousing*, if you will, so maybe not Dad of the Year. I hold on to that to fortify my loins against the onslaught of incredibly hot alpha daddy male.

A door opens farther on down the corridor and Gage Simpson walks out. I have a good vibe from him—and he clearly has some sort of vibe from whatever is happening in this corridor. He flashes that famous hot stuff grin and passes us by.

Roman mutters something.

"What's that?"

"I said that's all I need." He seems to shake himself awake. "We good here?"

"Uh, you bumped into me and started drilling me."

"Drilling you?" Said as if I don't know the meaning of the word—or all it's possible meanings.

"Questions. Talking. I should get going." I gesture toward the bar, but then I say the dumbest thing. It comes out of nowhere, or somewhere deep and dangerous where secret dreams are stashed away. "Would you have called me?"

"Called you?" He frowns as awareness dawns. "After the diner?"

The moment is suspended, an asteroid hurtling toward the earth, and I'm waiting for someone to blow it to fragments.

"Probably not," he finally responds.

Wow. I did not expect that to hurt so much. *Don't ask if you're not going to be happy with the answer.*

With a curt nod, he's gone, and I realize he's taken a little piece of my stupid heart with him.

Eleven

Roman

I pick up the pace, pounding the lakeshore path to slough off some of this negative energy. I shouldn't feel this way. I've been doing just fine for the last few months, not thinking about my ex, devoting all my time to my job and my family. I didn't need anything else.

Then I ran into her at that diner and now it feels like all I need.

If it was just sex, it should be easy enough to come by. Now that some pathway in my brain has opened up to the possibility, and I recognize that I won't be getting it with the first woman I've been attracted to in years, I should be able to take the next step.

Fire up the apps, right? Because I sure as shit am not relying on Luke or Chiara to get me a woman. I need to go with one of those hookup sites, the ones that encourage you to declare your intentions up front. No dating, just fucking.

I want to think I can do that. That my identity as a dad, a family man, a leader of men and women, doesn't change the fundamentals of need. I should be able to hook up, get my kicks, and move on.

I run faster, wondering if I'm trying to outpace the part of me that doesn't want that. That wants to eat pie with a certain redhead and talk silly stuff that wriggles inside to the deep stuff. The other night I actually shared some of drama with her in Dempseys'. Two minutes in her presence and I want to tell her things I don't speak of with anyone else.

Which is not good. After I recovered—or didn't—from the shock of her asking if I would have followed up after that first night, I'd said the only thing I could.

Probably not.

Because what would be the point of telling her otherwise? Of giving any hint that but for our current employment situation I would probably have been in her bed at that very moment, sliding into the hot, wet heart of her while my fingers tunneled through that gorgeous red hair and my body lost itself in the mindless joy of fucking hard and deep.

No. Better to cut off that avenue of thinking altogether. This way, we can both move on to other people.

Hopefully, for her, that won't include anyone at the firehouse. Danny Acosta is definitely interested, and while relationships between co-workers on the same shift technically should be reported, they happen all the time on the down low. Anything between a supervisor and his direct report is trickier, and usually requires a shift or house switch so there's no impact on operations or accusations of favoritism—or even retribution if it goes sour.

Not that it would ever get to that point, but it's good to think through the logistics and how it would affect my job and the life I'm trying to rebuild if I were to think about taking it further. So yeah, good thing it went no further than a kiss.

Shaking the screws loose, I leave the path and head up Foster to Clark, but because it's busy and I want to maintain my pace, I cut down Catalpa. Which is how I find myself outside Fern's Diner.

Pie after a run is probably a really bad idea, but coffee? The Starbucks on Clark is just a couple of blocks away but I like the idea of sitting at the diner's counter for a few minutes. I could say I'm doing it to support a local business or because the place has good memories for me. But really I'm doing it as a warning: *messing with Abby Sullivan could turn everything you're trying to build to rubble.*

I should go home and shower first but once I do that I'll be back in the real world and I won't want to come back here. It's a little cooler today and I've barely broken a sweat, so I'm probably not offensive to anyone in the fragrance department. While weighing these decisions, I hear a voice I'd previously been imagining in my more illicit fantasies.

"You trying to decide if it's too early for pie?"

I check the reflection in the window: Abby is standing there with that crooked half grin and those blue eyes, big in her pale, freckled face. She's wearing an open running jacket and shorts, and one of those cropped tanks that shows amazing cleavage, the existence of which I should not even be acknowledging. For a moment, I wonder if I conjured her out of my dirty imagination.

Bravely, I pivot to face her and avoid looking at her legs, which are long and toned. I bet she has freckles on the soft skin of her inner thighs. I bet my tongue would love to find out.

"I was trying to decide if I'm too sweaty for company."

She looks me up and down, then steps in closer. "You're probably good. Or I could bring something out for you, like water for a dog."

"So kind. Think I'll risk sitting at the counter and trying not to offend anyone."

"Or have breakfast with me and we get to score a booth!"

Her lean-in is conspiratorial. Unlike me, she smells fantastic, like pears or something. Maybe her shampoo, but probably all her. "Fern doesn't allow singles in the booths. Only two or more."

"You want to use me like I'm the car pool lane of diners?"

She shrugs. "Maybe I can pick your brain about my supervisor."

I stuff a smile down to where I'm currently repressing my lust. "Asshole, is he?"

"The worst. You probably know exactly how to handle that type."

"Takes one to know one. Could probably give the new kid some of my hard-earned wisdom."

It was the best of ideas, the worst of ideas ... but it didn't have to mean anything more than two co-workers chatting about their jobs.

A couple of minutes later we're seated in a booth, perusing menus. The same server who waited on us a week ago stops at the table and grins.

"Well, well, well, what do we have—"

"Nope," Abby cuts her off. "We have nothing."

The server—her name tag says 'Ethel' but I'm guessing that's supposed to be funny—screws up her mouth. "We don't?"

Abby shakes her head. "This is Roman. He's my boss at the firehouse. Roman, you remember Tessa, instigator and pie purveyor?"

Tessa's expression assumes a knowing look. "And the other night, you two—"

"Were unaware that this was in our future," I finish for her. In case she thinks to say something that hints at what could have happened after we left the diner. I don't need to be reminded of that kiss or all the lost potential because if I think about it too hard, I'll go fucking crazy.

Or crazier.

"Coffee?"

"Coffee," we both agree, relieved that we've navigated that slice of awkward. We order breakfast—me the huevos rancheros, her the three-egg skillet.

I stir my coffee and wait a second to let things settle.

"How was your run?"

"Unsatisfying."

She looks up. "How come?"

"I thought I could let off some—it doesn't matter. I'll probably hit the gym later to finish what the run couldn't do."

"Yeah, I know we're expected to put in a couple of hours working out on each shift. I usually run as well on off days."

There's just one Splenda packet in the sweetener caddy. I dig it out and pass it across. "Let me know the next time you're out. If you're looking for a running partner."

I'm clearly on a death wish for my balls.

"Think that'll make your runs more satisfying?" She grins and my pulse booms.

Jesus, what am I doing here? She's giving no hint that I upset her the other night at the bar when I told her I wouldn't have called her. We've worked a couple of shifts since and she's adjusting well, working in sync with the crew, chatty when she needs to be, listening when appropriate.

In other words, she's definitely over the awkward hump created by whatever energy existed between us before. I need to find a way to scale that mountain as well.

She wants advice. I can do that. "So, how did you find your first week on the job?"

We chit-chat about the work, our firehouse colleagues, city politics that affect CFD, and the differences between Chicago and New York. Tessa arrives with our food, so we spend a couple of minutes taking first bites and commenting on our excellent meal choices.

After a moment, I ask, "Tell me how you got here. To Engine 6."

She wipes her mouth with a napkin. "It's in my blood, I suppose. My parents—well, you know." She touches that pendant around her neck, a reflexive gesture.

"You get that from your mom?"

"Yeah, I did. She was wearing it the night she died." She bites her lip. "It's strange to be stationed at her house."

"You asked for that assignment?"

"I did. Maybe that's putting too much pressure on myself but I feel like it's another way to stay closer to her. Once she died, my dad didn't really like to talk about her."

That's got to be tough. My heart keens for her, but before I can offer anything more than a sympathetic look, she flips the conversation.

"What about you? How did you get into the service?"

"Not a family thing. I grew up in the Bronx and got into a lot of trouble as a kid."

"What kind of trouble?"

"The usual. Stealing, joyriding, vandalism. Had a local cop straighten me out and point me in the direction of the FDNY. But really the impetus to get my act together was my daughter being born. Kids tend to change your mindset and becoming a dad at twenty-one is a real wake-up call."

She nods, assessing me with those electric blue eyes that seem to know all my secrets. "And you got married."

"Yeah. As soon as I saw Lena in all her red-faced, wrinkled, new baby smell glory, I was a goner. I liked Tori—her mom—well enough and thought that was the best way to make a stable environment for my daughter. But my ex wasn't really the marrying kind. Her heart was never in it and we split up a couple of times. Tried again for the sake of Lena, then this last time, it just didn't stick. Or rather the split did." I rub my mouth. "How do you do that?"

"What?"

"Make me spill my guts like I'm in therapy? There are fifty million reasons why I should not be laying this on you."

"The boss thing? We can be friends as well, can't we?"

Friends. Maybe that's what I need. Someone I can talk to, who won't judge. But I have a feeling I'd be crossing the line before the friendship bracelets are woven and wrapped around our wrists.

"Enough about me. Tell me about this asshole CO of yours."

She grins at my deflection that happens to bring it right back to me. "Oh, where do I start? He's kind of grouchy, one of those abrupt New York types, y'know?"

"I'm sure he has his reasons."

"To make my life miserable!" She splays a hand over her collarbones and makes a dramatic face that pulls a laugh from me. I like that she's not bitter about the punishment I set her.

"I just want to learn," she adds. "And I don't want to miss an opportunity."

"Then you know the score. Watch and listen."

"That's what Alex Dempsey said. She left me a letter, talking about what a good LT you are."

That's unexpected. Alex Dempsey is a great firefighter. A bit of a hothead like her brother Luke but she has excellent instincts.

"They're good people, the Dempseys. Good at their jobs, too. You can learn a lot from Gage."

"And from you."

I'm strangely humbled by this. Mentoring my crew is one of the great pleasures I get from my work. I don't want to put any of that in jeopardy by playing favorites or disrupting my concentration.

"So, can I ask something?"

I look up in surprise. Nothing good—or safe—ever follows that kind of query. "Sure."

"Someone said you had a run-in with my father at a scene. What happened?"

Didn't expect that. I'm not sure if I should tell her because I hate the idea of her going back to her dad about it, but neither do I want to lie.

"About two months ago we were on a callout to a house fire in Logan Square. Our truck was first on site and we were setting up when someone pulled up in an SUV. A civilian." Her eyes spark in recognition, already suspecting where the story is going. "Or who I thought was a civilian."

"Really?"

"Uh huh. It was dark. I'd never met him, though I'd seen photos of him in his uniform. He didn't look like his photo."

"Does anyone?" She bites her lip. "Sorry, not trying to excuse it. So he tried to take over the scene?"

"In a manner of speaking. Demanded to know what my plan was. I told him to step aside to let us do our work."

She grimaces. "Did no one else clue you in?"

"They were busy, doing their jobs. Anyway, he said he was the commissioner. At this point I recognized him but I was so pissed that he was stepping into the middle of an active call that I basically told him to remove himself from the scene or I would have him removed."

Her hand flies to her mouth. "No!"

With hindsight it sounds amusing. The dressing down I got when Commissioner Sullivan stopped by Engine 6 the next morning wasn't quite as funny.

"Anyway, he let Venti have it." Venti is the nickname for Captain Matt Ventimiglia, Engine 6's head honcho. "Said I needed to be more respectful of authority and that I was on my last warning."

"What about a first warning?"

I blow out a breath, unsure about how much I should get into here. I figure I can come at it by the back roads.

"How well do you get along with your father?"

That surprises her. "Why do you ask?"

"There are rumors swirling about his support—or lack of—for your candidacy in CFD. That it's caused a rift."

She studies me from beneath the veil of her lashes, probably wondering how much I can be trusted. I see the moment when she relaxes enough to open up.

It's exhilarating.

"It's not really a secret that he doesn't want me in the service. He's erected roadblocks at every opportunity, told the instructors at the academy to put me through my paces, made it clear I shouldn't get any special treatment. In fact, I should be pushed harder so I wouldn't feel exceptional or think I had an in."

It's not far off from what I'd been told. "I assume this stems from fear because of what happened to your mother."

"That's what he says. Sure it's a dangerous job but anything could happen to me off the job. This is what I want. It's all I've ever wanted. I was born to do this."

Her desire to succeed is a living, breathing thing. I hear from guys all the time who say they want to save lives, make a difference, score with chicks. Abby wants this because it's in her blood.

"So you two aren't talking right now?"

"He didn't even call me when I started at Engine 6." Her father's resistance has really hurt her and again, something lurches in my chest. "You've met him, he's not an easy man."

This is true. I suppose I needed to know more about their relationship before I explain how he has the ability to really fuck up my career.

"You asked me about a first warning or why Commissioner Sullivan said I was on my last. I left FDNY under somewhat of a cloud. Got into it with my captain there because of some personal stuff, so that follows me."

The New York brass would have been happy to move me to another firehouse after how I screwed up. But by that point, my marriage was over, my family was in ruins, and my sister offered me a lifeline in Chicago. I did the necessary recertifications and training at Engine 6, and when the time came to appoint a new LT, I jumped at the chance. My experience in the service outweighed my mistake in taking on my captain with a fist.

"I was lucky to get the transfer. I started at a lower rank but got the promotion fairly quickly. I can't screw up because this is my last shot. My kid needs stability."

She's staring at me, all big-eyed sympathy and I want to curl up in a ball and rewind to five minutes ago when she didn't know this about me.

"You need the stability, too."

"What? No, that's not—sure, but we all do. Well, maybe not you, Ms. Adrenaline Junkie who climbs mountains for fun."

She laughs, that husky sound that goes straight to parts of me that would stand out in running shorts. "That's just for extracurricular. For my job, I need it. I want to know where I stand and that if I do my job well, I'll be rewarded. Treated the same as everyone else. So I won't be doing anything that threatens that."

From that statement, I deduce that Abby Sullivan will not be:

Gossiping about firehouse politics with her dad.

Kissing me like I'm her reason for breathing.

Giving her CO grief that makes him want to meet her challenge with a good, hard fuck against the wall of my office.

We both have things to lose. I'm acutely aware of the

damage that could be done if we indulge this ... whatever this is.

And hell if it doesn't feel like something. Sentient and alive with heated potential. A knot behind my breastbone affirms that the wrongness of wanting Abby doesn't quite cancel out the rightness of that kiss.

Of all the thoughts I've had today, that's the most dangerous.

Twelve

Abby

I feel like I've managed to emerge from a deep, dark abyss of longing into the cool, fresh light of normality. That breakfast with Roman assured me I can exist in the same space as this guy and not be constantly confronted with a missed opportunity. Clearly he wants to put the kiss behind us, which is awesome. I love moving on. I live for a forward trajectory. Hooray for progress!

After two weeks on the job, I'm finding my groove, learning on every shift and bonding with my crew. And if a small part of me aches (which I insist is sexual, and therefore transitory) when I see Roman in the lounge at the start of each shift, I ignore it and throw myself into the Morning Debate with gusto. When asked if I'd rather talk like Yoda or breathe like Darth Vader, firmly in the Yoda camp I am. This morning's question posed the stumper of whether we'd rather have spaghetti for hair or sweat mayonnaise. Spaghetti all the way, baby. I'll even condition it with tomato sauce as long as I don't have to sweat Hellman's.

We kicked off the shift with an RTA—road traffic accident—and an assist with an elderly woman who got trapped in her basement, the poor dear. After lunch, another Gage Simpson culinary masterpiece, we're on our way to a cat-in-tree call in Ukrainian Village.

I know it's not a cat in a tree, but people keep insisting it is and no one's giving me the skinny, so I keep quiet and listen while Danny smack talks Paul Wozniak, aka Woz, because of some woman who's giving him the runaround. Gage is driving the truck, Tyler is beside him, and the lieutenant is sitting opposite me with his eyes all gunfighter-squinty and one ear on the conversation.

After some back and forth about how Woz's lady friend spent much of the previous evening flirting with some guy who was not Woz while they played pool, Danny declares his Zeus-like judgment.

"Total skank."

"Hey, watch your mouth," Roman immediately shoots back, much to the surprise of the entire crew.

Danny flicks a worried glance my way. "Uh, sorry, Abby."

"No need to reel it in for my sake." While I'm not a fan of anyone referring to another woman in such derogatory terms, neither do I want my presence changing the crew dynamic. Team bonding and building are important. The crew shouldn't have to censor themselves because of the shape of my genitals.

"They need to reel it in for my sake."

All eyes fix on Roman when he says that. I feel foolish, like I've gone along sheep-like just to gain approval from the people with penises.

Wozniak sniffs. "Yeah, when you have a daughter, I get why that kind of language would offend." He slides a smug glance of *you're in trouble now* at Danny.

"What's it got to do with having a daughter?" Roman's

expression is hard and flinty and a total turn-on. *Not now, hormones.* "Are female relatives a necessity in order to reconsider your frame of reference and the junk that comes out of your mouth, Wozniak?"

"Ah, no, that's not—I mean—" He looks to Danny, who uttered the offending comment in the first place. No help from that quarter. "Sure, I have sisters and a mother and—"

Roman growls, now even more annoyed at Woz's take, which is rotting with each unfortunate word out of his mouth. "And you live on this earth with women who are people deserving of your respect, no matter whether you're related to them or work with them or are dating them. Not to say you can't gripe and grumble about your woman, but I don't want to hear any of those gendered insults. Got it?"

The truck draws to a halt and Wozniak mutters, "Yep, Lieutenant. Got it." The word *lieutenant* drips with so much sarcasm we're practically wading in it.

We pile out onto the sidewalk with Roman barking orders. "Sullivan, you're with me. Bring the first-aid kit."

"Yes, LT." I look around, still not sure what the situation is. No smoke, no fire, no sign of a vic in distress. "What've we got?"

"I think you're going to enjoy this one."

I follow him through a side gate into the backyard of a three-story walk-up. There's another gate, waist-high and closed, and a woman standing on the street-side of the fence.

"Hey, miss, how are ya?" Roman asks.

"Better than my idiot brother." She thumbs over her shoulder in the direction of a large tree taking up a sizable portion of the yard. "He didn't want me to get you guys involved but hell if I'm going in there."

Roman calls out, "How you doin' up there?"

"Just fine," someone calls back.

From the tree.

There's a guy sitting on the first rung of thick branches, about six feet up. Now I get it: cat-in-tree. That's when I sense movement in the yard. "Wait, is that a ... pig?"

Sure enough, looking remarkably unbothered by the situation, a pig is chewing on a leafy plant near the back of the yard. This isn't some cute pot-bellied citified animal, though. It's large, hairy, and mean-looking.

I murmur as low as I can, "Did we get called out to save a guy from a pig?"

Roman's mouth twitches. "Nobody ever calls the fire department for doing something smart." He looks over his shoulder. "Simpson, where's animal control?"

"On the way." Gage finger-quotes that. "ETA forty minutes. Short-staffed, and apparently there's a snake problem on the South Side."

"'Course there is." Roman shouts out, "Sir, are you injured?"

"The monster bit him!" As soon as the sister opens her mouth, the pig squeals.

"It's just a scratch," Guy-in-tree says, his voice taking on a wheezy whine. "Betsey is feeling a bit off today because that *witch* was taunting her." The "witch" is the sister, I'm guessing. "You better keep those animal control people away! Don't hurt her!"

"She ate one of my Chicago Rebels socks," the sister counters, resulting in another shriek from the pig. There's definitely history between this woman and her brother's porcine buddy.

"Stay here," Roman mutters as if anyone was thinking of going anywhere. He hops over the gate in a fluid movement, no awkward scramble for him.

"If it's rabid ..." Gage offers, stepping into the space beside me that Roman vacated. He yells toward the tree, "Has your pig had its shots?"

"I don't believe in that kind of thing. Goes against nature," the owner calls out. The owner who's stuck in a tree, mind you, because the pig he's keeping in a tiny Chicago backyard has driven him there.

"Great, we have an anti-vaxxer pig guy." Gage says to Roman, "Don't get bit!"

"That's your advice?" Roman shoots back. "Christ, you should be in the fucking fire department."

I lean on the gate, watching the pig with one eye and Roman's careful approach with the other. "So we've got a wild pig, maybe a boar—"

"You think that's a boar?"

"I told him it was, but he didn't care!" The sister again.

Gage is on his phone and soon has pics. "You're right, a boar. Is that even allowed in the city limits?"

"There's no municipal ordinance prohibiting it," the sister says, ever informative. "I checked."

Gage is aghast. "Really? We're leaving these decisions to the Chicago citizenry? *The people*, in case you haven't figured it out yet, Abs, are the worst decision-makers on the planet."

"We are indeed in the stupidest timeline," I observe. If someone wants to keep weird animals in their back yards, they'll do it. It's almost unAmerican *not* to.

Roman is standing below the tree. "Can I see your injury?"

The owner shows his arm reluctantly, as if he doesn't want to drop Betsey in it. Too late, mate, it's a bloody mess. Tree Guy sways but manages to hold on to a thick branch.

"Catch him," the sister yells after the fact, which only gets the pig more riled.

"Ma'am," I say. "You might feel better if you moved back to the street."

Gage is less tactful. "Your voice is pissing off the pig."

Roman orders, "Need a ladder in here!"

Wozniak and Danny are behind us with the ladder. "Open the gate," Danny calls out.

"Not a good idea." I'm already scrambling over. "We can't risk letting this animal loose." Right now, it's calmly sniffing some shrubbery at the other end of the yard except for the odd shriek whenever his nemesis, the sister, opens her mouth. Maybe it's already satisfied its bloodlust by taking a bite out of Pig Guy's arm. I'll take my chances but don't want to risk him running amok in the neighborhood.

"She's right." Following me, Gage hops over the gate and directs the crew to maneuver the ladder over the fence.

We two-man walk the ladder over to the tree and settle it against the trunk. Roman turns to me. "All right, Sullivan, up you go."

"Really?"

"Yeah, you spent four years as a paramedic and it's time you earned that fine salary the city is paying you. Be like your hero, Tom Cruise."

I barely have time to register the fact he's referencing a conversation we had in the before times because he's already indicating how this will go. "I'll brace the ladder and Simpson is going to run interference on our bite-y friend."

Gage slams his dark blond eyebrows together. "And by run interference ...?"

"Throw yourself in its path if it comes for us."

"Thought that's what you meant."

Roman flashes a half grin and wow, I almost fall out of my own mental tree.

"No heroics, Simpson, just let me know if it makes any sudden moves. First, take a walk over to the gate and tell the New Wave Feminists to manage the crowd."

I hide a smile, knowing he's talking about Danny and Wozniak. Over at the gate, a queue of onlookers is forming behind them. A few faces can also be glimpsed at the windows of the second and third floors of the building. Firefighters often have an audience but we don't usually think about that while the adrenaline is high and we're working to save someone. This feels different, the kind of call that might make the news.

I can't wait to tell Sam and Jude.

"Sullivan, why are you still here?"

"Okay, got it." I head up the ladder, my supplies over my shoulder. When I reach Tree Guy, I pull my bag to the front and settle it on a ladder rung. "Hey, I'm Abby, what's your name?"

"Colin." The name is given reluctantly. Probably one of those anti-government types who hates the idea of the authorities being involved in his personal business. "You're not going to hurt Betsey, are you?"

"Not if we can help it. Right now, we need to take care of you. Let's take a look."

It's an animal bite, all right, and will definitely need stitches. For now, all I can do is clean it as best I can, apply antiseptic, and wrap it up so no more dirt gets in.

"How we doin' up there, Abby?" Roman's voice is low and soothing and designed to keep everyone, including the damn pig, calm.

"Just fine. We're almost wrapped up and ready to come down."

"I'm not going down," Colin says because of course he wouldn't want to make any of this simple.

His sister decides now would be a good time to get re-involved. "Colin, stop being an asshole and get out of that tree!"

"This is your fault," Colin spits back. "You know she doesn't like anyone who doesn't respect her!"

Okay, time to call this. "I understand you might be a bit worried but you're going to need stitches and I can't do that up here. We need to get you out to the street to work with the paramedics."

Colin looks torn, which is some mighty weird ambivalence for a guy trapped by his pig in a tree. But it seems circumstances are about to overtake us.

"Shit, she's on the move," Roman says quietly.

I have my back to the pig, but during the next eight seconds, all I hear is a thundering gallop and then a loud, "Oh, fuck!" from Gage. The weight of the ladder shifts and I look down to see Roman is three rungs up.

"Hey, there, you okay?" I want to laugh about this because Roman is obviously not okay. He had to leave the safety of the ground because it was no longer the place to be. The sound of running and gasps from the crowd Danny and Wozniak have not managed to control has me itching to turn. Out of the corner of my eye I see Gage clamber over the fence to safety.

Roman shakes his head and flashes me another heart-stopping grin. So much for moving on. That grin hurtles me back to that night and undoes all my hard-won progress.

"This might take a while, Sullivan."

I'm starting to see that it might.

Thirteen

Abby

"Hey, Mom," I whisper to the image on the wall. "How's it going?"

She doesn't answer, but that's okay. It's enough to know she's watching over me. Or at least I hope as much.

I've stopped off to visit her on each shift for the last couple of weeks, trying my best not to look like a weirdo if someone happens by at the same time. All's quiet right now, a lull after our triumphant return to the firehouse a few hours ago. Betsey the pig was finally taken into custody, Colin was patched up by the medics, and we spent the return journey giving Gage and Roman shit for running scared as soon as the pig decided to go for a jog.

I felt useful today and my arm still tingles from where Roman patted it afterward with a gruff, "Good work, Sullivan." Before today, I was doing so well, ignoring the sensual pulse that hits my body whenever I see him, but now my mind and hormones are muddy again. Having the hots for my boss sucks and has the potential to interfere in my grand plan.

I've wanted this career for as long as I can remember. Mom would come home, bringing with her smoke-scented hair and clothes, and stories about the jobs she worked. In those days, there was a clearer delineation between firefighters and paramedics, and firefighters worked more fire suppression calls. There were no separate bathing facilities for women, either, so she preferred to wait until she got off her shift. She would make me breakfast, sitting with me before school, asking if I had done my homework.

I would lie and say I had. Really, I'd been up all night listening to the emergency services scanner, trying to pinpoint which calls my mom was on. And in the morning, I was finally able to breathe easy because Jo Sullivan had returned to me safe and sound.

Until the morning she didn't.

A movement startles me. A girl of about eleven or twelve is beside me, staring at the wall.

"Hi, there," I say.

"Hey," she says back. "I'm Lena."

"I'm Abby."

She takes my offered hand, shakes once, and releases. A grown-up grip. With her dark-haired pixie cut and cool hazel-green eyes, she looks like she should be casting spells. Her T-shirt says "I Paused My Game To Be Here."

"Are you new?" she asks.

"Yeah, a couple of weeks. How about you? Signing up for the fire service?"

She raises an eyebrow. If I'd had any doubt about her identity, that eyebrow would have clued me in. "I'm eleven so, no. Though my dad says I can do anything I want except ..."

"Firefighting?"

"Day trading. He says day traders are bro-tastic douchebags."

I laugh because that's completely true. Out of the mouths of babes and Lieutenant Rossi.

"You want to follow in your dad's bootsteps?"

"Maybe. It's kind of a cool job, but I really want to be a video game designer."

"That sounds amazing."

She smiles, and there it is: heartbreaker alert.

"Only my aunt Chiara thinks I'll have a hard time meeting a girl if I go into video games." That must be the matchmaking sister who was eager to push Roman "out there." "She thinks everyone would be better off with a girlfriend so it might be better to go into a more female-centric profession. Like dental assistants or ..." She eyes me, anticipating my contribution.

"Soccer?"

Approving nod. "Or softball. Chiara and Devi met at a softball game. That's where all the quality lesbians hang out according to my aunt."

"Good to know. If you're a lesbian."

"I don't think I am but I'm keeping my options open." She squints at the wall, her gaze fixed on my mother's photo. "Who's that?"

"Joanne Sullivan. She was a firefighter who"—*uh, don't talk about dead firefighters to the little girl of a live one*—"worked at this station about 20 years ago."

"She died. That's what happened to everyone on this wall."

I swallow my emotion. "Yeah, she did. She was my mom."

Something flickers in her eyes. "My mom's not around either."

I know she's not dead but maybe it seems that way when you can't see her regularly. "Sucks, right?"

She shrugs.

"Lena!" We both turn at the sound of his voice, me a little too eagerly. I have to stop doing that, like I'm a puppy happy to see my owner.

"Hey, Dad. We brought cake."

"You did?" Roman cuts a glance to me, then back to his daughter. "How'd you get here? Teleport?"

"No," she says patiently. "Aunt Chiara brought me, but she's finishing up a phone call in the car. I made lemon pound cake." She holds up a bag that's been sitting at her feet. "Abby's going to have some."

"I am?"

"Of course. It's cake. It'll make you feel better." She sends an unsubtle glance toward the wall.

Roman divides a look between us. His eyes stray to my mom's photo, then back to me for a beat. There's an odd comfort in it. He says to his daughter, "Come on into the lounge then."

"Could we go to your office?" Lena grasps his hand. "The lounge is noisy."

"Sure." He looks down at their joined hands, and something on his face softens. Something in my reproductive area, too. A moment later, he looks over her head at me. "You still in, Sullivan?"

"Free cake? Hell yeah." I mouth *sorry* as that sounds a bit profane in front of the kid.

Roman smiles his forgiveness and lets his daughter drag him toward his office.

🔥

Two minutes later, we're seated with cake on plates. Real, fancy ones that Lena has brought from home. She even has a cake knife and slice. A woman after my own heart.

I grab one of the forks from the table. "You usually travel with cake prep, Lena?"

"You never know when there'll be a cake opportunity. A cake-ortunity." She grins. "I like making up words."

"That's a cool one. Anything with cake in it usually is."

I take a small sliver of cake just in case it's bad. You never know with kids or even adults. I needn't have worried. The lemon zest explodes on my tongue while the lightness of the sponge fills me with the joy of cake.

"Holy bake-off, that's good!"

"You sound surprised," Roman deadpans as he pops a larger chunk into his mouth, indicating complete trust in the process.

I ignore the snark. "You're very talented, Lena."

"You guys started without me?"

A dark-haired woman appears at the door, the famous Aunt Chiara, I assume. She has gorgeous hazel eyes like her brother, though right now, they're a touch red and bloodshot.

I stand. "Have my seat."

Roman rises at the same time. "Abby, sit. Chiara, I know you'd prefer the boss chair."

"Wow, it's like we're related or something." Chiara takes Roman's chair, twirls around in it, knocks over a garbage can, and raises her arms in victory. Leaning across the desk with an outstretched hand, she says, "I'm Chiara, the elder of this twinset."

"You're twins?" I shoot a quick look at Roman who has taken up a casual lean against the wall with a look of concern directed his sister's way. He catches me and I avert my glance back to Chiara. "Clearly you got the looks."

Lie. They're both gorgeous.

"Oh, I like you."

"I'm Abby. Cake person. Hanger on. Somehow managed to angle an invite to the best party in town."

Lena digs into her cake. "Abby thinks I should play softball with lesbians."

"Didn't say that exactly," I mumble around another morsel of delicious cake.

Chiara smiles and there it is, a mirror of her brother. They're both dark and striking. Lena looks just like her dad, too, except more mischievous. Pixie-like.

I'd never call Roman a pixie, at least not to his face.

"So, Abby," Chiara says, "you're the new recruit, right?"

I nod, still chewing. "Yep, been on the job for all of two weeks."

"How are you finding this guy as a boss?"

I avoid looking at him, though my awareness of his presence has risen by several notches now that we are in the company of others. I have to fight every instinct not to run my eyes over his painful beauty, and that effort is costing me heartbeats and substantial peace of mind.

"Could be worse," I say diplomatically.

"Don't know about that. He was so bossy when we were kids—"

"And you caught up real quick," Roman says.

Lena turns to me. "It's true. Aunt Chiara likes to order people about."

"Defamed!" Chiara points a fork at the resident baker. "I am sweetness and light, kind of like this cake. Good job, favorite niece."

"Only niece," Lena returns with a grin.

I snag Roman's gaze and try not to get caught up in that soft pride he wears as he regards his family. I give myself three seconds to enjoy it but I retreat too late. He catches me again, sending my body into a heated glow.

I search for something to cool me down. How about the comedy stylings of B-Platoon? "Did you hear about your dad and the boar?"

Lena's eyes light up. "There was a boar?"

"Oh, yeah. Your dad got stuck on a ladder trying to escape from it."

"Hello, I was trying to protect *you* on that ladder."

I smile up at him. "Sure you were, Lieutenant. More like trying not to get eaten." I turn to my captive audience. "This guy on the West Side had a boar in his backyard, but really the boar had him. It bit him and chased him up a tree."

"Then chased *us* up a tree," Roman adds in that laconic way of his.

We spend a couple of minutes regaling the crowd with the Tale of Betsey the Boar, taking it in turns to describe the CFD's valiant efforts to corral it.

"Thought we were done for..."

"Never seen Gage Simpson move so fast..."

"Think bacon will be on the breakfast menu tomorrow..."

And so on, until Chiara and Lena are laughing their heads off, and I realize something like twenty minutes has passed.

Happy that I've managed to overcome any awkwardness in the presence of the man I have a serious hard-on for, I place the cake plate down on his desk. "I'd better head back to work. I have a truck to clean."

"Orders from your meanie boss, I suppose." Chiara smiles at me. "Nice to meet you, Abby."

"You, too." I hold out a fist bump for Lena. "Good talking to you, Lena. Thanks for the cake."

She gives me a light tap back and nods, her mouth still full.

"Lieutenant." I offer the *hey-co-worker* chin jerk to Roman and leave, feeling weirdly honored to have been part of that for a few lovely moments.

Fourteen

Roman

I try my damnedest not to look at Abby as she leaves my office, and I assume I'm doing a pretty good job until I clash eyeballs with my sister.

"She seems nice."

"Sure, she's a good candidate."

"Candidate for ..." She leaves it hanging and gives me that knowing look I understand so well. "Hey, Lena, we should rinse these plates off and leave the cake for the rest of the crew. Run along to the kitchen and I'll follow."

"Okay, though I assume 'we' means 'you' in this case." Lena stands and hugs me. "I know when Bossypants wants to talk with you alone."

I hold on to her, glad that she's still showing me affection. She'll start to see me as the enemy soon enough so these moments are ones I cherish.

"See you tomorrow, fragolina. And thanks for the cake. Another winner."

Chiara blinks at me once Lena has left. "What's with you and the probie?"

"We call them candidates here." Ignoring the meat of her question, I run a hand over my mouth, which is about the guiltiest I can possibly look.

"She's cute, funny, and seems like a tough cookie. Pretty awesome combo."

I don't need anyone telling me how great Abby is. "She's the daughter of the CFD Commissioner, so I need to watch her ass like a hawk and ensure nothing happens to her. It's like having a British royal on my crew."

Chiara opens her mouth but I strike first.

"Why were you crying?"

"What? No, just—" She deflates right before my eyes. "Devi met someone in Paris."

"Fuck, really?"

She nods and then next thing I know she's in my arms, sobbing into my shoulder. I knew things were tricky between them but I figured it was the pressure of long-distance and that it would work itself out.

"She wants a divorce."

I close my eyes and hold even tighter. I know this pain and I would never wish it on anyone, except maybe the asshole who slept with my wife and my good friend who covered it up, both of them colleagues at my old firehouse in New York.

"You don't think you two can figure it out?"

She shakes her head. "I—I don't know. I don't think so. She's found this other person and even if she admits to making a mistake, she still thought this other person was better than me for a while." Leaning back, she thumps her breastbone with her fist. "Than me, Roman! If that's the road she's gone down, where I'm not her number one, then fuck that noise."

Her burst of anger seems to lift her out of her gloom. It'll be a while but she'll make it through, and I'll be right there with her.

"Anything you need, pulce."

She slaps my arm. "You know I hate that!"

"Why? It's exactly what you are. An annoying little flea."

She growls, affirming my sis is back, if only for the moment. Deliberately, she returns to her seat, places her hands together in her lap, and looks up at me.

"Now that ridiculosity is out of the way, we're back to you and the probie. I felt this weird vibe between you two."

"It's nothing. It can't be."

Dark eyes go wide. Damn, my mouth is getting me into trouble again.

"Because she's your underling? Some stupid fraternization rule, I suppose." She twitches her nose, thinking it through with whatever weird logic she feels like applying to this situation. "But I've never seen you all cozy and flirty, finishing each other's sentences. Not even with la diavolessa." Chiara likes to assign demonic traits to my ex. "Is it because you haven't had a woman in a while so this one you're in close quarters with is getting you all riled up?"

"I'm not so desperate for female companionship that hanging in the firehouse with the only woman here has me foaming at the mouth."

"So you're a rock against the winds of temptation!" She thumbs over her shoulder. "Except when you're not."

This situation is too explosive for me to confide in a coworker, and all my friends happen to work here. I need a woman's opinion even if that woman is my sister.

"It's complicated."

"Tell me about it." She waves at me. "No, really. Tell me about it."

"Remember the night I got stood up but I met someone else at the diner?"

"Yeah, you were all bright-eyed and tipsy on good vibes and hot kisses ..." Realization hits her dramatically. The hands go up. The eyes flash vividly. "No! You didn't know who she was?"

"Nope. Two days later, she's here, starting her new job, and I'm her supervisor. So nothing can happen. Lives depend on it. Literally."

She opens her mouth. Closes it again. She wants to fix it because that's what family does but even she has to see what a bad idea this is.

I hold a hand up before she can start making a case. "There was a connection, but that's it. I'm not missing out on anything. Her showing up here is the universe telling me it's not meant to be."

She snorts. "That's the message you're getting from the universe? I think you need to recalibrate your transmitter, bro."

🔥

I head toward the lounge, deciding at the last second to make a detour to the truck bay, to check on how that wash-down is going. Abby's there alone with a bucket of soapy water and a sponge, giving Attila the truck a good going-over—which has me thinking dirty, dirty thoughts. I take a deep breath, calling my lust to heel.

"Where's Wozniak?" This is definitely a two-person job and I'm fairly sure he's on the roster.

She turns in surprise, half soaking herself in the process, or just enough to dampen her tee over her breasts.

Her chest. It's a chest and we all have one.

Thankfully the fabric is dark, though I can still make out the tear-drop silhouette of one beautiful—no, I see nothing.

"One of his kids called upset about something, so he stepped out to calm her down."

I nod. "Working off that cake, are you?"

"Yeah, I might just manage if I wash another ten trucks. Worth blowing any diet, though. Your kid's got talent."

"She does."

"Spit of you, too."

I enjoy the confirmation. Tori never liked that Lena looked more like me than her. Said it made us closer, which made her jealous. Kind of a weird thing for a mother to think of her daughter, but then Tori doesn't have any genuine maternal instincts.

"And your sister's a hoot."

"Try living with her."

She dips her sponge in the bucket. "You must be close."

"I must need cheap childcare."

She chuckles, that dirty sound that tightens my groin. "She still charges you?"

"The cost is having to listen to her wisdom about my love life." As there's no sign of Wozniak, and I feel lazy standing around, I grab the sponge from the other bucket and start working from the other end. "After my divorce and the move to Chicago, it was important that Lena have good influences in her life. Strong female role models."

"I'd say your sister qualifies."

"She'd be the first to say so. With great humility, of course." Smiling at the thought of Chiara being humble about anything, I soak the hubcap and get scrubbing. "My ex was more interested in Lena when she was a little girl. Could dress her up, treat her like a toy. Once she developed a personality it didn't really play as well to Tori's strengths."

"Lena's too individual for that," she says with a certainty I appreciate. She swipes a stray, dampened curl out of her eye. "So how often does she see her mom?"

"Rarely. I was awarded full custody."

"Oh, I see." Curiosity lights up her face and I wait to see how she'll phrase whatever comes next. It's sweetly diplomatic. "That must be tough on her. On them both."

"It is for Lena. Tori's not really interested in being a mom and she'd been looking for an out for some time."

I'd questioned for a long time why Tori couldn't step up. Wondered if it was my fault and if Tori's ambivalence about being a mom was tied to her attitude toward me. Lena's a daddy's girl, that's for sure, and my wife didn't like that. She wanted all my love in a way that wasn't healthy. Her neglect of her daughter was the final straw, and now she has her wish: she doesn't have to be a mom.

Or a wife.

At least not to me. But she'll be hitched again to my ex-FDNY colleague in a month or so, and is still giving me grief about letting Lena travel to New York for the wedding. I've been avoiding the subject with both of them in the hopes it would just disappear, which is kind of how I'm working through this Abby problem.

"So you're the man of a house filled with strong women," Abby says. "You must *love* coming to work."

I snort a half chuckle. "I do. But not to get away from my girls. I just love my job."

We're closer now, both working the sponges about a foot from each other. That damp curl has slipped over her eye again and she blows on it, which is so damn cute. I can't help myself: my wayward hand shoots out to push it back and hold it behind the delicate shell of her ear.

Just helping a co-worker see better, that's all.

"Need a hair pin or something," she mutters, the color rising in her cheeks.

My brain fills with lurid thoughts about where else she might be blushing. How I might raise color with my mouth on her breasts, her stomach, that soft, pale skin between her thighs. The pink, pulsing flesh there that I can already taste …

"Thanks for helping out," she says, cutting into my fantasy. "I've no idea where Woz has got to, not that I miss him."

"Why, has he done something?"

"No. I mean he's a bit inappropriate but nothing I can't handle."

I let that soak in. I have a duty to protect my crew, but an even more special one toward candidates who are the most vulnerable of the bunch. "You know you can talk to me about anything."

"Thanks for the offer. I'm okay. Really."

"Sure, but my door's always open, Abby. Unless you feel it would be awkward to talk to me because of what happened before." Or the fact I'm practically slobbering over her right now.

"No, not at all. I mean, we've moved on from that, haven't we?"

Have we? Sure, I'm going with that for my sanity. But even now, a foot apart, hidden by the bulk of the truck, it feels like we haven't moved on at all.

Fucking Chiara and her faulty transmitter analogy. I don't want to think the universe is telling me something, that Abby's presence in my firehouse is a sign of something positive. I can't act on it so what's the point in even allowing any excitement for the possibilities?

I say the words, though they mean nothing. "We have."

She tilts her head. "Who do you talk to?"

"Don't worry about me."

She considers that—and me—for a moment. "You're doing something right. The crew loves you, your daughter adores you, even your sister probably thinks you're the best brother in the world. Maybe your life is peachy." Said with a side of *who are you kidding*.

The air is charged, electric with something I can't identify.

Well, I can. It's sex but more. It's connection.

"Well, I'm not sure how much the crew loves me, my sister most definitely does not adore me, but my sweet girl? I hope she still likes me. I've got to appreciate this time with her before she figures out it's cooler to hate me."

"Just be there for her. That's what she needs." She returns to the truck, sponge at the ready, only now she's attacking the paintwork with even more vigor. There's emotion fueling that cleaning action.

"You talk to your dad lately?"

The sponge pauses. "He left a message the other day, asked me to call him."

"And?"

She shrugs. "I didn't. He barely spoke to me at my academy graduation and two weeks later he gives me a call?"

"Maybe he's had a change of heart. Dads do that all the time."

"You're taking his side?"

"Never." Her smile ignites something inside me, something I haven't felt in forever. Maybe never. Every time she flashes it, my heart flutters in recognition.

Damn universe.

Damn Chiara.

Fifteen

Abby

Sunday dinner at Aunt Kathleen's in Bridgeport on Chicago's South Side is a tradition I leaned into during my academy training, once Dad and I were on the outs.

My besties have leaned into it, too. One day I invited Jude and Sam over, and quicker than you can say corned-beef-and-cabbage, the boys had earned regular spots at my aunt's table with knee-melting smiles and enough charm to fell a middle-aged Irish woman who should really know better. Now they visit, even when I'm not around.

Today is the first Sunday we all have off, so we've come to pay homage to the Queen of Bridgeport in exchange for an excellent home-cooked meal, Harp lager, and Portuguese egg tarts from a Hong Kong-style bakery in Chinatown (a Jude discovery). I've been hoping for some easy downtime with my nearest and dearest, an opportunity to forget about my inconvenient attraction to one hot-as-Hades commanding officer.

Fat chance. All anyone wants to talk about is Roman

Rossi, given that he's a "foreigner" ("all the way from New York," per my aunt), a blow-in ("whose dick did he suck to get that promotion?" in the wise words of my cousin Jackie's husband, Johno, he of the shamrock-tattooed ass), and a stone-cold fox.

I didn't say that. Jude did.

Jackie, who got a good look at him in Dempseys', is in full agreement.

And now my aunt, who's looking at his finally-posted photo on the CFD intranet, is making her own pronouncement: "Wouldn't throw him out of bed for eating Taytos."

Taytos are Irish potato chips. We're in the living room, hoovering them up through our chip-holes while we wait for the roast to be done.

You've got to give it to the CFD official photog—they sure know how to make an already hot prospect look even more enticing. In his firefighter dress blues, Roman's grumpy-seriousness is on perfect display, made all the more attractive by that crease at the bridge of his nose, the one I want to rub so I can smooth away the stress that's buried there.

Those sparks of connection between Roman and me, the embers I've tried to douse with water, were healthily glowing while we cleaned that fire truck, and when he pushed that strand of hair behind my ear, I almost combusted.

I wonder if he's home with his family—"my girls" he said, be still and all that—ready to tuck into a Sunday meal. Maybe Lena baked something and they're chilling. Seeing him with his daughter a couple of nights ago melted something inside me. Then hearing about his ex and how she bailed on motherhood was hard. I can't judge a woman I don't know but I can sympathize with a man who's trying his damnedest to do right by his daughter.

Bonus feels: It makes me miss my dad.

"He's already managed to piss off Chuck," Johno says after a swig of beer.

"Wouldn't be hard." Kathleen eyes me. "You spoken to your dad?"

Great, my other no-go topic. "I left him a message on Friday. I haven't heard back." Roman had observed that my dad might have had a change of heart, so I returned the call, and now he's it. My gaze strays to the mantle, where my aunt has a zillion photos in frames. My mom and dad look so happy on their wedding day, her long red hair cascading down her back, him gazing at her with such ardent love. She was already three months gone with me, but there was nothing shotgun about it. No one doubted their commitment to each other.

"It's hard for him," my aunt says. "You know that."

"Ma, stop blaming the victim!" Jackie rolls her eyes at me and gives the "hark at her" head tilt I know like the back of my hand. "It's not Abby's fault that Uncle Chuck is such an asshole."

"Less of that language from you. I'm not blaming her, I just want you all to get along. And I don't want to lose *any* of my kids. I agree with your uncle there!"

"You're not going to lose anyone," Sam soothes while my aunt shakes her head and runs a hand through her graying red hair. My mom probably would have looked like her if she lived. These moments with her are always bittersweet.

At Sam's querying look for me to keep the peace I didn't even upend, I launch into the usual platitudes about my safety. "So far I haven't seen any dangerous action. It's all little old ladies who can't get up and bad drivers."

"You used the Hurst tool yet?" Johno asks after a particularly loud burp.

"No, not yet."

And he's off, soon joined by Sam and Jude, who, of course, have both had multiple opportunities to rip open cars with the Jaws of Life. Not that I want anyone to be in significant danger on my shift, but it would be nice to see more variety.

Feeling left out, I follow my aunt into the kitchen and watch as she bastes the roast. I could offer to help but she'll only shoot me down. Once, while setting the table, I put a fork three millimeters too far to the right and she turned into Carson from *Downton Abbey* telling one of the footmen what a failure he was.

When she stands and shuts the oven door, I hug her from behind. "You okay?"

"Of course I am." But she relaxes into me all the same and pats my clasped hands. "I told him he needs to get that Halligan out of his ass and call you."

"Well, he did and now we're playing phone tag."

She turns in my arms and cups my face fondly. "He'll come around. Jo would be so proud of you."

"I hope so. I feel her at the firehouse. Or I think I do." I shoot a look over my shoulder to ensure we're alone. "I talk to her photo at 6 when no one's around."

"Of course you do. I talk to her as well. And you know what she says?"

I have my suspicions but I wait expectantly all the same.

"When is my Abby going to settle down?"

Jesus, I'm twenty-five. Of course, my mom was married at twenty-four and dead by thirty. "My mother talks to you from the grave and that's her big concern?"

"Maybe we're both worried!"

"She's doing her best, bless her heart." Sam stops in and helps himself to a rosemary-spiked bread roll. "Chatting up strangers over pie and discussing pretentious movies by text." He laces an arm around my neck and kisses my cheek with a crumb-laden mouth. "She just can't seem to get any further, Kat. No follow through."

"Snitch." I push him away. "At least, I'm not 'looking for the one' in every bed in Chicago."

"Abigail Josephine Sullivan! Don't be so crude." My aunt slaps Sam's hand as he goes for another roll. "And you need to stop stuffing your face with bread, Sam Killian. You'll ruin your appetite."

"What can I do to help?" Sam asks before his gaze alights on the sink. "Hey, did Johno not fix that faucet?"

Sam roots around for the toolbox under the sink and starts getting handy with a wrench and a washer.

Kathleen circles back to the Great Question. "So why aren't you seeing anyone?"

I give Sam a death ray glare for telling tales out of school. Before I can answer, not that I have a response that will work, he weighs in. "She says it's because she's too tough for any guy. But that's not it."

"It's not? Enlighten me, oh wise one."

He tightens something with a grunt. "No guy is alpha enough for you. At this rate, your best bet is a cop or another firefighter but we all know your opinion of them." He winks at Kathleen. "I've heard ten-foot pole mentioned and she's not talking about what he's packing, Kat."

"Samuel Killian, that's very naughty!"

The woman loves it.

So I don't want to date firefighters. I'm open about that and I don't see what the big deal is.

"Statistically, firefighters are the men you're going to meet." My aunt looks at me. "What's wrong with firefighters?"

"Yeah, Abs, what's wrong with firefighters?" Jude has just walked in because I don't have enough people telling me who to date.

"All the ones I know are cocky, arrogant womanizers. Or man-izers," I concede for Jude's sake. "I'd *love* to dip my toes in that cesspool."

Roman's not, though. He's only recently started dating after his divorce, and the way he cares for his family—while not completely antithetical to tomcatting around—shows he's a guy with values.

I'm a whore for a guy with values.

With the faucet fixed and my love life dissected, the boys head out to watch the Rebels hockey game on TV.

Kathleen assesses me. "There are womanizers everywhere. And your father wasn't one. Neither was your uncle."

My uncle Frank, God rest his soul, was also a firefighter. He died of lung cancer three years ago, and it nearly destroyed my aunt. I've seen how a love lost crushes a person. I've felt it.

"So there are exceptions." My boss seems to be an exception to every rule I have. The last thing I need is to be thinking of more reasons to want him.

"You think this is the way to protect your heart, Abby?" She runs a hand over my cheek. "Your mother wouldn't want you to be afraid of love."

No, she wouldn't. But she'd expect some level of self-preservation. And where Roman Rossi is concerned, protecting myself is absolutely key.

Sixteen

Abby

It's about 4 a.m. when our truck pulls up outside a warehouse on Elston. This area is a mix of residential and industrial, and right now a couple of people are on the street looking at the smoke billowing from a third story window.

CPD are already on site and one of them approaches us.

"Building's currently not in use but it's been known to house squatters."

Roman nods and turns to us. His eyes flicker over my face before moving away quickly. It's the first shift we've shared since that connection at the fire truck wash-down, and I'm trying to be cool.

"Simpson and Brooks, hit the hydrants and get us connected. Wozniak and Sullivan, start the room to room on the second floor. Acosta and I will head up to the third."

If I'm disappointed about not getting the extra attention I so obviously seek from the LT, I try my best to hide it. Easy enough to do as we mask up.

"Remember to take it slow on the air," he says, mostly for my benefit, no doubt. "Nice, even draws."

I nod and pull the mask over my face.

Once inside, it seems eerily quiet. No sign of life, not even of a fire, except for the fact we saw that smoke coming from the window above. The first floor looks like a reception space that's never been occupied. Gage feels for light switches, but when he tries something the space remains in darkness. Following the glow of my flashlight, I check the corners, looking for the stairs. Roman is already moving toward the northeast corner, where he wedges the door open.

We head up the stairs, our pounding boots creating tinny echoes against the corrugated steel. The second floor is one long corridor with doors leading off it.

"Wozniak, you and Sullivan are here. Head downstairs as soon as you're done and check on basement access. Stay frosty." And then he's off to the next floor with Danny in tow, and I'm left with Wozniak.

"Okay, Sully, let's do this."

Still no sign of fire on this floor, so this seems like a pretty standard room check to ensure no one is trapped inside. We open doors and scout rooms before reaching the back of the floor. Nothing behind the last door but a couple of old desks and a swivel chair.

"All clear here," Wozniak says. "Come on, let's check the basement."

We head back toward the exit, where the air feels warmer than before. Something else is odd, a crackling sound, that's loud enough to get my attention.

"You hear that?" I ask.

Wozniak turns but before he can say anything, a shower of plaster rains down on our heads. I move back against the wall just as chunks of the ceiling fall into the corridor.

Burning chunks.

I look up, worried that Roman and Danny are close to that damage.

"Come on, Sullivan, let's book it!" Wozniak yells just as another flood of ceiling crashes into our path. Flames are licking the edges and then suddenly it goes up in front of us, blocking our exit.

Or almost blocking it. There's a narrow path through so I shove Wozniak and yell, "Go! That way!"

He yanks my arm and pushes me ahead. Seniority, I suppose, rather than a nod to my gender. The fire has now taken hold and I'm praying that (a) the ceiling will remain intact until we get out and (b) this turnout gear is as fire-resistant as they say.

That's when I hear a thud behind me.

Wozniak is down, felled by another ceiling drop. The debris is on fire as it falls and whatever hit Wozniak has knocked the wind out of him.

"You okay?" I tug his arm, then look ahead, planning the next few moves on the chess board. Would Roman and Danny have heard or seen what happened or is this just in the space between the floors?

"Yeah, fine. Make sure your air is on, Sullivan."

"Got it."

Wozniak tries to stand, crumples, and shakes his head. "Get the LT."

"No way, you've got to get up and come with me now."

"On your radio, Sullivan."

"Oh, right." I check the exit with my flashlight. All I can see is smoke, which seems to have conquered the space in seconds. As firefighters we know fire can move faster than humans but it's awe-inspiring and terrifying to witness it up close.

"Lieutenant, this is Sullivan. Can you hear me?"

"Copy, Sullivan. You okay?"

"Ceiling came in on us, we've got a smoker, and Wozniak is down."

"Unconscious?" He sounds so calm.

"No, but he's ..." I shake his arm because his eyes are closed but he doesn't appear to be out. "Breathe, Wozniak." I check his air gauge. Fuck, it's at zero. How could it be at zero? Is the tank damaged? "I think he's out of air and we're blocked."

"Which floor?"

"Second."

"On my way."

"Copy that."

I give Wozniak another shake and his eyes flutter open. Another tap of his gauge. "Are you getting any air?"

His head turns back and forth. "Must be faulty."

Still no sign of Roman.

"Can you stand?"

I help him up and place an arm under his, guiding him along a few inches. We step over smoking debris, though really I step over it. Wozniak is dragging, and I suspect he might have hit his head. He slumps against me, practically pinning me to the wall. The smoke is thicker here and he's running out of air.

Roman, where the hell are you?

Time seems to be slowing down because there's no sign of the cavalry. But the heavier smoke tells me that time is also marching on relentlessly, that contrary bitch. That's the last time I wish for more variety in the callouts.

I need to take action. I whip off Wozniak's mask and slip off the breathing apparatus. If there's no air, it's just another weight he can't afford. I place my mask over his face and seal it.

Breathe. I think it rather than say it as I want to hold onto my own breath for as long as I can.

His eyes flutter as nature takes its course, his body's impulse to inhale kicks in, and the air hits his lungs.

"Abby! Call out!"

I've never been so glad to hear another person's voice. "We're here!"

Roman appears like a golden god in a haze of smoke. It takes him all of two seconds to assess the situation, given that I'm tethered to my crew-mate. I've still got my SCBA tank on my back and Woz is breathing through my mask.

"Put your mask back on, then head to the exit," Roman barks.

"But he needs air and—" I cough because now I'm inhaling black smoke, absent oxygen.

"Now, Abby." He pulls the mask off Woz and shoves it in my hands. "That's an order."

I do as he says, gasping at the precious air from my SCBA as the mask is resealed. Woz is more alert now, and Roman takes over supporting him. Before I strike out, I pick up Woz's tank, the one I relieved him of earlier when I thought we'd have to fight our way out of there.

I move on ahead, feeling as though I'm pushing through a physical wall of smoke though it's really just that: smoke. I'm trying not to inhale while it makes my eyes itch and water, even with the mask. Too long without it, I suppose. I look behind, my chest flashing in panic because I can't see them. But then Roman's there, a beacon in the dark, and I realize it's going to be okay.

🔥

Gavin the EMT takes a look at my eyes. "You feeling better?"

I nod, not wanting to speak because I know my scratchy throat will hurt.

"Gav, give us a second."

Roman is at his shoulder, a tower of strength that I wouldn't mind sinking into now. He's mad at me. I talked back in there and that's a no-no during a working fire. During any time. Gavin winks at me, like I'm going to be okay and the big bad boss isn't going to remove my intestines and string me up by them. I know better.

With Gavin out of my sightline, I peer up at my lieutenant and boy, I like what I see. All that hot, scowly, alpha business that really shouldn't be attractive when the anger is directed at you, but what can I say? Women, we are complicated.

"I specifically ordered you to re-mask and leave and you give me your opinion?"

"Wozniak was stuck and—"

"And it was my job to get him out. Not yours. You're a fucking candidate, Abby, and there is a chain of command. I make the assessment and you follow orders. How is this hard?"

"It's not. It was just an instinctive reaction."

"Like giving him your air?" His voice changes to low and measured. There's anger there, but also genuine concern. I feel like a kid being taken to task by one of my parents—my father, actually, which isn't how I want to think of Roman.

Daddy issues, clean up in aisle five.

"He seemed to be concussed, his air was out. Was I supposed to leave him there and come find you?"

He opens his mouth. Closes it again. It evidently costs him dearly not to be able to respond with a comeback that fits his narrative.

Finally he gruffs out, "I'll be talking to that fucker about his equipment. Where is it?"

I point at the tank behind me. Roman picks it up, fiddles with the regulator, stares at the gauge for a couple of long, painful seconds, then lays it on the bed of the ambulance.

He inhales deeply. He's still angry but I don't think it's

with me anymore. I'd hate to be in Wozniak's shoes when Roman goes off on him, concussion or not.

"Get on the truck. We're heading back to the house."

He turns his back on me and I feel worse than I did ten minutes ago when the smoke burned through my nostrils and down my throat.

Seventeen

Abby

Back at the firehouse, we jump off the fire truck and start the strip down.

"Wozniak, my office, now," Roman barks out.

Full of sympathy, everyone looks at the guy who is about to get reamed. I touch his arm. "Good luck."

There's a Band-Aid over his eye, and while I had thought he was concussed during the fire, it turns out he's fine. Just winded, which probably means he's not in great physical shape.

"Thanks," he says to me. "And you know, thanks for what you did back there. You shouldn't have had to. I checked that equipment."

Maybe he did, maybe he didn't. In the few weeks I've been here, he's the one most likely to screw around and cut corners. He left me cleaning that truck, and as much as I tried to cover it's obvious that Roman has his number.

He hangs up his turnout gear, then follows the lieutenant with his head dipped.

Tyler nudges my shoulder. "You okay?"

"I don't know. I mean, I feel okay, but I also feel like I really messed up. I just couldn't leave him there without any air."

"You sure about that?" Gage's tone is drier than a James Bond martini.

I bite my lip. "Who screwed up here?"

"Wozniak, without a doubt. Ten to one he didn't check his gear when he came on shift."

"Is it true he wanted the LT job and Roman got it?"

Gage raises an eyebrow. "Look who's up on all the flavors of the tea. Yep, he passed the exam after his third try and expected he was a shoo-in, but Roman came in with twelve years' experience, five as a lieutenant in New York. He did the CFD mini-academy and aced the city recertification. We'd be dummies not to find a spot for a guy of his caliber."

No doubt Roman is a better leader than Wozniak, but the friction I've seen in the past few weeks could be down to the fact Roman got what Woz rightfully sees as his. There's bound to be bitterness, but Woz really needs to get his act together.

This incident isn't going to help.

When Woz comes back into the lounge, looking like he's been dragged to hell and back, I suspect the energy between them has only become blacker.

🔥

About an hour before shift end, Tyler puts his head around the door to the lounge.

"Venti wants to see you, Abby."

I haven't spoken to the boss much, but he seems like a good guy. Kind of gruff, one of those heart-of-gold types. I head to the office and smile at Billie.

"Go right in," she says, but there's no smile in return.

The first person I see is Roman, standing by the window in an at-attention pose, hands behind his back. I've never seen him look so serious, not even when he called Woz into his office to haul him over the coals. The captain is behind the desk and on the other side is Fire Commissioner Chuck Sullivan.

My father.

"Candidate," he says, an unmistakable edge to it.

"Sir."

"Close the door, Sullivan," Captain Ventimiglia says, "and have a seat."

I do as I'm told. What the hell is my father doing here? My back's to Roman so I can't see his expression.

The last time I saw my father was three weeks ago at graduation. In that time, his hair has gone grayer, the lines on his face more grooved. The buttons of his uniform are straining slightly, so he must have put on a few pounds. Even though I know his presence here is likely not conducive to a happy-families reunion, I'm still glad to see him and know he's all right.

He heaves a sigh. "I understand there was an incident at a callout this morning with you not following CFD protocol."

I slide a glance to the captain, wondering why the Commissioner is getting involved. Should I defend myself or land Wozniak in it? And did Roman really report me for not immediately following his order?

"I made a judgment call in the moment. Lieutenant Rossi has already put me straight."

"You gave your air to another firefighter, putting yourself in danger. What the hell, Abigail?" That little burst of emotion surprises me so much I start.

Before I can answer, the captain speaks up. "Candidate Sullivan understands she made a mistake."

"Mistakes get people killed."

No shit, Dad.

"She wasn't sure how long it would take for us to get there," Roman says. "She showed good instincts even though it wasn't strictly kosher."

My neck prickles with his scrutiny.

"You're limited to light duty for two weeks," my father says.

"What?" I jerk my gaze to the captain, who remains unmoved. "But I can't learn if I'm not on callouts."

"It'll give you time to review the procedures again." My father again.

"Would you be getting involved if this was a firefighter not related to you?"

The captain's eyes widen, a clear signal to me to keep a lid on it. But I can't help it. My father has barely spoken to me in months and now he's here as soon as the grapevine reports I made a mistake? Who told him?

I twist in my chair to face Roman, who's still standing by the window in a military stance. He meets my gaze without giving me an inch. Did I once think those eyes beautiful? I take it all back. All I see now are cold, flat discs of censure.

Somehow I manage to choke the next words out. "Is there anything else?"

"No, Candidate. You can go." The captain sounds conciliatory, maybe even a little weary.

I can't look at Roman as I leave because if I do, he'll need a tank of air to breathe through the rage I'm sending his way.

Eighteen

Roman

I've no idea why Commissioner Sullivan feels it's necessary to interfere with the workings of my crew. I'm trying to see it from his perspective—the man lost his wife on the job, after all—but this micro-management BS is untenable.

Venti and the Commish are shaking hands. I can tell the cap isn't loving this either but he's a hundred times more diplomatic than I could ever be, which is why he's in charge of the firehouse and I'm not. He mumbles whatever crap Sullivan needs to hear while my head does a half-decent impression of a room filled with noxious gas in need of emergency ventilation.

Knowing that leaving before I blow would be best all around, I push off from the windowsill and head toward the door.

The commissioner doesn't let me off so easy. "Lieutenant? Walk me out."

Fuck.

I hover at the door, not making eye contact with Venti

because if I do, I won't be able to rein in my feelings. I already don't like this guy. We had a run-in and while it should have been smoothed out by now, it's only become aggravated by the presence of Abby.

She acquitted herself well during that incident. Really well. So there was some flapping of the gums, but that's to be expected. I don't think Abby is capable of not giving her opinion, but she's no fool, and for the most part knows when it's best to keep it zipped. What concerns me more is not the danger Woz put her in—and believe me, that grabs my gonads—but my reaction to it.

I wanted to kill him.

And I wanted to kiss her.

I came *this* close to touching her earlier at the scene, checking if she was okay. To cover my inappropriate reaction, I got all pissy with her. I had to. Now her father is here trying to tell me how to do my job.

Billie isn't around so I assume the Commissioner will say his piece in the outer office but instead he starts walking and doesn't stop until we get to the Wall of the Fallen. It's a canny move.

"You've lost people?"

He means in the service. "I have."

"My daughter doesn't want to hear it from me but I'm doing this for her own good."

Of all the self-serving bullshit. "Your daughter is a member of my crew and there's a chain of command here. I prefer to sanction crew members in my own way."

"You think she shouldn't be punished?"

"I think she should be educated. Like all my crew."

Sullivan rubs the back of his neck, drawing attention to some scarring there. It's a tired move and for a second my heart pangs in sympathy. But then he opens his mouth.

"I heard she was put on latrine duty her first day."

"You hear a lot." I still have no idea how news of an early morning run made it to him. I hadn't even filed a report yet and I can't imagine Venti shooting the shit with this asshole about the fuckups of his crew. He knows it undermines me.

Someone in the firehouse is feeding Sullivan information.

"She's not good with authority."

I wonder why. I don't say that aloud but it's written all over my face. At his eyebrow arch, I continue. "Commissioner, what exactly do you need from me?"

"I need you to take care of my daughter."

Somehow I don't think he means the way I'd like: both of us naked, figuring out the perfect spots that turn each other to jelly. Probably shouldn't be thinking of sex with the daughter of the man who could have my head on a pike in front of the Quinn Academy if he's feeling chippy.

"We look out for everyone here. Your daughter is safe on my crew."

"But she could be safer. Do you think she has what it takes to go the distance? Or is she just here as some sort of messed up way to honor her mother and screw with me?"

Now I'm truly pissed. This dysfunctional families bull shouldn't be a factor in the running of any firehouse.

"Listen, sir, I don't care about this personal crap except insofar as it affects the ability of one of my crew to do her job. Plenty of people have succeeded while running on spite. If that's what gets her engine running, then I won't question it. If there's nothing else?"

I'm already walking away.

"You're on probation here yourself, Rossi. You think I've forgotten your attitude problem from a few months back? There's a lot of scrutiny of anyone who comes in from another service because you haven't learned to do it our way."

I halt, not liking the threat in those words. "The captain

has nothing but praise for my performance. We meet once a week to discuss it."

"Let's hope it stays that way. I know moving here was a big deal for you and your family. Just keep an eye on Abby and if she steps out of line, report it to me."

I turn and walk back. Dead wife or not, I will not be threatened in my own firehouse.

"Are you that desperate to have her run out of CFD, Sullivan? I won't do your dirty work for you."

He pulls on the edges of his jacket. "Like I said, do your job as her superior officer and keep her out of trouble."

"You're underestimating her, you know that? There've been a couple of hitches, but nothing that can't be smoothed out. Abby has what it takes to succeed at this job: the drive, the smarts, the passion. She just needs a few people with a bit more experience to have faith in her to put it all together. Try support instead of sabotage. Goes a long way. Sir."

He has no comeback for that, and I have no intention of waiting for one. I don't even watch him head out because I'm back in Venti's office before the Commish has put a key in his car's ignition.

"What the fuck just happened here?"

Venti shakes his head. "He's got a bee in his asshole about his kid. We always knew there'd be extra scrutiny once she was assigned here."

"How the hell did he hear about the run this morning? I haven't even had a chance to write up an incident report. And he knows about an off-the-books set down I gave her a few weeks ago."

Venti leans back in his chair. "So he has eyes and ears here. It doesn't surprise me. The man cares about his kid."

"And you're going to put up with him coming in here and telling us how to run this firehouse?"

Venti squints at me. "I get where he's coming from. If it was my Evie—"

"Well, it's not." Evie is the cap's daughter and is currently dating Tyler Brooks, which apparently caused some drama a while back. "Abby Sullivan is doing just fine and I sure as hell am not allowing anyone else to tell me how to be her CO. I will not be treating her with kid gloves, either. As for this light duty business, you're seriously allowing that?"

Venti looks at me long and hard. "What was the incident report gonna say?"

I resent the implication that it wouldn't tell the truth. "What happened. She gave her air to Wozniak and she probably saved his life. Not that he deserves it, the lazy prick."

"So, she did the wrong thing for the right reason. She needs to be made aware of that and if the CFD commissioner tells me I need to limit her to the firehouse, then that's what needs to happen. It's not that far off the mark, Roman."

Give me strength. I could tell him about the veiled threat Sullivan just made about my future with CFD, but I'm not sure I'd be getting any sympathy from that quarter. We might both be Italian but Venti isn't about to take my side against the brass, not when he's this close to retirement. Besides, word is he and Sullivan were academy buddies back in the day.

So, fucking great.

I know this much. I won't be spying on Abby for her dad or giving her any special treatment. Still I can't help thinking I've just dug myself a deeper trench of trouble when it comes to my future at the Chicago Fire Department.

Nineteen

Abby

I'm still fuming over what happened this morning. My light duty was effective immediately, so for the last hour of my shift I was relegated to a bunch of shitty jobs around the station while the crew headed out on one more run. Apparently a floater from the pool would fill my spot for the next couple of weeks.

The whole situation stinks to high heaven.

Roman pulled me aside later and told me he didn't agree with the decision but it wasn't up to him. Fine, whatever. If he isn't going to go to bat for me, so be it.

My father didn't seem the least bit regretful about imposing that punishment on me. Obviously he's been looking for an excuse to come down on me, and now he has it. He must feel like a million dollars.

I'm at home, trying to nap, and failing, when a text message pops up from Diner Dude, the first one he's sent me since the night he gave me his number and I shot him that text to tell him I'd made it home safely.

You okay?

I consider ignoring it, but after several false starts, I decide to go with an informative, *Fine.*

That good, huh?

His response produces a mirthless chuckle from me. He used to be married, so he can probably translate the language of "fine" proficiently.

He doesn't wait for me to respond. *You want to get breakfast?*

I want to punch something.

That can be arranged.

My intercom buzzer sounds, making me jump. Is Roman here?

I shouldn't want to see him, but a part of me—the part that craves his approval, and fuck my life, his comfort—needs to hear his voice, even if it's telling me I screwed up.

I press the door admission button and take a quick look around. The place could be tidier—oh, what do I care? I only need to impress him at work and it seems I can't get that right.

I stick my head out the door just in time to see him crest the rise of the stairs in running shorts and a gray tee, but no appealing sweaty damp patches, so he hasn't put in his exercise yet. The clean masculine scent of soap and spice hits me hard.

He stops a foot short of me and leans a hand on the wall. The pose is anything but casual; he seems to be taking charge of my hallway like he takes charge of everywhere else.

"What's up, boss?"

"You need to vent and I'm here to listen."

"I screwed up. I know that. Woz probably could have survived another minute. I shouldn't have given him my air, I should have trusted you'd be there, and then I should have listened when you told me to go. I thought I was taking the initiative."

Those dark eyes take my measure. "You pushed the

envelope but for what it's worth, I think you did fine. Wozniak shouldn't have put you in that position."

Okay, this is what I need to hear. Sure, Roman was telling me all this earlier, but I was too pissed at my father to absorb his words.

"I can't believe my father got involved. Or that he even knew so fast."

Roman does that scowly thing and he looks like he has something to say but decides against.

Dread fills my chest. "Did—did you tell him?"

"You think I'm on check-in terms with your father? Nah, sounds like we have a chatty Kathy at the firehouse."

"A spy?"

"If he wants to keep an eye on you, he's going to have a mole in the house." He moves in closer, and my nostrils are filled with him. "Abby, this is not the end of the world, just a slight setback. You're going to be a great firefighter one day."

"It doesn't feel like that right now. It feels like I'm pushing, trying too hard because ..."

"Because ..." He leans in. A door down the hallway opens and Mrs. Dumont puts her head out and gives me the nosey parker nostril twitch.

"Would you like to come in for a second?"

"Sure."

I stand back to let him in, and get the full spicy effect of just-showered male. I'm obviously in a vulnerable state right now because it makes me weak. Time to buck right up.

I gesture toward the sofa, really to send him away from me. "Take a load off, Lieutenant."

"Roman. Outside the firehouse, call me Roman." He settles in the corner of my sofa, elbows on knees, hands clasped, his face turned toward me in expectation. "You said you felt like you're trying too hard. Why is that?"

"I want to impress you." Taking a seat on the opposite end

of the sofa, I quickly add, "The team. My father. Anyone who's ever said a woman can't do this job. That *I* can't do this job. I realize it's self-inflicted pressure—"

"Partly. You're representing your gender in a traditionally male-oriented job and that's a heavy load to carry, but it's not yours alone. Have you talked to Alex Dempsey?"

"Not yet. I don't want to go running to her with my problems."

"Then come running to me. I need to hear it when you're feeling overwhelmed or unsure about your place at Engine 6. In CFD. All of it."

That offer sounds seductively dangerous, a warm pit I would gladly sink into. It's one thing to talk about your professional problems with your supervisor. With our dynamic—and let's face it, blistering chemistry—the capacity to cross the line is all too real. But if I'm to succeed in this career, I need to set all those reservations aside. I'm a pro. I can do that.

"You know my background. And you know my dad doesn't want me to do this. Then the fact I'm Chuck Sullivan's daughter places a target on my back."

He hums his encouragement, so feeling encouraged, I go on.

"People think I got a leg up, which is not true. I've had to work harder because I'm a woman and harder again because I'm the daughter of the Commish. There can't be any perception of favoritism or giving me a pass because of either of those things. So now I'm here and it's not like Fire Academy. Now every decision determines fates. I'm good at this job, or at least I know I can be, but I don't want to be a distraction."

He steeples his hands together over his lips and gives me every iota of his attention. I remember that look from the diner, the way he considered my words carefully before he spoke. There's nothing sexier than a man who listens.

"I don't want you to be a distraction, either."

I bite my lip, which sends his gaze in a dark, delicious dip there. Knowing that he's similarly affected eases something in my chest. Like we're in this together, fighting the good fight to not jump each other's bones. It'll take two to tango and as long as one of us remains strong, we should be able to push through this.

He clears his throat. "You did really well at the Academy. Wyatt Fox says you were one of his best students and that guy never gushes about anything."

"You talked to him about me?"

"He tends bar over at Dempseys' some nights and it came up." He flashes a wisp of a grin, so fast I almost miss it. "Okay, I asked him. I needed to know what you're capable of and he told me you were top of the class in practically all areas. So you have to get out of your head and stop second-guessing your instincts. You have good ones. That call was out of left field because you don't usually have to cover the ass of a more experienced firefighter. His mistake put you in danger."

He sounds quietly angry, and I'm suddenly very aware of how hot that is. How attractive having a man like Roman in my corner might be.

How dangerous.

"I'm sorry I pushed back. On the call and then later when you tried to explain. I was just so angry about my father's interference."

"I didn't like how he talked to you. That wasn't right."

I wanted Roman to hear me and now that's he listening and empathizing—well, be careful what you wish for. "He's getting his dream, to sideline me. I appreciate you standing up for me, though."

His eyes warm. "I want you to succeed, not because you're

a woman or have had a rough go being the daughter of some big shot. But because my crew needs you to succeed. I'll always have your back."

"You will?"

"Of course, Abby," he says so gently it makes me want to cry.

"I—I appreciate it. I've already learned a lot from you. I want to continue learning."

He studies me, which means I'm stuck—gloriously stuck —returning his heated regard because any other option would mean I have to back down. I can't do that because anything less than toe to toe with this man will signify weakness.

He unfolds from the sofa, which is really for the best because I was about to do something incredibly stupid there, like climb all over him.

"My offer still stands," he says.

"Offer?"

"Breakfast."

That text seems like ten years ago instead of ten minutes. Can I do the friends and co-workers thing? I might be brave in a working fire but I'm not sure I'm brave enough to spend time with Roman Rossi, pretending I'm not dying to stick my tongue down his throat. Pretending I don't want to feel his strong arms around me and all the wonderful comfort that comes with that.

"Maybe another time," I say.

He nods again, understanding in his expression. He knows the sparks between us are likely to ignite if we spend any non-work time together. By common instinct, we move toward the door, sadness dogging my steps. This feels like the end instead of a brand-new beginning to the story of us.

He stops at the door and turns.

"Remember you asked me about whether I would have called you?"

You mean when you crushed my heart as flat as a pancake? No, haven't given it a second thought.

I snatch a jagged breath. "You said probably not."

"I lied."

Long pause while my heart trip-hammers against my ribs, almost cracking a couple in the process.

"You lied?"

"Yep. I had every intention of calling you. I've been out of the dating game for a while and wasn't sure how long I was supposed to wait, what the protocol is these days. I obviously waited too long."

You mean, we could have already done the deed and moved on? Once I'd found out he was a firefighter, I wouldn't have wanted to date him anyway. I can't risk that level of closeness, but I would have been very open to something more casual.

Tripping down that rocky road would help no one just as the man telling me this now doesn't change a thing.

If anything it makes it worse.

I gave him an out—said no to his breakfast offer and made it clear that he and I breathing the same air outside the firehouse is madness. Now he's here, dangling something I can't have.

"If you'd called me, it wouldn't have changed anything."

"You sure about that?" He moves back into the apartment, so fast he's in my personal space like it's his personal space. I look up into that sculpted face and hold my breath. "I said I wouldn't have called because it seemed like the easiest way to move forward," he says, every word a carbon copy of the thoughts rolling through my frazzled brain. "Put it behind us and deal with the new world order. But it was a lie."

My heart's not doing so good. Still, he continues, stringing together more words than I've ever heard from his lips.

I am spellbound.

"I wish I'd done more than kiss you because I can still taste that cherry pie on your lips, I can still feel your gorgeous breasts against my chest, I can still hear those breathy little moans you made when our tongues tangled. I wish I'd spent the night with you so I'd have that memory of how good we could be together."

I have no words. And if I did, what would be the point? Nothing can resolve this to our mutual satisfaction short of banging each other's brains out.

The burning look he delivers says he understands completely. Great, I'm totally simpatico with a man I can't have.

I'm still melting under his scrutiny when he leaves three seconds later.

Twenty

Roman

I walk out of Abby's building, crushed with disappointment, though fuck knows why. I stopped by to tell her I had her back, to let her vent, and make sure she was okay.

Instead I blurted out that if we were living in a different universe, I'd have called her for that date.

Excellent leadership skills, Rossi.

The minute she turned down breakfast with that look of such misery I knew what she was feeling. What we've both been feeling since she walked into my office at Engine 6: how the fuck can we pretend we don't want each other?

She's been doing a better job of it and clearly has the right idea. *Don't spend a minute of unchaperoned time together.* That's what she was saying when she basically told me to walk my ass out the door.

But I had to open my big mouth. I couldn't go another second letting her think I might not have wanted her from the start. Maybe she could tell with the way I've been practically drooling all over her, but I needed to say the words. Actualize the hell out of it, and if in actualizing, if in making the words live and breathe outside my head resulted in sending a call up to the universe, then maybe my sister and her dumb New Age shit have the right idea.

So I said it. I told her my wishes and dreams in the most inappropriate manner. And then I got the fuck out of Dodge before I acted on those fantasies.

It was supposed to make me feel better, a cathartic admission.

Instead I've only gone and made it so much worse.

These tangled traps occupy my mind as I let myself into the apartment. It's Tuesday, so I should have the place to myself, except I hear voices in Chiara's kitchen, and there I find my sister and daughter seated at the table.

"What's going on? Why aren't you in school?"

Lena looks up at me with red-rimmed eyes. My heart drops.

"She got into a fight," Chiara says.

"Are you okay?" I touch a hand to her head and she ducks away.

"I'm fine." She leaves the kitchen.

Chiara blows out a breath. "The school called you but couldn't get through."

I turned off my phone before I went to Abby's. "I had it off for a while and forgot to turn it back on."

"Lena talked to Tori and the bitch blabbed. Told her you won't let her come to the wedding."

"Shit. Tori wasn't supposed to say anything. Why the hell would she do that?"

"Because she knows it would look terrible if her own daughter isn't a bridesmaid. Tori is all about the optics."

I turn on my phone and sure enough, I have several messages, a couple from the school, the rest from Chiara. Nothing from Tori, though.

I scroll to my contacts. "Excuse me while I shove those optics down her throat."

"Maybe hold off and deal with Lena first. She was upset and got into a physical altercation at school. Have you forgotten that part?"

I take a breath. While I was fantasizing about getting my rocks off, my daughter was having a meltdown.

"Yeah, okay. I'm sorry you had to leave work. Thanks for picking her up."

"Sure, I'm here to be the backup. I think she's taking the move and changes really well, but the fact her mom is so hot and cold is really hard on her. I know you're trying to protect her but maybe you should let her go to the wedding."

"No fucking way," I growl, and especially not now when Tori tried to end run it. "I'm going to talk to Lena. Go back to work."

Chiara looks like she has more to say, but instead takes the wise approach and leaves.

I knock on Lena's bedroom door. There's no answer so I put my head around. "Fragolina?"

She's curled up on her side, her back to me, looking at her phone screen. She makes no effort to face me. I understand her hurt and I hate that I'm the bad guy here, but sometimes you have to be. That's pretty much the definition of parenting.

Taking a seat, I run a hand over her shoulder. She doesn't flinch, so I take that as a positive.

"You okay?"

She shrugs and my heart breaks at seeing her so closed off.

Only when her mother is involved does she recede like this and become smaller. I'd vowed she'd never feel like that with me.

"What was the fight about?"

"Nothing."

"Want to tell me what your mom said?"

She turns over, fueled by indignation. "You know what she said. She wants me in the wedding and you never told me!"

"True. I didn't want you to take part."

My candor surprises her. "But, why? She actually wants me there. It's like you're trying to keep us apart."

"That's not the case. I—I just don't want you … to go." As I can't defend my bitterness toward Tori, I add another string to the bow. "Who'd look after you?"

"Aunt Kayla. Aunt Lisa. There's a whole other side of my family I can't see because you moved us out here! Because you got mad at everyone."

I dig my nails into my palms. I've never described it this way to her, and I sure as hell know Chiara wouldn't. "Is that what your mom said?"

"She said that you both made mistakes but that we wouldn't have had to move if you hadn't gotten into a fight with Uncle Rick. You'd still have your job and we'd still be in New York. And I'd be able to go to Mom's wedding."

Yeah, a lot hinged on one thrown punch. Tori knows what preceded that, how her affair with my colleague and the cover-up by my captain, "Uncle Rick,"—who was supposed to be my closest friend—sent me off the deep end. Sure, I could have taken it, suffered the indignity of my whole crew knowing I was fucked over by people I cared about. But I didn't and here we are. Tori has no right to use my reaction to her bad behavior as leverage in her mind games with our daughter.

"I don't want you to go, Lena. If I can't go with you—and I can't—then you can't go at all. That's all there is to it."

Her look is pure tween hatred. I'd hoped to stave this off for longer but now I'm in it good.

"It's not fair."

"Maybe not. But sometimes we have to do things we don't want."

"Adults always say that to justify their own bad decisions."

Does my daughter know me or what? Yet I hear a thread of her mother's thinking in there.

So maybe I'm the king of bad decisions. Tori, my job in New York, this wedding business. Abby.

Abby, who I almost caved to not fifteen minutes ago, the worst best mistake I almost made today.

"I'm sorry you can't go, Lena. We'll do something else."

My daughter growls and turns her back on me.

🔥

Two days later, I walk into the Engine 6 gym, surprised to find Luke pondering the weights.

"Shouldn't you be headed out to make a baby?" Luke's shift ended thirty minutes ago but there's no end in sight to the wagering on his powerful sperm.

"Just getting some time in. Baby-making takes stamina. Spot me?"

"Sure." I go through the routine of making sure Luke's windpipe isn't crushed all while thinking on how best to approach my dilemma.

"How's it going with your candidate?"

"Torres?" Luke counts off with the barbell in his secure grip. "Guy's great. Nice to have another joker on the crew, and he's definitely pulling his weight."

While I'm pleased to hear we have a good guy in the house, I was hoping to hear there's friction or trouble in paradise. Maybe I should come at it from a different angle.

"You hear the Commissioner put Sullivan on light duty?"

Luke sits up, grabbing his towel to wipe at the sweat dotting his chest.

"Yeah, she was spittin' nails about it. Not that I blame her. Kind of a sick call."

"I wonder if the fact she's on my crew gets his goat."

"Because of your history with him?" Luke considers this. "You think he's going to go harder on her because you're her CO? Or you think he doesn't trust you to have her back?"

"Maybe both. She did push back during the call—makes me wonder if maybe we don't work so well together."

Luke considers this. "Rossi, are you trying to get Sullivan transferred off your crew?"

"No." I take a seat beside him on the bench, and murmur, "Maybe."

He knows there's nothing wrong with her. She's going to make a great firefighter so the only reason I want her off my crew is as plain as the nose on my reddening face.

"You want to f—uh, date her?" Whatever he sees on my face is not good. "You're fucking kidding me? It's been barely a month!"

"How long did it take you and your lady to know?"

"Day One. She walked into the Engine 6 locker room and I was in a towel. End of story." Cocky grin. Fucker. "Of course, we had to go through the motions of pretending there was nothing because of work stuff. So, been there." He twitches his nose. "What does Abby think?"

"We haven't—uh, discussed it. But I'm pretty sure she's interested."

Luke narrows his gaze. "So you're investigating the options behind her back? She won't like that. Hell, I don't like that."

"It's not—listen, I'm trying to think of options so I can

present them to her. Really, I should be forgetting the whole thing because I've got enough drama at home."

"What drama?"

"My ex wants Lena in the wedding party as a bridesmaid. I told her no and that she couldn't discuss it with Lena, but she found out."

"Your kid did?"

"Yup. Now it's World War Three and I'm the bad guy. Just when I think things are starting to even out. Chiara's marriage is imploding and—" I rub my forehead. What the hell am I thinking trying to carve out a path to date a candidate on my crew? "Forget I said anything."

Luke waits a beat. "There's nothing wrong with looking for a little happiness for yourself. Back when Kinsey and I met, I'd gone through a pretty bad divorce myself. And I threw myself into taking care of the kids. Alex and Gage were old enough to look after themselves but I used that as an excuse to not make any sudden moves. I almost fucked things up with Kinsey but when I went all in with her, told her she was number one, she met me halfway and it changed everything. It's okay to want things, Roman."

"As long as everyone's on the same page." I check the door to make sure we're alone. "The thing is, this attraction I feel for Abby is trouble, you know. Not only because she's on my crew but because I need to keep things stable. I'm on shaky legs here as it is and I want to fuck with that for someone I barely know?"

Laying it out there like this is the cold ice bath my horny muscles need.

I have too much to lose to let a piece of very fine tail derail me. Abby obviously has ten times more sense than I do.

"Pretty sure I did not say or imply any of that," Luke says.

I jump off the bench and head to the treadmill. "You

didn't have to. I just needed to talk it out and now I have, we're good."

"Are we?"

I set the treadmill to its most punishing route. May as well practice for the days and weeks to come.

"Yeah, we are."

Twenty-one

Abby

I'm a couple of minutes late for my shift, likely because I'm not eager to tie myself to a mop for the day. I have company in my tardiness. Wozniak is in the locker room and looks a little sheepish on seeing me.

"Hey, Sully, how's it going?"

"Could be worse."

I could be wallowing in memories of an inappropriate hookup with my superior officer—oh, wait! I'm not and I have nothing and no one to keep me warm.

"Yeah, this whole warehouse business is really fucking us both over."

That's an interesting take. The only person who seems to have been screwed sideways here is me. I wait on tenterhooks to hear how this affects another straight white male.

I don't have to wait long.

"There's an LT position opening up at Engine 70 that has my name on it but now this incident is being blown way out of proportion. Rossi is being a total asshole. Just loves playing the big man on campus."

I'm not about to get in the middle of this. I have to work with both of them so you won't hear me taking sides, though if pressed, I know exactly where I officially land.

I'm a Roman girl all the way.

I stash my backpack in my locker and close it. Woz is tying his shoelaces and I can feel him staring at me, expecting a response.

I keep it as neutral as possible. "Well, I'll be thinking of you while I'm fumigating the equipment room."

"See? There you go. We workers are getting trod on. You should take this light duty shit up with your union rep, Sully."

And say what? I saved this lazy dickwad's life by skirting protocol and my father the commissioner thinks I'm not ready for prime time? Oh, sure.

Woz is on a roll. "You know Rossi came in here, up shit creek after he punched out his CO in New York and somehow he manages to jump the line straight into a management position. Guy's on thin ice, though, I heard." He whispers, "With your dad."

That day over breakfast, Roman had hinted he left FDNY on bad terms. So that's the story: he punched his boss and is now on a last warning with Chuck. All the more reason why we're a terrible idea.

"I wouldn't know."

But I know this: I've never wanted to pummel someone as badly as I want to pummel Wozniak right now.

"Just sayin' that if Rossi gives you trouble you can always sic your pater on him. Use those connections, Sully."

"Okay! See ya at breakfast." Christ, I need out of here.

I head to the kitchen-lounge for morning meal. Some of the A-platoon are still there, sharing stories about what happened during their shift, so I spend a couple of minutes listening in and trying to center myself for the twenty-four hours ahead. Mopping and inventory. Yay.

Grabbing coffee, I become supremely aware of a looming presence to my right. Roman has appeared in all his hot Italian glory, mug at the ready as we both go for the coffee pot.

"Go ahead," he says.

"Oh, you were first."

"All yours, Sullivan." He steps a foot or so back to give me plenty of space. The symbolism is not lost on me.

I pour a cup and add a drop of creamer. He passes the sweetener caddy over. "Looks like we're out of your brand."

Damn, no Splenda. Another sugar substitute will have to do. A warm flush overtakes me, my body far too pleased with the notion that he remembered my preferred brand from the diner. He opens the cupboard above and takes out a yellow Splenda box, shakes it, and growls.

"Who left an empty fucking box in the cupboard?"

No one fesses up. Roman mutters "fuckers" and pops the empty box in the recycling bin. He adds Splenda to the shopping list on the fridge.

"You don't have to do that. I can bring more in from home."

Another grunt in response that finds an answering call between my thighs. He picks up the coffee pot and pours into a mug that says "World's Best Dad/Firefighter."

"Lena gave you that?" Excellent deduction!

He tilts it and looks at the label like it's the first time he's seen it. A fond expression suffuses his face.

"Yeah. Though she probably doesn't think that anymore." At my look of concern, he shakes his head as if to say there'll be no confidences today.

I don't take the hint. "Is everything okay?"

He opens his mouth but we're interrupted by Danny who's just breezed in a couple of minutes past shift start.

He picks up the caddy. "No Splenda?"

"We already had this convo," I say. "All out."

Danny shakes his head sadly, then nudges me. "Hey, Simpson is having a cookout on Saturday. You going to that?"

"I hadn't given it much thought."

He offers me his widest grin. "You should go, then we could hit a club afterward. Make a night of it."

Please do not ask me out on a date while Roman is here. And what is with all these club kids?

"Not sure I can make it."

"What?" Gage turns from the stove where he's cooking up a big hash and egg scramble. "Is someone actually considering *not* attending the event of the season? Abby Sullivan, was that your whine I heard?"

"This is the first I'm hearing of it!" I slide a glance at Roman, which is the worst thing I could have done. I'm not sure what I expected—some combination of yearning and anger, maybe, if that's a thing. Instead I get the Rossi cool appraisal, the armor in place, and not a shred of softness for Yours Truly. Hastily I look away.

"I can probably make it." To Danny, I add, "But no promises for after."

"Worried about dating a firefighter?"

"I have no intention of dating anyone I work with. That's just a disaster waiting to happen." Are these words actually coming out of my mouth?

"Okay, I promise not to catch feelings," Danny says with a cheeky grin. "Let's keep it physical."

"Acosta," Roman growls. "Be very careful."

Danny reddens. "Hey, I'm sorry, Abby. You know I have nothing but respect for you."

"Sure, not a problem. But I'm serious about not dating anyone here. It's just too messy."

Neither can I imagine being with anyone other than Roman right now. The man has imprinted on me. He is Splenda and no other sugar substitute will do.

The crew give Danny shit for all manner of infractions, until Roman raises a hand and calls for the Morning Debate. "Whose turn is it?"

"I think it's me." I've been ruminating on a good question and think I have it. "Would you rather experience life in slow motion or fast forward?"

"Slow motion!" Tyler chimes in. "I love my job so I wouldn't mind if it took longer to get through the day. We might have more time on a call as well."

"No, no." Danny's frowning. "Fast forward is better. That way we can get all the dangerous and boring calls done quicker."

"What about you, LT?" Gage asks.

Roman considers it for a moment. "Probably slow. I can think of a few moments in my life I'd want to last longer."

Gage looks wistful. "Yeah, I'd love to have these early years with my kids slow down. It's happening too fast."

Roman nods. "You want to savor it while you can. Other experiences, too."

All I can think of is that kiss, how it took control of my senses for a brief time and how my world stilled to that one perfect moment. How I'd love to do it again, slower this time, and then let Roman torture me with his tongue all freaking night.

Is he thinking about that kiss as well? Is that a moment he'd want to last longer?

Those words he said in my apartment are still ringing in my ears. *I wish I'd spent the night so I'd have that memory of how good we could be together.*

"Okay, food's up, ingrates!" Gage serves up a couple of whopping great bowls of breakfast eggs, and the crowd goes to town, grabbing their fill.

Unable to resist, I take a quick peek to see what Roman's up to, only to find he's no longer here. Sometime during the breakfast distribution commotion, the lieutenant left the lounge.

🔥

People think that firefighters sit around all day waiting to be heroes, but ... sure, there's some of that. Mostly, we're filling our time with a laundry list of duties that include checking equipment, doing inventory, mopping and cleaning, and running drills.

Another is buying food for the firehouse. Tyler asked if he could swap chores with me because he wanted to do the grocery run with Gage and check out engagement rings for his girlfriend, Evie, daughter of the captain. (Apparently Gage has a very discerning eye when it comes to diamonds.) I'm in the bunk room, sweeping in preparation for a mop down, and hoping to God I don't find anything I can't unsee under the beds. One day last week I found a stiff sock, and we all know what that means.

I'm debating my sweeping strategy when a call comes in from CFD Media Affairs.

"Hello?"

"Hi Abby, this is Maria Fernandez. How are you?"

"I'm good, Maria. How about you?" Maria reached out to me when I first started to tell me that any press enquiries about my joining the fire department should be referred to them. I've had one or two calls from the media, but hardly the tsunami of interest she hinted at.

"Good, good! So, it's coming up on the twentieth anniversary of your mom's sacrifice and ..."

I don't hear the rest. Of course I knew it was coming, I even knew the date, and I had planned to reach out to my father in the hope that the anniversary would provide us with a common bond, but I've had other things on my mind.

Roman-shaped things.

"Sorry, Maria, I missed what you just said."

"The memorial service? We thought to hold it at Engine 6 instead of the Quinn. It's a historic firehouse for a number of reasons—one of the oldest in the city, your mom's tenure there—"

"The Dempseys."

Maria huffs. "Well, we don't really consider *that* historic. The kind of headlines they used to generate didn't always reflect so well on the department. Thank God they're all married off. It seems to have muted the drama." Her voice moves from conspiratorial to cheerful. "But we don't need the Dempseys when we have Abigail Sullivan, daughter of our Commissioner and a revered, trailblazing firefighter! The Commissioner thinks that holding the service at Engine 6 will keep the focus on the true heroes—the men and women who serve every day on the front lines."

My father approves of this? "So where do I fit in?"

"We'd like you to speak. Just a few words about following in her footsteps, what it means to you to be there, that kind of thing. We can even provide you with some basic text that you could tailor."

"I don't know, Maria. I really just want to do my job and this kind of attention sort of detracts from this. I'm not doing anything special."

"You'll be there representing the old and the new, the history and the future of CFD. Just think of all the little girls who might watch and be inspired!"

Inspired to be held back and put on desk duty, but still somehow get to wield a mop. *You too can live the dream, girls!*

I let her bang on about media synergy and holistic marketing for a minute or so, and then beg off when I can't stand it any longer.

I ponder what I just heard. How can my father be on board with the public relations aspect of this if he won't even support me doing the actual job? I wonder what Roman would think—then I realize that he's the last person I can talk to about this. Confidences can only lead to an intimacy I can't nurture.

But I do have something to run by him. I lean the mop against the wall and take a walk.

"Knock, knock." I lean against the entrance to Roman's office, my fist raised. "Hey, Lieutenant."

He turns from whatever he's reading and looks me up and down. Subtle, but an unmistakable check out. "Hey, Sullivan, everything okay?"

"Yeah, I just wanted to say thanks for earlier, what you said to Danny. I'm sure he didn't know how far he was pushing it."

"Oh, he knew. He shouldn't harass you like that in front of the crew when you're less likely to cut him off because you want to be polite." He narrows his eyes. "Of course, if you want to go out with him, that's your business. It's not against the rules."

No. The rules are just for me and Roman.

"I don't want to date him. Or any firefighter."

He doesn't respond, merely watches and waits.

"It's not personal." The words are gushing from me now in direct proportion to my fast-rising color. "I've just seen how difficult it is to be married to one. How much it hurts to lose someone in the service, so it seems like tempting fate to put two firefighters together like that. Double the potential for disaster."

My heart's thumping hard. I'm not saying this to warn him off—we're already never going to happen. But I want him to know I won't be dating anyone at Engine 6. If I could and we weren't already crazily problematic, I would definitely go on that date with him.

"I see," is all he says.

Subject change needed. "How come you skipped breakfast earlier?"

He taps his pen on the desk, obviously trying to decide if I'm worthy of his confidence. "I had a call from Lena's school. She got into trouble a couple of days ago. Fight with another kid."

"Oh no! Is she okay?"

"Yeah, she's fine. Physically, anyway. I have a meeting there tomorrow, and I think we'll figure that part of it out. But she's pretty mad at me." He pauses, probably weighing whether to tell me more. My silence is rewarded. "I won't let her attend her mom's wedding."

"Ah, that sounds tricky." I know that Roman is on less-than-ideal terms with his ex. A curious eagerness to be his shoulder grips me. Surely we can be friends. I'd like that because something is better than nothing where this man is concerned. Sure, that's risky but everything about this situation is, and apparently I live for danger. "Is it because you don't want to go?"

"I'm not invited, which is perfectly fine. Only I can't let Lena go alone. That side of the family are a bunch of booze hounds." The pen tap becomes more pronounced. "But that's not the issue—or the entire issue. The problem is that Tori wants to dress Lena up like a doll for this shit show. Trot her out and pretend that everything is A-okay." He waves a hand. "Sorry, you don't need to hear this."

"No, it's fine. So what does Lena want?"

"She's eleven so it's not relevant."

"Oh dear."

He points at me with the pen. "You're not a parent so I won't be taking that attitude from you."

His teasing affront makes me smile and gives me confidence I can be honest with him. "Listen, it sounds like she wants to go and maybe your feelings on the matter shouldn't come into it. As long as you can guarantee her safety while there."

He eyes me with that Roman brow of sex. "In other words, it's not about you, Rossi."

"I never said that, but yeah? Of course, you're dealing with a minor and you want her to be safe and not in the middle of any toxic situation. But ask yourself if your resistance to this is because you want what's best for Lena or what's best for you."

"Jeez, one round of mopping the bunk room and you're the grand old oracle of wisdom?" His half grin, an expression I'm starting to adore, confirms he's joking.

"I should open up an advice booth! Like Lucy in Peanuts."

"Charge more than five cents though. Inflation."

I smile. "No charge for you. I expect quid pro quo on all you're going to teach me once I'm back on active duty."

He stands and approaches, stopping just a few inches short.

Yet too. Damn. Far.

"I'm working on that, by the way. No promises, but I'll be talking to Venti today about getting you reinstated sooner."

"I'll keep thinking it'll happen. The power of positive thinking." Can I positively think his lips onto mine? My entire body is awash with the masculine scent and heat of him.

He's close and so very present, and while his mouth is moving, I've no idea what's coming out of it. It takes me a second to realize he's said something about Danny.

"What's that?"

"If Acosta hassles you again, let me know."

"I'm sure he won't. I think he got carried away with the crew present."

"Easy enough where you're concerned." His eyes drink me in. "And you're right, dating a firefighter is tricky, not just because of the workplace dynamics but it's tough on families. Your dad went through that with your mom, so I see where he's coming from. Why he's so protective. I'd be the same with my kid or with any woman I was involved with."

He's staring at me now, so serious, so Roman. Is he trying to tell me it's a good thing we're not exploring this attraction because one of us getting hurt or killed could result in unbearable pain for the other? Or is he saying that he feels protective of me?

"Best not to get involved at all," I mutter, though the words sound weird and a million kinds of wrong.

"Listen, I know you probably have regrets about that kiss but—"

"I don't, Roman. Not a single one."

He huffs out a breath. "Good. I'd hate to be one of yours."

There's a double meaning there. Regret for what we've done and regret for what we can't. It's provocative and I want to take him up on the promise imbued in those words.

His chest heaves. I take a step. It's perilous, but I seem to be living on the edge lately. My fingers twitch with need, my skin tingles with want.

Most troublesome of all, my heart starts an erratic beat. It's not merely excitement or a sensual pull, though all of that is present. It's a yearning for connection with this man who would hate to be one of my regrets.

The siren goes off, announcing, "Engine 6, Ambulance 59 ..." and the code for the call, one I can't go on.

Roman collects himself, and I realize it's probably-maybe-possibly-definitely for the best. "Okay, Sullivan, back to work."

Twenty-Two

Roman

I put my head around the door of Lena's bedroom. She's on her computer, but quickly shuts the screen down when she sees me.

"Hey, you still mad at me?"

She rolls her eyes, but there's affection there. "Yes."

I take that as an invitation to come in. Really, I need to take a shower and get some Z's after a killer shift, but this has to happen first. Abby's advice resonated with me.

"I didn't have time to clean up."

"It's okay. I kind of—" She stops and squares her shoulders. "What did you want to talk about?"

She sounds so grown up, as if the events of the last few days have added weeks or maybe months to her age. I hate to see those moments escape me.

"Let's talk about your mom's wedding. Other than being a part of it, how do you feel about it?"

"How do I feel? I don't wish you two were getting back together, if that's what you mean."

"Not really, but good to know. We've never really talked about your mom and ... Mark." Mark Levinson, my former co-worker at Ladder 43. I practically choke on his name. "I guess I haven't wanted to talk about them but I've not really considered how that makes you feel."

I take a seat on the bed and wait for her to sort through her emotions.

"I don't like what she did. The affair. It wasn't fair to you ... or to me. But Mom's never been the kind of person who thinks about how stuff affects anyone else but herself. So I guess it didn't surprise me."

My girl has always been so intuitive where her mom is concerned. I hate that she has to be.

"And now they're getting married," I say. "I didn't think you'd be interested in going. Getting dressed up." I'm trying to frame this differently.

It takes her a few seconds but she considers this. "I'm not. But Mom said she has a dress for me. I don't really want to wear that but ..."

"But ..."

"But if Mom wants me to be part of the wedding, to be a bridesmaid, it must mean that she ... wants to see me, right?"

The heartbreak I hear in my daughter's voice knifes me in two. Lena was—is—pretty hurt about Tori's behavior during the divorce. Her mother never fought for her so Lena took that the way it was intended: her mom didn't love her enough. Now it sounds like she's prepared to wear a dress that would make her feel unlike herself if it means pleasing the woman who's held her at arm's length since she was born. My little girl would stuff her feelings down deep to show her mother she could be the daughter she wanted.

I'm so fucking angry but I have to show a different side of myself to Lena. I have to make excuses for my ex-wife's behavior so my daughter will be less hurt. "Of course she wants to see you. Wedding or no wedding, she wants to see you. But she's been planning it for a while so it keeps her busy." Even to the point of canceling Lena's last visit to New York.

"I thought this would be a good way to show her I'm making the effort."

You don't have to show her a damn thing.

But I don't say that. I want my daughter to have a good relationship with her mother, so if this is the way it has to happen, then she gets to be in the wedding party.

"You still want to go, even though you have to wear some stupid dress?"

"I'd suffer through it so Mom can have her big day."

Her generosity floors me. I throw my arms around her, absorb the warmth and goodness of her. "I wonder where you came from, little one. I know you look like me but you're far too good to be related to this dummy."

She sniffs and smiles into my neck. "I just turned up."

"Sorry I stink." In all the ways.

"I like this smell, when you've just come home. It makes me proud of you."

I close my eyes, gratitude that I have this special being in my life flowing through me.

"You want to go to New York for the wedding, we'll make it happen."

She lifts her head. "Really?"

"Yes, really."

But I'll be talking to Tori about how it's going to go down. I'm not looking forward to it, but if it makes my girl happy, I'll walk through that fire.

Twenty-three

Abby

It's my day off. I've already hit the climbing wall at First Ascent in Uptown, laundry is in the dryer, the Roomba is doing its thing, and the sun is shining its ass off. (Not that the great outdoors is calling my name or anything, but a sunny spring day, even spent inside, has a distinctly cheering effect.) I'm catching up on Season 3 of *Sex Education* and wishing I could carry off Gillian Anderson's style or have as much sex as the show's "teenagers" when a text comes in.

Hi Abby, it's Chiara, Roman's sister. I have a favor to ask. Could you call me?

I hit dial. "Hey, everything okay?"

"Oh, thank God you're there. Alex gave me your number. Are you busy right now?"

I pull a potato chip out of my cleavage. "Not terribly."

"Could you pick up Lena from school? I got held up at this stupid meeting at work."

"Sure, but where's Roman?" We have the same days off.

"He's instructing at the firefighter academy today."

Oh, I didn't know that, but then he's not obliged to tell me anything.

"Will he be okay with me doing this?"

"Why wouldn't he be? You're a trusted member of his crew and you live close by."

"Gage not around?"

She laughs. "Yeah, I tried him and Brady first but they're not picking up. Probably having sex."

Well, thanks for that lovely visual. "Of course I'll do it. I just don't want to make anyone uncomfortable."

"As if you could. Lena thinks you're really cool! Look, I have to head back to this meeting. Lena gets out at 3:15."

I check the time. It's 3:10. "I'd better get going."

"Yep! I'll text her and call the school to say you're on the way. Thanks. Byeee!"

Okay, then.

Seven minutes later I'm waiting outside Sacred Heart School on Sheridan as the kids flood by me in a river of navy and white uniforms. I spot Lena, who raises a hand in greeting.

"Hey, you, how's it going?"

"Good." Puzzled, she's clearly wondering why I've been chosen for this monumental task.

I launch into an explanation. "I live in the neighborhood so I could get here the fastest. Your aunt really thought she'd make it."

She walks alongside me. "I could have made it home by myself. Or gone with my friend." She waves at another girl, getting in a car. "That's Milly. She lives in Rogers Park."

"I guess you could have, but here we are. It's just a couple of blocks."

I let her take the lead because I realize I don't actually

know where Roman lives. On the way, we chat about her favorite subjects—history and English—her favorite video game—"Super Mario 3D All Stars"—and her favorite candy—peach Kit Kats. (A friend sends them from Japan.)

We reach the door to a nice-looking duplex on Greenview. It's closer than I thought, about three blocks from me. All this time, he's been practically my next-door neighbor.

"Are you coming in?" she asks. "We have pizza."

Chiara had already texted to say I should stay until a responsible adult returns so this is moot. All the same, I maintain the illusion that the kid has a choice here. "I love pizza."

"Everybody does."

Once inside, she sits at the kitchen table and I join her as she pulls cold pizza from a box. Within a couple of minutes, temporary tattoo sheets have made an appearance and we spend some time choosing. (Well, Lena does. I'm clearly not qualified to be anything but a blank canvas.) While she lays on the first one, she asks in a very young voice, "Do you miss your mom?"

The question takes my breath away. Only a child can ask it in such stark, unrelenting terms.

"All the time. How about you?"

"She's not dead. I mean ..." She colors. "She's still around. She's getting married soon. Dad's letting me go but he doesn't really want me to."

Roman changed his mind about Lena attending her mom's nuptials? I wonder if that has anything to do with our conversation earlier this week.

"It's probably a bit awkward for him."

"He doesn't still love her."

Good to hear, though I shouldn't have an opinion on that at all. "Still, might be awkward. He's probably worried about you traveling to another city."

"That's not it. It's because he worries Mom will get mad at me because I don't usually like to dress up." She picks out another tattoo—it looks like a dragon with sun rays around its head. "My parents used to fight about me all the time. About how I didn't wear dresses or how I did my hair."

Her hair is short, feathered over her temples and hanging over her left eye. She always looks super cute.

"If you don't want to wear a dress, who cares?"

She raises a knowing eyebrow, just like her dad's. "That's what Dad would say, but Mom said they weren't raising a boy. Dad would then tell her she wasn't raising anyone. Which would get them fighting again." Her nose twitches. "All their fights were about me."

I take the tattoo sheet from her and scan it. "You might think that, but believe me, the fights were about other things that had nothing to do with you. They probably didn't see eye to eye on a lot of stuff, and that's what you remember because you assume you're the center of the universe. Like we all do."

That pulls a Roman-like grin from her and my heart catches. "That's what Dad says. 'Copernicus called. You're not the center of the universe.'"

"Cute." I recall Roman mentioning that was one of his mom's sayings, and my heart yearns for that simpler time when my mouth was full of pie and sex with a hot guy was in my future. "So I'm going to take this one, if that's okay." I hold up one that has an egg-shaped robot vibe to it. "It looks like Zingbot from Big Brother."

"You watch Big Brother?"

"Yep, never miss it. You?"

She nods enthusiastically. "Dad thinks I'm not old enough to watch it but Mom and Aunt Chiara let me. Chiara applied to go on it. I think she would have been really good."

"I can see that. Who's your favorite player? I'm a Janelle stan."

Her eyes go wide. "Me, too! Best player in BB history."

"Iconic. Always sidelined by some ridiculous guy alliance."

She nods wisely. "You want to play video games?"

"Sure!" I haven't played video games in several years but I used to be pretty good. "I have to warn you—I'll probably smoke your butt."

She's amused by my certainty. Ten minutes later, it's clear my confidence is severely misplaced as I fail to make my way around the racetrack even once in the latest adventures of Crash Bandicoot.

"That was a lot easier in my day," I say, after my vehicle bursts into a ball of flame. Again.

"When? In the eighties?"

I point the controller at her. "I'm not an eighties kid. I'm barely a nineties kid. The nerve!"

She grins and I grin back at her. Such a sweet kid.

"Hey, anyone here?" Oh dear. I had really hoped Chiara would return first.

"We're in here, Dad."

Roman walks into the den, all alpha-daddy swagger (it's a thing!) and my breath leaves my body because he's ... him. That's it. I can't deny the attraction. It looks like I'm destined to turn to goop in this man's presence, so maybe I should just learn how to manage the craving.

"Hey, Lieutenant."

His brows pinch together. "Is everything okay?"

"Yeah, didn't Chiara call you? She asked me to pick up Lena." Lena's moved on to a community version of the game where she can be challenged appropriately by her peers who are half my age.

"No, she didn't." He sounds annoyed to be out of the loop or more likely that I've been co-opted into childcare duty. I'm definitely getting anyone-but-you vibes.

"She had an important meeting. I'm just around the corner, so it was no bother."

He nods toward my arm. "Sure about that?" I have three new tattoos—a pink pony, a purple robot, and a blue dragon. Or maybe it's a dinosaur.

"Best tattoo parlor in Chicago." I stand up, wiping crumbs from my thighs from the cookie Lena made me eat. Where "made me" means "offered-and-was-gone-in-three-seconds." "I should go."

"Stay for dinner," Lena says, barely looking up from her game. "Dad's making the spicy-ah-meatballs-ah."

"Oh, no, I can't. I have ... something else on."

Lena is disappointed enough to pause the game, and I get how hard it must be to look at a kid who wants things.

"See you around, Lena."

"Okay." She pouts but I won't be swayed. Besides I have no choice; I can't be in the same room as Roman.

Wait a second, that's not true. *Yes, I can*. I am a fucking professional, but I do have something on. Roman follows me to the door, where I stop, "Well, have—"

"What's happening to—"

We blink at talking over each other, then grin ruefully. This shouldn't be so awkward.

"What's happening tonight?" he finishes. "A date?"

"Yes, actually. Well, a drink at a bar but not until later."

"Mr. D-Bag of the unsolicited ab shots, is it?"

"Connor the connoisseur of abs and Kurosawa, I think you mean." He mouths an *ah* that makes me chuckle. "Yeah, we're finally going to meet in person."

"The abs have worked their magic at last." He rubs his mouth. "Thanks for walking Lena home today and hanging with her. That was really nice of you."

"I'm not sure why Chiara called me."

"I think we both know why."

Now it's my turn to mouth an *ah* in agreement. "What makes her think that's a good idea?"

He leans against the wall, his head near a picture of the three of them—Chiara, Roman, and Lena—in a candid pose. "She picked up on a vibe between us."

"Were we that obvious?"

"Only to my sister who's looking to matchmake at every opportunity. I think she's worried I'll head back to New York. She likes me being here."

Back to New York? The notion chills me. "Is that likely? I thought you'd ... finished there."

"I'm going nowhere."

There's a definitive stamp in his voice that immediately affirms his intention and conveys solidity and trust. Having a man like Roman in your life—in *my* life—is hashtag goals for sure. It doesn't have to be as a boyfriend or lover, either. He can fill myriad roles: mentor, boss, running partner, cheerleader.

Friend.

The silence stretches as our gazes lock in challenge. Apparently, we're both desperate to prove we can spend time together and *not* do what comes naturally: touching, tasting, and so much more.

That *friend* notion is looking less and less likely.

"So a drink date?" he finally says. "I think you might need to coat your stomach. Don't want you getting light-headed."

"Hmm, those abs *are* something else."

"Keep it in your pants, Sullivan."

That pulls a laugh from me, one of my deeply awkward ones, but something wicked flashes in Roman's eyes. He likes my laugh, I can tell.

"I guess I could throw a frozen entree into the microwave," I say casually.

"Or help me with my spicy-ah-meatballs-ah." He plays up

the fake Italian accent and I'm swooning again, loving when he drops the guard of Lieutenant Serious.

"How spicy are we talking?"

"As spicy as you need it."

Although I should demur, I can't say no to that.

Twenty-four

Roman

I should have let her go. Thanked her for her service and sent her packing to her frozen entree and date prep with a guy who isn't me. Instead I used my kid's request for my own selfish wants. I can't stop Abby from seeing some other man but I can make it damn difficult to not think about me while she's doing it.

It's an evil plan. I'm not usually a games-player but I can't be forthright about my motives here because I'm not supposed to have any.

I'm supposed to ignore those freckles across her nose.

I'm supposed to ignore the lushness of her curves and the way she fills out that blouse.

I'm supposed to ignore that dirty, sexy laugh that she seems to be using, oh, ten times more than before. That sound is a sex act in some countries and should be illegal in every state of the union.

Whether because we've entered a different phase or we're both hovering in this will-they-won't-they limbo, the vibe is flirty and loose and easy, and I'm enjoying myself too much to question it. One dinner with my kid as chaperone can't hurt.

"What can I do?"

I look around. No sign of Lena all of a sudden, which means I'm solo and in deep ass trouble. "As I've lost my usual helper, you'll have to do."

"Sorry to disappoint. I can't cook but I can chop onions or parsley or—"

"Open wine?"

She grins and my heart knocks so hard it hurts. "I can definitely do that!" She grabs the rabbit corkscrew thing and sets about opening a bottle of Shiraz sitting on the side table.

"Glasses in the cupboard above the sink." My hands are already deep into the minced veal and pork so I'd usually grab them. Instead I track her as she reaches up, full breasts straining against the thin cotton of her blouse as she takes down two glasses.

I don't have to watch.

I want to.

Swallowing a bolt of lust, I return to the raw meat mixture coating my hands. It should be enough to dampen my ardor, but do you think it is?

That would be a negative.

"Should I get you a straw? Or maybe a sippy cup?"

I arch an eyebrow. "I can wait a couple of minutes. Almost done here."

With the meatballs in the frying pan, I wash my hands and pick up the glass.

"Thanks for inviting me," she says, suddenly diffident, another look on her that I didn't expect. I like it.

Hell, I like all her looks. Smartass, go-getter, feisty, annoyed, soft, strong. I especially like that look on her face when she's just been kissed to distraction.

"Thanks for staying, despite the underhanded tactics of

my evil twin." After taking a sip, I move the meatballs around in the pan, then check the sauce which is bubbling nicely.

"You guys must be really close."

"We are. It's been the two of us since my parents passed when we were in our early twenties."

"What happened?"

"Car crash. One minute they were celebrating twenty-five years of marriage, the next, gone when some idiot went the wrong way on the Long Island Expressway." It was part of the reason why I stayed with Tori despite the warning signs. I needed to get it right, keep my little family together and honor my parents in some way.

A quick look finds her nodding in sympathy. She lost her mom, so I know she gets it.

I clear my throat. "When Chiara got a job out here about six years ago, it felt like I'd lost a big part of myself. She's always been the person I turn to."

"Did your ex-wife get along with her?"

God, no. "They hated each other. No one was more pleased to see Chiara move out of New York than my ex. Oil and water, y'know. But really it boils down to Chiara being very protective of me and Lena. She never thought Tori was good enough for us."

"What did you think?"

I flick a glance over my shoulder. The last thing I need is for Lena to hear any of this.

"Tori's happier now. I think we all are."

Abby senses my discomfort and leans in, ensuring only the two of us would ever share this. It feels so good to be this close to her, even if it's a by-product of my sob story.

"You were together for a while?"

"Ten years that was ten years too long, to be honest. We shouldn't have married but I couldn't bear the thought of not being with my kid. And in the end, it turned out marriage wasn't so necessary for that after all."

"Your worst decision, maybe?"

I jerk to attention. "What?"

"That night at the diner you said sharing that pie with me was your second worst decision. You wouldn't tell me your first."

Huh, I didn't expect to be thrown back into that moment when Cherry Pie and I connected for the first time. Or to be seen so clearly it rattles me. "I guess I'm not one for giving up on something, even if it's not good for me."

She colors, which cheers me big time. We can both play the perceptive game.

"Lena was talking about her mom's wedding before you got home. She said you changed your mind."

"I did. Turns out it's not all about me."

"Hmm, funny how that works."

"You're an inspiration to us all, Sullivan."

She chuckles, takes a sip of her wine. "She mentioned that she was worried you were upset because you guys used to fight about her."

"About Lena? Partly." Lena is usually quiet about that, so maybe she needs an ear outside the family.

"She implied that you guys parted ways because of your conflict over her. I told her there were probably lots of reasons why you would fight. I'm sure you've told her the divorce wasn't her fault but kids seem to internalize that."

I nod slowly, thinking it through. I probably haven't been as open with Lena about the reasons for the divorce. She knows about the affair but we were kaput long before that.

"Yeah, I was looking for something different from my marriage. A partner in all things, not just someone to party with. Tori had different notions about that." Getting a bit too in the weeds there. "Thanks for talking to her," I say, my voice so low that it pulls her in closer. Close enough to smell her scent over the hearty tomato fragrance in the kitchen.

After getting over the initial shock of seeing Abby in my home, I took a moment to enjoy the sight of her playing video games with my daughter, eating her baked treats, connecting with her through those tattoos. That's what Lena needs—people who love and accept her unconditionally. Tori hated that Lena was a gamer, thinking it another sign that we were raising "a lesbian."

I can surround myself with good people who will be good for my daughter, even someone like Abby. As a friend.

"Chiara and I try to talk to her about these things, but sometimes we can't help letting our feelings about Tori filter through. She's smart and sensitive, and picks up on that. Because I find it hard to sound neutral, I sometimes choose to say nothing at all."

She peers up at me, all blue-eyed loveliness and my instincts to kiss her are so fucking strong I almost buckle. Instead I move the conversation to uber-personal territory because if I can't lay my lips on her, maybe I can emote some other way.

"Tori's marrying one of my co-workers back in the firehouse."

She grasps my arm. "Roman, I'm so sorry. Were they—?"

"They were. Everyone knew but me. He wasn't a particular friend but my captain at the firehouse was and he covered it up. It was a whole thing."

"I bet it was. So that's why you separated from FDNY and came out here."

"There was a bit more to it. I punched my captain—my friend—and though I could have moved to another ladder, it's the kind of thing that follows you. To be honest, getting out of New York was good for us both, though it was tough on Lena to start."

"Of course it would be!" Her hand still lays curled around my arm, like she can't get enough of my heat. My gaze dips to her forearm, covered in Lena's tattoos. Lena has been going mad for those lately, which are apparently all the rage with her friends. I want to kiss them, then kiss Abby everywhere else.

"Starting over like that is huge and you're doing this to make the best life for your kid."

That she gets it feels like the sun shining light on a dark place. "Chiara was going through some stuff at the time with her wife and needed a shoulder. It seemed like it would be good for all of us."

"Family is everything to you. I get it. And then you landed right back into the fire when you ran into my dad."

"*That* I can handle. What's trickier is having the hots for a direct report who happens to be that man's daughter."

She doesn't even blink, and neither do I. Look at us, maturely acknowledging the problem.

With a sip of her wine, she eyes me over the lip of the glass. "When you flame out you do it with style, Rossi."

"That I fucking do." Back to the meatballs because yet again,

It's gettin' hot in here.

"Hey, I have something for you to do."

So take off all your clothes ...

"Oh, yeah?"

"Can you maybe ... boil some water?"

She grasps at her throat dramatically, leeching the tension from the moment. "I resent the implication! I haven't burned a pot of water in months."

I direct her to a pot and instruct her to fill it three quarters of the way.

She places it under the faucet. "Hmm, I wonder how the clear liquid stuff comes out."

"Cute."

She shrugs. "I know. Playing up my inner blonde sure appeals to the boys."

"Not this boy. I'm all about the competence porn."

"Well, you're not my audience."

Lie of major magnitude. If I had my way, I would be her entire fucking audience. We share a look that basically affirms what would be happening if we were different people in a different universe.

With a heavy sigh, I throw some salt in the water, the meatballs in the sauce, and pick up my wine for a healthy swig. The notion that I need to be always moving takes hold, like it can protect me from the wild, inappropriate thoughts running riot.

In action, the dreams can't slip through.

"So you're not a cook?"

"No, though my aunt Kathleen tried her best to teach me. I practically lived with her and my cousin Jackie after my mom died. It was tough for my father to manage me and work the shifts he did."

"I understand that. One-parent families need a support network, especially when the parent works long hours. That's one of the reasons I came out here. Lena needs more than I can give her."

She shuffles closer, touches my arm. "From what I've seen, you're an amazing dad. And you obviously had her welfare in mind when you moved to Chicago."

"And the free childcare," I joke.

Her hand is still on my arm, the warmth of her seeping into my bones. Deeper. To the marrow. "She's doing okay, Roman. She's got people who love her and that goes a long way."

My chest warms at her praise. "I'm glad you had that support, too. With your aunt."

"Yeah, I was lucky. Some people might say I wasn't

because of what happened to my mom, but I landed in a good place. And Dad and I were close in the years after. I didn't want him out of my sight. I'd wake up terrified he wouldn't come home." She punctuates that with a frown.

"You okay?"

"Yeah, I'd forgotten how upset I used to get. I'd be up early, waiting for him to come off shift. Insist on making him coffee even though the poor guy really just wanted to hit the hay. But I thought I was looking after him because he didn't have my mom anymore." A softness overcomes her expression along with a crimp between her brows I want to kiss better. "It seems like an age ago."

"Not that long. Maybe cut him some slack. You're always gonna be his princess." Here I am defending that asshole again, but we're both dads. I can empathize with him there.

"Bet that's what you thought when you heard Chuck Sullivan's daughter was posted to Six. Some prima donna who needs constant attention."

"Yep. Turns out it's true."

She pushes at my shoulder. "What? I'm not afraid of hard work or getting my hands dirty."

The mention of "dirty" and "hands," even in that innocuous context, charges the conversation—an exchange that does not need any more electricity.

"No, you're not. In fact, you're a revelation, Abby."

She's surprised me every step of the way. With how hard she works, how great she gets along with anyone, how she's never once traded on her family name. I'm proud to have her on my crew even if every second I'm with her makes me itchy with need.

My admission makes her blush. Does she have any idea how special she is?

"Can I be honest with you?" she asks before I have a chance to say something stupid.

"Always," I reply, hoping she'll nail down the stupid for both of us.

"I know we've said we can't and I understand all the reasons—truly I do—but I still think you're the hottest guy I've ever met. Inside and out. Neither of us wants what's happening between us to affect our careers but I'd like to think we could be mature enough to handle it. I mean, it's just ..." She lowers her voice. "S-e-x. It's no one's business but ours."

My cock stirs. Or at least it stirs more than usual because it's been in a constant state of awareness for the last half hour.

Right on cue, my perfect little cock-blocker of a kid skips in. "Is dinner ready?"

"Here she is, the Queen of Perfect Timing."

Lena gives me an *oh-dad* look. "I had homework to do."

"I've never seen you so enthusiastic to hit the books. Set the table, please, and show our guest that we're not heathens."

"She knows."

Does she? I eye Abby, feeling quite the heathen as a result of her last statement. Is she suggesting we do this and screw the complications?

It's just s-e-x.

It's never just sex, but maybe I'm too old to accept a statement like that at face value. Maybe I need to take a page from the book of my juniors, the advice of my sister, and the encouragement of everyone telling me to bang someone already.

Only this is not the woman I should be breaking my sex drought with. She's a direct report, the daughter of my boss, and a whole lot of fucking trouble.

And hell if I don't want a little trouble right now, especially when Trouble gives me that come-and-get-it scorcher of a look that tells me all I have to do is say yes.

We're tearing into the garlic bread when my sister shows her sorry matchmaking face.

"Hey, gorgeous people!" She beams at me and I want to murder her. "What'd I miss?"

"All the work," I say. "But you're in time to see the fruits of your meddling."

She's washing her hands at the sink, fake bafflement on her face. "*Med-del-ling*?" Like it's a foreign language.

Annoyed, I grab a bowl for her and ladle up a serving with an extra meatball I hope lodges in her throat.

Chiara squeezes our guest's shoulder. "Thanks so much for helping out, Abs!"

Abs? I exchange a glance with Abby, who gives me a quick grin that melts the frost compacting my heart.

"Happy to. And I got the better end of the deal." She licks her lips. "This is amazing. How come you don't cook like this at the firehouse?"

"And steal Gage's thunder? I'm not getting into that kind of piss—" Quick glance at my daughter. "Kind of contest. Besides it's nice to have someone cook for me seeing as I do all the cooking here." Pointed look at my sister. Tonight, I am the master of nonverbal communication.

"I refuse to allow the patriarchy to determine who should be in the kitchen," Chiara says as she digs into the spaghetti and shovels it in her mouth. Smashing the patriarchy has clearly never tasted so good. Barely two chews and a swallow later, she's back. "Mom did all the cooking when we were kids and I vowed I would not be that chick. But now my wife is eating another woman's croissants so maybe I don't know what I'm talking about."

Abby looks concerned, which is pretty damn empathetic of her and just affirms what a good person she is.

"But Aunt Devi will be coming home soon, right?" Lena shoots a worried glance my way.

Chiara raises both hands. "Of course she will! I just miss her, that's all."

Lena doesn't like to hear about people going through relationship problems. It's a little too close to the bone.

Deflecting, Chiara smiles at Abby. "So Abby, tell us all about how you became a firefighter. I heard you used to be a paramedic?"

"Yeah, I was. Still am. That's a pretty traditional path. Once you're in that lane, Fire Academy seems like the most logical step."

"And your mom was a big shot, huh?"

"Yep, one of the original cohort of women firefighters in Chicago twenty-seven years ago. The first group were twenty women, assigned in pairs to ten stations, so they could look out for each other. Some of the stories I've heard about the resistance to their presence would make your hair stand on end."

Chiara swallows another mouthful of pasta. "Like what?"

"Red pepper on their sheets, dirty underwear in lockers, risqué reading material to try and create an atmosphere of harassment. Some of the women quit but my mom didn't."

I love hearing the pride in her voice. It's a hard act to follow but so far she's kicking ass.

"And for a hetero lady, it can't have been all bad," Chiara says, because everything is about relationships with her. "Those are pretty good odds!"

"Oh, yeah. Of course they were all catches, every one." She flicks a shy glance toward me, then away again.

"She met your dad there," I say, then immediately regret it.

Abby meets my gaze directly now. "She did. When I was born, he wanted her to quit. Only one superhero per family allowed."

"Did she?" Lena is listening intently. "Because she should be able to do whatever she wants."

That's my girl.

"She stayed home with me for a couple of years," Abby goes on, "but then she came back to the fire department. It must have been hard for her, but she and my dad figured it out."

Her brow rumples as she thinks on that. I suspect she wants to say more, talk about how a firefighter marriage strained at the seams, but that would only make the conversation too serious.

"She must have been really brave," Lena says. "Like you."

"Oh, I'm not brave. But she was. She was a total badass."

I think her daughter is just like her.

Twenty-five

Abby

Roman won't let us help with the dishes—I offered, his sister scoffed—so we sit at the table, enjoying the sight of a man taking care of business. Lena is playing video games, having claimed she's finished her homework.

"I could get used to this," I say, as I drain my glass. When Chiara goes to top me up, I call it. "Can't. I'm supposed to be meeting someone."

"Who?" Chiara's mouth turns down. "A date?"

"Sort of. Roman doesn't approve."

His shoulder muscles stiffen at the mention of my plans. It takes all my willpower not to reach out and run my hands over them. It's not even sexual—or not a hundred percent so.

He turns, drying his hands on a dishtowel, an eyebrow scooted in disapproval. "He's into Kurosawa."

"What's that? Some weird BDSM thing?"

I laugh, seeking to ease the tension that bunches up my internal organs whenever I talk about other men around Roman.

"He's a celebrated Japanese filmmaker," I say to Chiara. "Connor's a fan."

"Connor? Have you gone on a date with him yet?"

"No. We've been missing each other. Our stars haven't aligned." I've actually ignored his texts for the last few weeks.

Roman bends over to pull a dishwasher packet out of the cupboard under the sink. His jeans tighten perfectly across his ass and I have to blink to come back from the heaven that image sent me to.

Chiara smirks at me. Damn.

"So, it sounds like stars are not aligning for a reason," she adds with a devious twinkle. "Maybe it's not meant to be."

"I won't know for sure until I meet him." I avoid Roman's heated gaze. "I really should get going."

Before dinner, I made it very clear to Roman that he just needed to say the word and I was his. In bed, that is. I truly believe we can handle this in a mature and adult manner.

I'm especially interested in all things *mature and adult* with this man.

"Thanks so much for dinner. This was really nice."

"I'll walk you out," Roman says, and when his sister grins, he scowls at her. Which is about as sexy as the man can get.

Hard-earned smiles, stormy scowls ... I love it all.

But it doesn't matter. He's walking me out and that's all there is to it.

"Thanks again," I say over my shoulder as we get to the front door.

He doesn't say a word, just opens the door, follows me out, and closes it behind him.

"You going somewhere?"

"Walking you home. Unless you're going out on your date immediately."

"No, I'm going home first. To, uh, take a shower." A cold

one from the way my body is reacting under Roman's hot and heavy gaze.

"Then I'll make sure you get there safely."

Safely? Impossible under the circumstances as every cell of my being is under sensual threat. We walk, neither of us speaking until the silence threatens to bury me.

Finally, I say, "It's strange that we're such close neighbors but never met before a month ago."

"Kind of nice, though," he murmurs. "I get to run into you at the diner and walk you home."

There's a sweetness to those words, like he genuinely believes those are perks instead of straight-up temptations. But perks of what? Friendship?

We exchange a few words about nothing I can remember and then we're at the front door to my building. The cicadas are singing, a light breeze ruffles Roman's midnight-dark hair, and this beautiful spring evening hitches my heart with its perfection.

"What?" he murmurs. "What's that smile?"

"I'm just thinking of what a lovely night it is." And how now I'm going to ruin it by going on a date with some random guy.

Roman stares at me, into me, and that light breeze ignites into a hot gust that envelops my body.

"Why are you looking at me like that?" I ask.

"I genuinely don't know what to do here."

He sounds a mix of forlorn and annoyed. I can understand that a man like Roman operates on a level where certainty is a given. He understands the world a particular way, its rules, its patterns, and how to keep his people and crew safe. My entry into his life has thrown him off course and he's looking for a way back to the straight and narrow.

I can't make up his mind for him.

"What do you want to do?"

"What I want is not possible, Abby." His gaze drills into me, strips me raw, and leaves me a spineless mess on the metaphorical floor.

"Tell me what you *don't* want, then."

I expect him to say he doesn't want me to go on that date. I *need* him to say that.

"I don't want to feel your smile on my face when you come in for your shift or the brush of your arm against mine as you get off the truck. I don't want my lungs to be filled with the scent of you. I don't want to hear your laugh because it—and everything about you—makes me so damn crazy I can't think straight."

"Roman—"

Whip quick, he moves in, his hand cupping my hip, the heat of his touch imprinting on me through the fabric of my top. With lips brushing my ear, his whisper is delicious and decadent.

"I don't want to feel like this anymore. So fucking desperate. So fucking needy."

I place a hand on his chest, an attempt at comfort, though whether it's for myself or for him, I can't say. Nothing has ever felt so solid and masculine, so perfect under my trembling fingers.

His proximity, the intensity waving off him wraps around me like a gorgeous, weighted blanket. One twist of my head and my lips will rub against his dark cheek. He needs a shave, just like that night at the diner. Perhaps we can pretend we're those people again. I want to feel that strong jaw between my thighs, the weight of him and the moment over me.

"You said it could be just S—" He breathes against the shell of my ear. "E—" Another touch of his lips against my temple. "X." He finishes with a rough sound in his throat that instantly gets me wet. "Did you mean that?"

I said it but now I realize that was me trying to convince myself—and him—to take a chance on us.

"I don't know," I whisper, though I really shouldn't admit that. We can't date, yet sex might not be enough.

He turns, locks eyes onto mine, and breathes a hot puff of longing against my lips.

"How about we pretend that's all it is?" His words are tentative as if he's testing their viability to exist in a real sentence.

"You mean lie?"

"Is it a lie if we're so ... upfront about it?"

Be honest about the fact we're lying, but pretend this means nothing all the same? If that's what it takes to feel him inside me once again, I'm prepared to strike that devil's bargain. I refuse to overthink it because that will produce a level of reason that's so inappropriate to how I feel right now.

I tip my toes, he inclines his head, and our lips line up perfectly.

There's still time to take a step back into sanity, but in this moment, pleasure and need are a two-punch with their hooks in me. I meet his kiss and fall into madness.

This kiss isn't a lie. Nothing that hot and deep could ever feel like an untruth. It takes a hold of my senses and wrings them out until I'm gasping. I hadn't realized how much I missed his mouth, the honesty of it.

"Still as sweet as cherry pie." He closes his eyes and leans his forehead to mine. "I shouldn't want this so bad. Nothing good comes from wanting something this bad."

"It's okay to want things, Roman." I've been telling myself that for years while I strive to take control of my career and the life I crave. We're not hurting anyone, though the closer I get to Roman, the more I realize that someone could emerge from this damaged.

Me.

"We have tonight," I say. "Let's make it unforgettable."

I seal the deal with another kiss, followed by a soft exploration of his jaw that previews coming attractions. Then I turn away, shaky as the leaves teased by the wind, and open the door.

In my apartment, my purse falls to the ground and when I turn Roman wraps me in his arms. Everything about him is solid, hard, and insistent.

I'm tall and well-built, but with Roman I feel soft and, well, cared for. He has my back at the station, on every call. The alpha protector thing is embedded in his DNA.

Who takes care of him?

Tonight, that'll be me.

I push him against the door, my hands shaking as I fumble with his belt. No slouch, he unbuttons my blouse, pulls it apart to expose my bra-cupped breasts ...

And groans.

"You are something else. A fucking vision."

My hands unzip and pull his jeans down. He helps remove them, kicking off his shoes and socks. I fall to my knees, then work my way back up along the inside of one thick, hairy, hard-as-stone thigh. His muscles bunch with each press of my lips to his skin, and when I peel his boxer briefs down to free him, his entire body stiffens.

"You okay?" I ask as I pull his underwear off. *Oh Lord, look at him.*

"Define okay."

"Not likely to collapse if I take this beautiful cock in my mouth." I kiss the underside softly, moving my lips over the throbbing vein.

I hear him swallow. "No, not okay. Definitely not okay." He curls a hand around my neck, moving his thumb over the corner of my mouth. "You don't have to—fuck!"

"I know." *You were saying, Lieutenant?*

I've always loved giving head. The taste, the feel, the power to give that much pleasure to someone while they are trusting you with their most precious possession. (Because let's be honest, guys *love* their dicks.)

I suck him deep, and apply myself to tasting every solid inch of him. The musky scent consumes me, the solid weight fills me up, and knowing what this does to him takes me somewhere special. He groans, a long and heartfelt sound, and in it I hear his pleasure and his gratitude.

"Abby, yes, fuck—that's so good." He tunnels the fingers of one hand in my hair, while the palm of the other at the back of my neck keeps me in place, focused on his pleasure which is also mine.

"Baby, I'm going to come," he warns, but I'm going nowhere. I suck harder, taking him deeper, and make sure he'll never doubt my commitment to his need. The first drop to hit my tongue is hot and salty, and I drink him down through his howl of release.

Breathless, I rest my head against his thigh and let him stroke my neck and jaw for a few precious, quiet moments.

"Up," he says, his tone raspy and rough.

Standing, I place my hands on his hips. His body feels like an anchor, something solid to hold on to. He curves his palms around my butt and pulls me in for a deep, wet kiss.

"Before this goes any further, I need you to do something for me."

I blink at this weird attempt at bargaining for my orgasm. "Something else?"

He rubs his nose against mine. "Dump your date."

"I could just stand him up." Though I'd never do that.

"I know what that's like. It's not nice. Break the date. Then let me show you why it's the best decision you could have made."

Neither of us seem to be so hot in the decision-making department, but I'm prepared to follow his lead on this. I reach for my purse and pull out my phone.

Twenty-six

Roman

I've made a ton of mistakes in my personal life, but I've always tried to keep it out of the professional. After the two collided in New York, I should know better but here I am again ...

... and I don't care.

Her hand on my chest. My mouth on hers.

One taste and I'm gone.

I cup her gorgeous ass and yank her close enough to feel how hard I'm getting. Again. Even though she milked my cock perfectly with that hot, sweet mouth. I should have made her come first but in that moment, letting her suck me deep just felt so fucking right. I hadn't realized how much I needed it, but somehow she knew.

Her arms circle my neck, and she kisses the corner of my mouth, an almost too sweet gesture for the level of lust I'm feeling.

Or maybe that gesture is just right. Lust is merely a word right now. My chest is swarming with a ton of other emotions, and lust is the least of it. I want to protect her, fight dragons for her, punch anyone who says she can't. Not that she needs me going into battle for her.

I lift her against me, needing to feel that heat between her thighs. She groans as her favorite parts meet my favorite parts in a hot as hell *how do ya do*. I take that sweet kiss and manipulate it to my liking—a dirty, deep, wet swirl of my tongue inside her velvet mouth.

Her moan makes me harder and my hardness makes her moan louder. We're a feedback loop of mindless, oh yeah, never-stop-baby desire. I'm acting like I haven't been with a woman in ... okay, that's about right. This is exactly how it's going down. I'm a teenage boy suddenly presented with the prom queen. Every reason for not doing this is dissolving in a melting pot of hormones and lust.

I flip our positions so her back's against the door and she's hitched up, her thighs over my hips. No position has ever felt so good but I've a feeling that lying on top of her in a bed might ace it. I leave her lips to ask, "Bedroom."

Really, it comes out more like, "Br-oom" because word formation has deserted me.

"Behind you," she gasps.

I shift her higher against me and head to the bedroom, while she kisses every part of my face. It's kind of sweet how much attention she pays to my cheekbones and eyebrows, nose and lines at the corners of my eyes, parts of me I don't feel are all that deserving. I suspect she's giving my mouth a break so I'll keep my eyes open and not break a leg on the way to the bed.

I lay her down. She blows a strand of hair out of her eyes and leans up on her elbows to watch as I peel off my shirt.

Those gorgeous blues glaze and darken.

"You are something else, Roman Rossi." She sits upright

and places both hands on my hips, her thumbs running along my V-cut. Her eyes never leave my face.

That's ... different. With my ex, there wasn't much of that eye contact. She was always pretty clear about what she needed from me. Hard and fast, not a lot of tenderness or connection. I spent most of my twenties in a weird dynamic of fucking my wife, but never making love to her. I tried, but she wasn't having any of it.

This already feels like a vast improvement. It shouldn't— or I shouldn't allow myself to hope.

I should want to urge her forward, demand she get down to business and let me get her off as fast as she did me, but apparently I'm enjoying the slowdown. And when she places her soft lips on my stomach, she hums, a vibration over my skin that raises it in gooseflesh.

I let out a sigh at the rightness of it.

"Let me see you properly," I ask. Beg.

Inching back, she unhooks her bra to reveal the most beautiful set of tits I've ever been privileged to witness. Her pale skin, mapped with light blue veins, makes my mouth water.

"Jesus, you are gorgeous." Gentling her back on the bed, I cup one perfect breast and brush a thumb over her nipple, weirdly proud when it peaks under my touch.

Looking up, I clash gazes with her. Her lips part, and I realize it's been twenty years since I kissed her. So I take her mouth with mine and commit to this moment and to her. No more hesitation. If I'm going to cross the line, I'm going all the fuck in.

I strip her completely, ensuring no more barriers—not clothes, not jobs, not that niggling voice telling me this is a mistake. I've taped its mouth closed. Finally we're where we need to be: skin-to-skin, exploring and touching.

She has a thing for my arms. She can't help running her fingertips over my biceps, squeezing the muscles.

"They are," I murmur.

"They're what?"

"Real."

She swats at my arm—another quick check she can't resist—and then she coasts a palm over my pecs. "These, too?"

"Yep. Think I need to do some checking of my own." I plump one supple breast and take it to my mouth. Then inside, swirling my tongue over the rosy peak before graduating to a lusty suck. She arches off the bed in pleasure and that response makes me fucking wild. Still sucking, I move a hand down her rib cage, her belly, through the thatch of curls to find her wet and hot.

I release her breast to speak. "Open up for me, ciliegina."

"Chili what?"

"Little cherry." I stroke through her pussy and take those shivers of desire as my due. All mine. "Sweet as pie."

Continuing to rub through her slick, hot heat, I figure I can multitask and kiss her pale, perfect skin. The muscles in her belly contract when my lips skim her skin. When my tongue gets a taste of the heaven between her thighs, she's moaning again.

"So sensitive."

"Not usually," she pants as I ratchet up the tension with a finger inside her. "Your hands, they're ..." She shakes her head, rolling her hips to suck me deeper. I add another digit, pushing and stretching her, seeking out the points that'll light her up.

Turning an index finger, I glance against her clit, just a whisper to test the limits.

"Yes, that's—oh, yeah, that's it, Roman."

I love hearing my name on her lips. I don't know why

that's important but it is. I need to know I'm the one she wants here, that I'm not replaceable.

I shake my head, wondering why I thought that. Knowing the origin but preferring to push it away. I don't need the ghost of my marriage haunting this bedroom.

I rub more, generating more slickness as my cock insistently pushes against her leg. Pre-come leaks, streaking against her skin and I suck in a controlling breath. Watching her fist the sheets and the eyes rolling back in her head assures me she's close but I like drawing it out. I had thought this would be quick, a desperate effort at release—get 'er done so we can rear view it and move on—but it no longer feels like that.

It feels fucking monumental.

I want to spend all day and night with parts of my body embedded inside hers, looking for all the ways to get her off, then switch to her wringing every last drop of come from me. I want it to last, then I want to start over and find new ways to fuck that neither of us have thought of.

I swirl my palm over her pussy, a slow, sinful, sensuous rub. It unwinds something in her and soon she's coming against my hand, grasping my wrist to hold me fast.

As if I'm going anywhere.

This is the only place I want to be.

Twenty-Seven

Abby

I don't think I've ever come so hard in my life.

Roman's dark hazel-green eyes glitter with lust and pride. He knows exactly what he's done and he's pretty in love with himself right now.

"That was—good," I murmur.

He kneels between my thighs and I get the best vista imaginable: Roman, all God of Thunder thighs, his lightly-furred chest, bronzed skin, the arms.

The. Arms.

I could craft art with those arms as molds. But the main attraction right now is getting Roman's attention. He's pumping his cock and while I know I probably should be helping, the sight is so arousing—and that orgasm was quite draining—that I'm happy to lie back and watch.

"Just good, huh?" he says with a smirk, referring to my downplaying of the peak I just reached. "Guess I'll have to figure out how to improve on that."

I sit up and curl a hand around his neck.

"Thank you."

He stops the motion of his hand. Looks shocked, to be honest. Has no one thanked him for an orgasm before? Isn't that listed in Emily Post's etiquette rules?

"You're welcome," he says quietly.

"Let me." I take his hand away and replace it with my own. He's hot and hard again in my grip, a weird contrast with the vulnerability I see in his eyes. I get the impression that Roman's not one for self-care. That everyone looks to him for their needs and he doesn't think over much of his own.

The tip of his cock is dotted with fluid and it looks like it needs some love. I run my hand over the shaft, letting the pre-come lubricate the motion. He pulses hard in my hand.

"Need to be inside you, Abby."

I couldn't agree more.

I grab a condom from the nightstand drawer and watch as he secures it and lies over me. The vibe has changed. Still sexy, but now more urgent. More of a recognition that we can't laze about all day in bed like a regular couple because there's nothing regular or couple-y about us.

This is about primal need, answering a call, and releasing a fire-truck load of tension.

He rubs his sheathed cock over my opening and I almost come again. I'm not going to last but I'm conscious that I need to. I need to prolong this time with him.

In this game of *would you rather*, I want the power of slow motion.

"You okay, Abby?" he whispers.

I nod, and he lays the sweetest kiss on my forehead before pushing in with one long, all-reaching stroke, and it's like my body knows he's the only one who fits right and makes itself ready for him. The moan that erupts from my throat doesn't sound like me. I don't usually sound so wanton and needy. Sure, I enjoy sex and I recognize that it's usually better with a partner, but I don't generally rely on that partner to complete me. I have my own hands, tools, and fantasies for that.

But with Roman, it's different. He rules my body with a quiet intensity that slays me. He's here with me, his gaze pure and searching, each thrust another question trying to get to the heart of who I am. The man seems to think he can know me this way, and that in knowing me, we become partners in pleasure. I understand that concept—I read romance novels—but I've never experienced it.

I cup his stubbled jaw, my thumb rubbing his bottom lip until he opens and takes it inside his mouth, and that additional connection jumps along the live wire between us, igniting every neuron in my body.

He stops his thrusts and sucks on my thumb. I'm so turned on I can't even get mad at the loss of momentum. He's still inside me, stretching and filling and I've never felt so owned. Such a part of something.

Releasing my thumb, he draws close and gifts me with a dirty, wet, deep kiss I feel down to my toes. While our mouths are still connected, he resumes fucking me slowly and thoroughly. I had expected it to be fast and furious, but this is so much better. This is a man who knows exactly what I need, and shit, that is scary.

"Feels so good, ciliegina. Even better than I dreamed you'd be." With each stroke, he takes a piece of me. "Need you to squeeze my cock with that perfect pussy. Take every drop. All yours."

My brain has no time to register, my body is already responding to that order and giving him what he needs. What we both need. We are joined as one in a filthy-sexy goal to make this the best sex either of us has ever had because this is our one shot.

It can't be this good.
It can't be this good.

It can't—oh shit, it's—yes—there, that's it.

It's that good. By the time I've figured it out, I'm flying, every part of me soaring into some unknown level of the stratosphere.

This gorgeous man, my alpha-boss DILF, with forearms I want to dip in bronze finally lets go and stills, his forehead against mine, his eyes shut against the onslaught of fulfilled lust. His groan of release is low and guttural and prolongs the aftershocks of mine.

When he opens his eyes, I see a softness there I would never have expected. But I should have known better. This man cares about people, and even though this is just sex—I'll be telling myself that on my deathbed—I suspect he feels some sort of tenderness toward me.

Which is wonderful in the moment, but might be detrimental in the long-term.

🔥

A long time later, Roman rolls on his back, rolls me into his side, and wraps me up for a cuddle.

This is not good.

I mean, it's great. The man has stellar cuddle technique and did I mention the arms? But I also know that we can't go back to the diner or to those people we were before I walked into Engine 6.

He takes my arm and applies a sweet kiss over my dinosaur tattoo.

"We should probably cover next steps," he whispers against my wrist.

Stretching, I run a hand through his soft, dark hair. "Thought you'd need time for recovery."

"Not those next steps. I'll be ready for action before you

know it." He leans up and looms over me, back to Lieutenant Serious. "I have to report this to Venti."

Can't we enjoy the peace a while longer? "Um, why?"

"Because all voluntary relationships at the firehouse need to be reported to my CO, anything that has the potential to interfere with the chain of command."

Every fire department treats voluntary and familial relationships differently. CFD might be looser because how else could you explain why the Dempseys have three siblings at the same house—and at one time had all five of them there? Close relationships like that are usually not allowed but Jude said they used some loophole about being foster sibs to get around it. As for other types of relationships—well, people are banging in firehouses all the time and everyone usually keeps it under wraps. But as soon as it moves to something serious: dating, living together, marriage, then that couple could not be on the same shift.

But Roman and I are not serious and neither do we have the potential to be. No one in upper management needs to know about this.

"I told you I don't date firefighters." I'm already getting flack for being my father's daughter, now I'll hear it because I messed around with my lieutenant.

How bad do I have it that the word "my" in front of the lieutenant makes my chest warm?

He opens his mouth but I'm having none of it. "I'm going to come out of this worse than you, Roman, and all because we banged. It's not like we're in a relationship."

The light in his eyes dims. I hate to be the one to cause it. "No, but it's enough to cause a distraction."

"It doesn't have to be. Because now we've done it and we can move on. No more distractions."

"So you think this one and done can be swept under the rug?"

I pick at the edge of the sheet then decide that more definitive action is needed. Pulling back the bedcover, I grab for my blouse and throw it on. The afterglow has chilled. "It has to be. I'm barely a month on the job."

I look over my shoulder. With an arm behind his head, he's lying there against my white sheets and fluffy pillows like a bronzed god of sex.

"I get the impression you don't want to date me, Abby." There's a teasing edge in his voice.

"This isn't personal, Roman. But the reality is that you're my CO, I'm your candidate, and declaring a relationship—even if I wanted to which I don't—means one of us has to switch shifts or out of the firehouse. We both know it won't be you. We both know I'll be judged—"

"I won't let that happen—"

"I'll be judged and that will be it. Besides, I want to stay at Engine 6 because it's my mom's house. And I want to learn from you. You're the best."

He parts his lips, arches that brow.

"I mean the best at firefighting!" The arrogant ass. Now all I want to do is jump in his arms again and knowing this effect on me makes me tetchy. "Do you think you can respect my wishes here?"

He looks offended. "Of course I will. This is totally your call, Abby. I'm not going to hassle you into a repeat of something you so obviously don't want."

That's not what I meant—but he's already on his feet, leaving my bedroom to grab his clothes, I assume. I take one last, longing look at that amazing body and commit it to some dark corner of my brain I'll dip into later.

I could explain that I'd love nothing more than to see him outside Engine 6, meet for breakfasts at Fern's, hit the lake path for a run together before hitting the shower for more fun, but it's better to draw a line under what happened. It was amazing sex, life-altering, even. I can't believe I think that, but it's true. Only, I can't say that to Roman. I can't even hint at the fact this might have been more than a pressure release.

He comes back in, jeans on, buttoning up his shirt. I'm crazily relieved that he didn't leave without saying goodbye.

I ask, "Are you mad at me?"

"Abby." There's no missing a hint of exasperation in his tone. He curls a hand around my neck and kisses me softly. "Does that seem like I'm mad at you?"

"I don't know. Maybe you bottle it up."

"I'm not mad, just disappointed. I think we rocked the fuck out of that bed and that we would be amazing together, but I understand this is difficult for you. Don't worry, I'll survive your rejection."

"Roman, I—"

He stops my protest with another kiss, this time deeper and so hot I want to pull him back under those sheets.

"See you around, ciliegina."

And on the last word—little cherry—he's gone.

Twenty-eight

Roman

Another day, another disappointment. Yet again, I'm leaving Abby's house with my head bowed, only this time it's because I pushed too hard.

I'd known going in that there was no future with my sweet Cherry Pie, that I'd be getting whatever scraps she threw my way. I had an inkling the sex would be great, though I was wrong there.

It was off-the-charts amazing.

When she wrapped her sweet lips around my dick without me even prompting, I could have cried at the generosity of it. When she came against my hand, my heart soared with pride. When I lodged my body deep inside hers, I knew I was in trouble.

Her thumb in my mouth, her big baby blues eye-fucking me, her tight, hot pussy milking me so good I saw stars—every single thing that happened was a fantasy come to life. And I probably could have gone for another round if I hadn't opened my big mouth.

We should probably cover next steps.

Excellent read of the situation. Top marks.

She was never going to go for it, but I had to give it a shot. I see her dilemma, though it goes deeper than just her worry about the workplace dynamics. She's said a couple of times that she can't date firefighters and there was that reference at dinner to how tough it was for her parents, both being in the service.

She's afraid.

Or hell, I want to think that's her excuse. That it's not personal. That she might like me a little.

I am a fucking teenager again.

Maybe the deep connection I feel is all on my side. Christ knows I've been wrong before. I should accept that she's done me a favor and I don't have to come clean to Venti, who would rip me a new one.

Now I just have to keep my eyes and hands to myself, treat the probie as the underling she is (no matter how much I want her sweet body *under me*), and act like this isn't a missed opportunity.

🔥

A day later, I'm still cranky. (I overheard Chiara telling Lena I was double-emo brooding because no one wants to date me. My twin's opinions are sometimes a little too on the nose.) I should be feeling on top of the world because I've banged my fantasy woman and cleared the pipes, but now I've had a taste and I want more.

Today I have to pin on my game face and play nice for my crew in a social setting. Turning the corner onto the street of Gage Simpson's house in Andersonville—we all live around here, it seems—it occurs to me that Abby will likely be walking over as well.

It's probably too much to hope that she won't show at all. That I can relax for a few hours and not have to censor my gaze and repress every filthy thought. I need to ignore the fizz in my veins every time I see her. Act as if she's just another co-worker.

I can do that. I have to do that.

Tell that to my mind as it turns to mush on seeing her in Gage's backyard.

With a date.

Good-looking, smiley, the kind of man that suits a woman like Abby.

"Lena!" Gage yells, then comes over and does a complicated handshake-fist bump thing with my daughter.

"Hey, Gage! I got a tattoo."

"You did? Let's see." It's a turtle with a rainbow coming out of its ass. "That's so cool," Gage says. "How long does it last?"

"Forever," Lena announces with authority.

"Awesome. And what else have you got?" He nods at the tray in her arms. She wouldn't let me carry it.

"Salt-caramel brownies for the party."

"Are you kidding me? I love brownies! Drop 'em off in the kitchen but bring me one back because the host gets dibs." He grins at me. "Where's your sister?" He and Chiara are pretty friendly.

"Lovely to see you, too. She said she might stop by later. More important cookouts to attend, apparently."

Gage mimics being wounded.

"Dad, can I go talk to Roni after I drop off the brownies?" Roni is Gage's niece and usually has some cool comic book art to share. She's just finished a screenwriting course at Columbia College in Chicago and is working on some script about female superheroes.

"Sure." I take a look around, my eyes skittering over Abby

who's dressed in shorts and one of those tops that exposes her shoulders and ties around the neck. Bet she got *that* knot right. Her legs are long and toned and the whole effect makes my body tighten.

On closer inspection, I recognize the guy with her as one of her friends from that night in Dempseys' bar. The relief that washes through me tells me all I need to know: I have a major fucking crush.

"Need a beer, LT?"

"Yes. Yes, I do."

He grabs me a Sam Adams, my usual, from a cooler—it sure is handy having one of your crew also being your regular bartender.

"Where are your little ones?" I need to get my mind off the topic of my candidate.

"Probably in the alleyway with some fireworks."

Gage grins just as his husband, Brady, comes out of the house carrying a blonde toddler with bows in her hair and leading another dark-headed little boy by the hand. Brady Smith is a scarred-and-tatted chef, a former Marine and a man of few words. Next to Gage, who has a golden leonine quality to him, he's dark and intimidating but the love is there, no doubt about it. Both of them adore their kids as well as their gaggle of nieces and nephews.

I blow out a breath. Between my sister and the family of Engine 6, Chicago was a good place to land. It could have been a lot worse. Even though Lena had to start a new school midyear, she seems to be settling in, fights notwithstanding. She needs the stability and while I might want to get unstable with my candidate, I sure as hell need to keep my dick in check to maintain that even keel.

"You okay? Or should I be keeping you and Sullivan separate?"

My skin chills despite the warm temps. "Now why ever would you say that?"

"I've seen how you look at her. I know it well." Gage casts a glance toward Brady, breathes out, and comes back to me. "You were pretty upset when Woz messed up on that call."

"I'd be upset if it were anyone. He shouldn't have put her in that position."

"No, he shouldn't. And she thought she was doing the right thing. Sometimes instinct is more important. What feels natural."

"Are we talking about Sullivan's decision to give her air to a crew member because he didn't check his equipment or is something else on your mind?"

Gage sips his beer. "If your gut tells you a relationship with Abby is worth pursuing, maybe you should pay attention to that?"

If Luke's been getting gabby, I will fucking murder him. And if not, then what does that say about how I've been acting around my candidate?

My. Candidate.

I push deep the thrill of possession those words inspire and return to the problem at hand. "I'm her supervisor, Simpson. That's not happening." Gut or not.

The same filthy lying gut that's screaming at me to take her, claim her, make her mine. But she's already cut me off at the knees, told me how she wants this to play out. I should be glad that a woman like that was willing to give me the time of day, if only for a couple of hours. Getting back into the dating game is hard enough after years in the wilderness of a bad marriage. So I had some fun with a gorgeous woman, who's not looking for anything serious. I should take it for the win it is and move on.

When I'm finally ready to go that route, I need someone who will make a good mom to Lena. Who thinks I'm worth that effort. Unlike Tori, who wanted us to act like we were still in our early twenties, no responsibilities, party animals forever. And then abandoned her vows and commitments so she could have a do-over with another guy.

"You and your guy, I'm gonna guess that wasn't always plain sailing. I mean, this is you, Mr.-High-Maintenance-get-the-hell-out-of-my-kitchen, we're talking about."

Gage grins. "Fuck, no. I went pretty hard at it and he took it slow. Dumped me a couple of times. Generally acted like an idiot. Him, not me."

This amuses me. Gage Simpson would always assume he was in the right.

"Yet here you are."

"Just kept trying. I saw something there and once I see it, I can't unsee it, y'know? A vision of me and Brady and our HEA."

"HEA?"

"Happily ever after, dude."

Right. Mine is with a sweet little girl and my pain-in-the-ass sister, not a hotter-than-sin redhead who could do things with her mouth I'd be dining off for months.

Like a slap in the face to my good intentions, Abby's dirty/sexy laugh carries over the heated air and lodges somewhere south of my chest and north of my quads. She's young, fresh, the complete opposite of a jaded punk like me, and I want her more than common sense should dictate.

I'd like to think there's a way out, that I can have my brownies and eat them, too. I'd like to think it isn't over before it's even begun.

Twenty-nine

Abby

Roman left my apartment approximately fourteen hours, twenty minutes, and twelve seconds ago. I hated telling him that there was no future between us, but was sure —okay, 80% positive—that I made the right decision. Now, I'm second-guessing everything.

Attending this shindig was low on my list, but it would have looked weird if I didn't show my face. I need to act like a normal human being, able to hang with co-workers and friends, and not get overheated at the sight of my commanding officer at the grill, chatting with Gage and not looking my way at all.

Which is fine.

I can't risk getting caught up in his heated orbit. I don't think I would make a mistake on the job—I'm fairly certain I have that part of the equation under control—but the rest is tricky. Telling people we're together in some way would be some drama-llama rigmarole, and what if it fizzles and fails? We'll have declared our intentions for no reason at all.

Everyone would know I'd crossed a line with my CO.

Everyone would look at me, thinking I'd found another way to get ahead. It was bad enough I got the stink-eye from classmates at the academy. I certainly don't need it because I'd screwed up and around with the man who can make or break my career over the next year. Neither did I want to risk having to leave Engine 6. It's my mom's house, and now mine.

Yet I couldn't stop thinking of his expression when I shut it down. Not crushed exactly—I'd never presume that level of hurt—but he hadn't liked it. He thought there was something here worth pursuing.

Part of me did, too.

So here we are at the Dempsey cookout, acting like strangers who haven't touched, sucked, and kissed each other's bodies like sex-starved weirdos.

Someone taps my back and I turn, hoping and praying. Not Roman, but neither am I disappointed. This is someone I really want to see.

Alexandra Dempsey-Cooper.

"Hey, sister-in-fire, thought I'd better introduce myself officially!" She opens her arms and I find myself hugging a legend in the Chicago Fire Department. This woman made headlines years ago for (a) carving a big shot's Lambo to ribbons with a chainsaw; (b) conducting a very public romance with the then mayor of Chicago, Eli Cooper; and (c) having her life loosely made into a movie by Oscar-winning actress Molly Cade, now Alex's sister-in-law. The movie got a million things wrong about firefighting but I still watched it eight times.

"I'm sorry I didn't come see you sooner," I whisper in her ear, though I have to fight through a mass of dark curls to do it. "It's been a wild month."

She sets me back and murmurs, "I bet."

"I brought you a little something." I barely have time to

raise the shopping bag at my feet and Alex is squealing loud enough to draw all eyes to us.

"Sweet Mandy B's?" She peeks inside the shopping bag filled with a half dozen of Chicago's finest cupcakes. "Oh, if I wasn't a married woman I would be proposing to you right now."

"You did say I had to pay the toll."

"True, true. Following orders to the letter. You will go far, youngling."

A bright-eyed, dark-haired little boy, about three years of age, tugs at Alex's maxi dress, which by the way looks amazing on her. The woman is all va-va-voom curves.

"Mommy, I need to go."

"Of course you do." She looks around, her lips curving when she spots someone. "Go tell Daddy. He said he'd take care of all the potty breaks."

"Daddy has the new baby," he moans with another tug of her dress.

"You're killing me, Smalls." She turns to me. "I'll be back in five. Be ready to dive into those cupcakes and tell me everything about your first month on the job, Sullivan."

"Yes, ma'am."

Ten minutes later, I'm relaxing in an Adirondack with a can of Grizzly Pear cider, a hot dog with all the trimmings, and a great view of the party—which does not include whichever spot is currently hosting a certain lieutenant.

"So Gage says you landed on light duty," Alex says on the heels of an orgasmic sound after she bit into a chocolate cupcake. A smidge of frosting sits on her bottom lip and she darts her tongue out to capture it. "What the fuck happened?"

Kids are everywhere but Alex is obviously no-holds-barred. I'm guessing each of these impressionable youngsters will be swearing like firefighters before the day is through, if they aren't already. I share my tale of woe, trying not to dwell on Roman's part in it. I know he was doing his job and was obliged to represent the incident as it happened.

"Wozniak is such a lazy ass. You should have left him there."

"Tempting. Roman—uh, Rossi—gave him hell. Wrote him up. Then somehow I got the short end of the stick." Roman hasn't been able to swing me back onto active duty just yet. Rubbing salt in that wound, Woz is here, currently yukking it up with a couple of guys from C-shift.

Alex smiles, a touch of evil in it. "You know, I gave my air to someone once against protocol and yada yada, I now have two children."

Chuckling, I glance in the direction of Eli Cooper, former mayor, now hot-shot lawyer with a specialty in representing military vets. He's holding his newborn son in a baby Bjorn and looking very, very fine. That Dad energy is sexy as all get out. I should know because another one is clamoring for my attention.

"Other than Wozniak being a useless dickwad, how's it going on B-shift?"

"Really good. Of course, I have mighty big shoes to fill, Firefighter Dempsey."

Alex kicks out her foot, wrapped in strappy sandals. "Size nines, but forget that. You're forging your own path. What about your dad?"

"He's waiting for me to fail. Says it's because of what happened with my mom—how he couldn't handle it if it happened to me. I want to be sympathetic but I can't let his fears control mine." I take a bite of my dog, and when I'm done chewing, ask, "You have four brothers in the service. Are they always trying to protect you?"

"You wouldn't believe the crap they gave me when I joined

up. Luke, especially. He took over as Dempsey dad when Sean died so he came out against it pretty strong. Even told me Dad wouldn't have wanted it."

"That had to be rough."

"It was. And it makes everything harder. You're dealing with family stuff and work stuff. How are you going to manage when you have to deal with sex-life stuff? The menfolk get all up in arms about that, too."

I snort, and when I next catch Alex's gaze, she's looking at me all cockeyed. "What have I missed?"

"Zilch." Roman is now talking to Eli and oh God, it happens. He takes the baby into his arms and starts rocking it like a hurricane crashing my ovaries. Too late for my composure, I look away.

"Is it that Sam guy? He's pretty hot."

"God, no. We're just friends." Sam's talking to the Cleopatra lookalike who came into the Dempseys' bar with Luke's wife, Kinsey. She's older than him but he's definitely shooting his shot. I can spot the Sam Killian charm-a-thon from fifty paces. "Who's that he's with again?"

"Madison Maitland. The first Mrs. Cooper."

"Your husband's ex?"

"Yep. She's pretty cool, actually. Practically one of the family." She grins. "So, if you're not otherwise occupied, I have the perfect man for you. Have you met Bastian Durand?"

"The hockey player?" He's a power forward with the Hawks and the last person I expected to be hearing about during a family cookout.

"Yeah, he's stopping by later. He and I are friends. He asked me out once but Eli was having none of it." A fond memory lights up her face. "So, anyway he's single and I think you two would be cute together."

"I'm not much of a hockey person." I'm pretty sure that

Roman is now rocking the baby. I can't actually see it because my eyes are working overtime not to travel that direction yet my whole being is acutely aware of top-notch Italian-American daddy action in my periphery.

"You don't have to be," Alex says in response to my hedging about hockey fandom. "He might prefer that, someone who's not the usual puck bunny star fucker. I'll introduce you guys later unless you have someone else on your radar."

Ignore the man with the infant. Do not look.

There's some sort of baby-babble coming out of Roman's mouth. My ear pulls a muscle trying to hear it.

It doesn't matter. He's great in the sack, that's all. Objectify!

When I smile vaguely at Alex, she doesn't smile back. "Fuck, no."

"What?"

"Listen, I've made *so* many mistakes. Witness me sleeping with the asshole mayor of Chicago and getting knocked up by him. Twice. But I have not done the doo-doo on my firehouse doorstep."

"What are you talking about?" I sound weak and defensive.

"Rossi?" She whispers his name like it belongs to a war criminal. "It can't end well, Abby."

"It's nothing. Just a little flirtation which I'm not even thinking of acting on." I can't reveal the truth, not after that reaction. Let her think it's gone nowhere.

"I'm serious, you can't—"

Her little boy, Logan, appears out of nowhere hopping up and down in that age-old dance we all understand.

"Again? Are you drinking from the keg on the sly, buddy?" She stands and grabs his hand, then turns to me.

"Let's talk later, after you've figured out which story you want to tell me."

"I don't know what you mean."

"Sure, sure." She smiles to take the sting out of her admonition and heads off to the house.

It is a truth universally acknowledged that a free chair at a backyard cookout doesn't go unoccupied for long. Within thirty seconds, I have company in the form of Lena. She's wearing a T-shirt with a drawing of a mustachioed firefighter and a slogan that reads "My Dad is my Hero." Aww!

"Hey, Abby."

"Hey, Lena. Nice tee and tattoo."

She holds out her arm, admiring the tat with the cool appraisal of a tween. "Do you want another one?" Before I can demur, she opens her Godzilla backpack and takes out a transparent envelope. I see something sparkly. "We have to do it in the kitchen where there's water."

Well, I walked into that.

Two minutes later, she's holding the damp plastic paper over my wrist and a moment later, I'm the proud owner of a glow-in-the-dark rainbow mermaid tattoo. Or I assume it will eventually glow in the dark. Right now, it has a Hulk-green sheen to it.

"Very cool," a dark voice says, and I look up to find Roman standing at the door, minus the baby, thank God. Not sure I could have handled that.

"Dad, you need to get one, too."

"I do?"

Lena is already wetting another tat and pulling her father over to the sink. "I've picked this one out especially." She holds it down then grasps my hand. "Abby can make sure it works."

Which is how I become assistant to the tattoo artist, my hand clasped over the plastic patch, feeling up the thick, muscle-corded forearm of my lieutenant.

"Sorry, she's kind of bossy," Roman says. "No idea where she gets it from." He's not pulling away, and neither am I making any effort to remove my hand which I insist is just ensuring the best quality tattoo application.

That's when I notice his nails covered in bright blue polish. "You had fun at the salon?"

He raises his free hand to showcase his manicure. "Don't think it suits me?"

I'm trying to imagine Roman sitting still while Lena paints his nails. The image melts the heart I'm supposed to be walling up against this man.

"It suits you. Just like this tattoo." I move my hand away from the image.

Roman squints at it, still covered by the plastic sheet. "This is what you picked for me, fragolina?"

"Aunt Chiara said you're a sparkly unicorn," Lena says. "Because there's no one like you."

Roman scoffs. "Doesn't sound like your aunt. And it certainly doesn't sound like me."

"Oh, I dunno," I mutter. "You're one of a kind. I think that's what we're getting at."

"*We're?* You're siding with my tormentors now?" His eyes do that crinkly business, which is just one more thing that gets my engine running when it comes to Roman Rossi. I do not need more reasons!

Lena has moved to the other side of the kitchen to organize the contents of her backpack, so I feel safe in teasing him. "Tormentors is a bit strong."

He sweeps his gaze over my halter top, his eyes lingering a hot fraction of a second on my cleavage. Did I choose my outfit with this man in mind?

I would never.

"Tormentors is pretty accurate."

I murmur, "These old things." The girls *are* having a good day.

"If the bra fits."

Oh my. I can't breathe for wanting him. I need to get out of this air-conditioned kitchen, which seems to be playing havoc with my nipples, and back into the sultry heat. It would be cooler than the space around Roman.

He shakes his head. "Sorry, I shouldn't flirt with you. Or anything else. That's not my usual MO, by the way."

Just with me, then. That night in the diner, he opened up to me, and several times since. As for last night ... well, wow. The lieutenant brought his dirty talking A-game. I love that he can't help himself around me. He knows it has the potential to be ruinous to us both, yet he can't resist.

And who doesn't enjoy being wanted by a man who would be willing to announce it in a formal way to his superiors? But the consequences are too risky. In these situations rife with imbalance, it's always the woman who emerges as the sorry one.

I once asked a friend at CFD HQ to pull my mother's file. Reading through her work history, it became clear that she was the one who had to make the concessions, who took two years off to give birth and spend those early months and years with me, who had to fight her way back into the department. All against my father's wishes. Aunt Kathleen told me he wanted her to stop being a firefighter and stay home with me. There was no question of him giving up his job or interrupting his career track.

Not that this thing between Roman and me has legs like that. We aren't headed down the path of matrimony, but the longer I mess around with him, the more potential I have to be hurt, emotionally and career-wise. And what if he got injured or worse? Do I want to spend every shift worried about him running into a burning building or soothing his fears because I was likely doing the same? I have enough of that dynamic with my father.

Yet, I can't deny this pull I feel toward the man.

I swallow and shuffle forward though I know it's a terrible idea to be so close.

"Do you think it's possible to go back to before?"

"Before what?" His head dips toward mine. "The diner? The kiss? Last night? There are several milestones to the story of us and I don't think we can unring any of those bells."

So we're already on a runaway train to disaster. Before I can pull the rip cord, he murmurs, "You look so fucking gorgeous right now, y'know that?"

"Roman."

It's all I can manage. He's all I can feel. My breathing picks up, jagged little pulls into my lungs.

"What I'm trying to say is that ..." The words emerge from his throat, low and husky, "I want more of this. More of you. Any way I can have you."

I've made it clear I won't be dating a firefighter, CO or not. Roman appears to be saying he'd be okay with less than that, which is the dream right there, isn't it? The best sex of my life with the hottest guy I've ever met, all with no strings.

"And you're okay with not reporting it?"

A muscle in his jaw bunches. Not okay but willing to compromise. "If those are the terms ..."

"The tattoo's done, you guys!" Lena's back in between us, pulling the tattoo sheet away.

"A rainbow-farting unicorn. Just what I've always wanted."

"Daaaad!"

He angles a hand around his daughter's neck, pulls her in for a full body hug, and kisses the top of her head. Those blue-tipped nails, symbols of the perfect love of a dad for his daughter, run through her dark hair. I love how tactile he is, how there's no pretense about how he feels. Maybe it's an Italian thing. When I first met him, I thought he was a repressor of emotions. Boy did I have that wrong.

Who wouldn't love to be under Roman's wide wing?

He smiles at me, and the answer thrums in time with my heartbeat.

No one.

Thirty

Roman

I kept my word and convinced Venti to cut Abby's desk duty short so now we're back, fully staffed and ready to rock every callout. It's been a week since the Dempseys' barbecue, and each night after putting my daughter to bed, I've been heading over to Abby's to put her to bed—and that beautiful body to use.

The sex is phenomenal and we're having fun. I've stayed away from serious topics so as not to spook her. I'm not sure casual is in my wheelhouse but with a woman like Abby, I'm willing to take whatever she can give me.

It's this or nothing, and I can't go back to nothing.

"Nice dinner tonight, Lieutenant."

I look up at the visitor to my office sanctuary, those bright blue eyes glinting with sexy intent. Not that either of us could act on our intentions at work, sexy or otherwise.

I don't usually cook at the firehouse—I used to at my old station in New York but I'd lost my appetite for it. Tonight I'd taken it upon myself to serve up my meatball special for the crew at 6. I know Abby likes my cooking, and if she won't let me close in any other way, I'll find another way in.

"Glad to serve. How's Baby Thor taking it?"

"The poor guy's pretending he enjoyed the break from the stove but I saw him on the Bon Appetit website planning how to take you down."

"This is exactly why I didn't want to get into this."

She leans against the doorjamb. Something is on her mind and I have patience in spades. After a few beats, she asks, "Have you heard about the memorial service at the end of the month?"

"I have." The CFD will be honoring the fallen with a service dedicated to all firefighters lost in the line of duty. "I understand they plan to do it here."

She wrinkles her nose. "I thought they'd use the Quinn. That's what they did ten years ago for the first major anniversary."

"That must have been tough."

"Yeah. I was sixteen, just a kid."

"You're still a kid. Her kid. You don't suddenly turn into a robot because now you can drink and vote." I've seen her stop by the Wall of the Fallen regularly and offer up a prayer to her mom. The vulnerability in that small thing always checked my heart hard.

Knowing that Abby won't be led, I let the silence linger for a moment, giving her the space to take this conversation in whatever direction works for her.

After a moment, she finds her way. "I remember her, coming home, smelling of smoke and perfume. It's a really weird combo that you don't ever forget. It was like she wanted to step into womanhood, into being my mom again, before she crossed the threshold of our house. That night—the night it happened—I was awoken by a bad dream. It was like I was sinking into something hot and sticky, and I reached out for Mom, but we kept missing each other. When I woke up, I heard voices and I crept downstairs. My dad was there, crying on my aunt's shoulder. The two of them were hugging each other and I asked what was wrong." She shrugs, shakes her head. "But I think I knew. In the dream, she should have pulled me out but she couldn't."

She looks so damn lost that every cell in my body itches to comfort her.

"You miss her like hell."

"I do. You lost your parents, so you know what it's like. How you have all this emotion, all these things you want to tell them."

I nod. "Someone once said that grief is a kind of unexpressed love, stuck inside you with no place to go. But you can find an outlet for it, Abby. Honor her every day on the job with what you're doing. Be happy in your choices."

Her eyes are wide, pulling me deep. "You think that's enough?"

"That's for you to decide. But I do know that she's watching over you, here in this firehouse and out there in the field."

"God, I hope not. Because ..." She waves between us and lets loose a nervous giggle.

"I'm sure she shuts her eyes when you get naked and busy. Like God does."

That brings out that dirty-sexy laugh I can't resist. After a moment, she goes quiet, then looks over her shoulder and steps inside my office. "They want me to say something at the memorial. Make a speech."

I lean forward in my chair, straining toward her in this small space where we can't touch, and clasp my hands together. "And you'd rather not?"

"I don't know. My dad did the honors last time and now,

if I do it, it would be because it's a PR move and I'm following in her footsteps—"

"Which you are to a certain extent."

Her fingertips stray to the pendant around her neck. "But also, blazing my own trail, or trying to. My father looks at me and sees her. Sees what happened to her, not the potential I have to do a good job."

I stand, dying to take her in my arms though we both know that's not possible. One touch will spark to a flame that neither of us can control. But hauling my body upright brings me a little closer to her which I hope is some comfort.

"You're not your mom, Abby. You are an individual with hopes, dreams, and ambitions all your own." I squeeze her arm because the words out of my mouth need a physical expression. It's supposed to make her feel better, but instantly I steal some solace in being able to touch her.

"I wonder what she would have thought. Would she have encouraged me or would she have been worried sick?"

"Likely both. Take it from a parent. We want our kids to go out there, shoot for the stars, leap over chasms, and do amazing things. We also want them to stay locked in their rooms, wrapped in a comforter, letting us love and protect them. Parenting is one long series of mixed messages."

She laughs. "Remind me to never get into the mothering game."

"That doesn't interest you?"

"Actually ... I was being flippant. One day, I'd like it, after I've made my mark." A pretty flush suffuses her cheeks and now all I can think of is Abby with a baby.

Abby with *my* baby.

I try to swallow back the image of that beautiful body of hers transformed with something we create together, but it's stuck, playing on repeat in my dumb brain. Like Gage Simpson incapable of unseeing his HEA.

"You looked like a natural with Alex Dempsey's newborn at the cookout," I say.

"Sure. Did you happen to notice all the women drooling when *you* held that stinky little bundle? It was like a collective panty-drop."

"Ah, so my daddy skills turn you on, Sullivan." *Bring it back to sex.* Better that than any strange detours to a future with Abby carrying my child.

She places a hand on my chest, which only makes it worse. My heart is thumping fast and furious.

"Big time, Rossi. And thanks for listening." She leans up on her toes to give me a quick peck, but I'm having none of it. I can't help the fever burning through my veins, the beat pulsing through me that demands I claim her, here and now. Her lips brush mine and my body combusts, answering the primal demand of man-needs-woman.

She lets out a rough, sexy sound and kisses me back with a passion that rocks me to the core. But she also has a boatload more sense because she pulls away, her fingers to her lips like it's the first time.

Last time, here, for sure. Because that cannot happen again.

"Sorry," I murmur. "I'd like to say I don't know what came over me but it would be a lie."

She blows out a long breath, one designed to grab the reins of our slippery control. "No, I get it. It's really tough to ignore."

A movement behind her snags my attention. Wozniak is standing just outside the door with a clipboard, and from his expression, he definitely saw too much.

Fuck.

A sweep of heat flushes her cheeks, and she tries a rueful grin. "Best get back to it."

"Sure."

She walks by Wozniak who barely acknowledges her. He makes a point of waiting for her to leave the corridor, then comes in and hands me the clipboard. "Equipment inventory. We need more batteries."

I scan the sheet, buying myself time to figure out how to approach this. Woz and I have always rubbed each other wrong. I don't blame him for seeing me as an interloper, the guy who took his job. But I also know I'm a better lieutenant than he could ever be. The lazy ass is always looking for a shortcut—maybe he thinks he's found another one.

Peering up, I find him watching closely. I could ignore it, assume he didn't see anything, but no one could have missed the raging sex hormones flying around my office and zinging off the walls.

Better to put my cards on the table. "Something on your mind?"

"*That* is a fucking shit show waiting to happen, you know that?"

I blink, not expecting that. I thought he'd make some snide comment about Abby.

"It's not your concern."

"You want to be in the Commish's crosshairs, that's up to you. But she's a decent firefighter and this doesn't look good for her."

He's feeling protective about the probie? I don't like the slither of discomfort rolling down my spine, the feeling that I'm the one in the wrong.

I don't like it because he's right.

I could tell him that I want her so badly I'm not thinking straight. That I want to declare to the heavens and anyone who'll listen that we're in a relationship but she won't have it. Or me. He might think I'm the one in charge here, but not at all.

"It's ... complicated."

"And only going to get more so if you keep that up."

"Thanks for your input."

He sighs, shakes his head, and leaves.

My heart thunders in my chest. Usually I have ice in my veins, so I try to assess what's behind this sea change. Because I just got caught making out with a direct report?

That's not it. It's something more serious, something I might not be able to undo.

I'm falling hard for this woman.

Which is pretty fucking annoying because she's not anywhere close to having that level of feeling for me.

Thirty-one

Roman

I come awake slowly, my eyes adjusting to the half dark. The blinds are open and the streetlights cast a striped stencil over Abby's arm, currently wrapped around my chest. All that pale, freckled skin looks good against my darker tone. I could look at this woman all night.

I don't know the exact time, but I know I have to leave. Placing a kiss against her temple, I move an inch to test the waters.

"Where do you think you're going?" she murmurs.

"I need to tuck you in before I go home and tuck Lena in."

Abby lifts her head. "You're adorable with her."

"Adorable?"

"As a kitten."

I growl, which makes her laugh and mutter "adorable" again.

She's the adorable one. The taste of her is still on my tongue. She looks satisfied and sleepy, and I'd love nothing more than to get her even more satisfied and sleepy. But I've already spent too much time away from Lena.

"My kid likes you. Keeps talking about how brave you are."

"No one braver than the woman cleaning out a firehouse bathroom."

This woman is quick as a whip, and while I know she was frustrated about the light duty, she hasn't let it affect her attitude. I love that.

I pull on my jeans. "Lena was right when she said you were brave and your mom was a badass. You are and she was."

"Tell it to my father." She wrinkles her nose. "By the way, you never told me what Wozniak said." There wasn't much talking when I arrived.

"Told me you deserved better. Sounded almost protective."

"Do you believe that?"

I wouldn't trust Wozniak as far as I can throw him, preferably off the top of a building. "Hard to say."

"You think he's the Eye of Sullivan?"

She means the spy. "Maybe. Your dad's all seeing, is he?"

"God, yeah. When I was younger, it seemed like he always knew when I'd been up to no good. He'd come home from work, ready to tear me a new one for something I'd done with my friends. Half the time, I'd no idea how he found out."

"A weak link in the gang. Someone always tattles."

She chuckles. "That's true. Probably Jimmy Corrin. That guy was always moaning about how everything we did would bring on his allergies. Go into the woods, allergies. Break into the creepy abandoned house, allergies. Take one of the parents' cars for a joy ride, allergies."

"Sounds like you were a ballsy little troublemaker. Or auditioning for a part in a Stephen King book."

"That's not far off! But I was the only girl in the gang, so I had to assert myself. Otherwise they'd have walked all over me."

"So you came up with all the wicked bad ideas?"

She shrugs, super cute. "Maybe."

I lean in to kiss her, and soon we're lost in each other all over again.

For the first time in my life, I'm not sure what comes next. Well, not the first time. After I found out that Tori was messing around with a co-worker and that my closest friend—my captain—had known about it, I'd fumbled through a raft of rage-fueled days for a while. No good at my job, no good at my life.

But I made a decision that had immense consequences. Punched out my friend, not even the guy who did the dirty with my wife. That's how I handled it because that seemed like the worst betrayal.

I vowed that the next woman I chose would be one who wanted me for ... me. The guy beneath the muscles, the man who cares about family, friends, and firefighting.

But a rebound fling isn't such a bad thing, I suppose. Roll out the training wheels for a real relationship further down the road. Or that's what I thought before Wozniak stopped by my office the other day. His possession of that knowledge has sharpened my thinking and made me acutely aware of everything I have to lose.

And I'm not talking about my job.

"What's on your mind, Diner Dude?"

"Well, Cherry Pie, I'm wondering if I'm a little bit crazy, medium level bananas, or wholesale bonkers."

"It does feel a little like that. Dangerous, but good."

Right, Ms. Adrenaline Junkie likes the sneak-around factor. Doesn't mean it can't become more. "My biggest concern is how this plays out at work. With Wozniak in the know, word will get out. Or he'll think of a way to use it. If he tries anything or makes a crack, let me know."

"So you can knock him into the middle of next week? That doesn't seem very smart after what happened in New York."

I suspect Abby would rather we call it quits than risk me getting into a fight with a co-worker that threatens my career.

"He has a point, though. That kind of dynamic changes a crew. There will come a time where I won't want to send you into a dangerous situation because I'm worried about you."

She sits up, eyes flashing with outrage, her beautiful breasts swaying. It's quite the sight and gets me semi-hard again. "You will treat me no differently, Roman Rossi."

My gaze dips to her chest. "Easier said than done."

She pulls at the sheet, probably realizing that any point might be better made with less nakedness. "You don't want to see *any* of your crew hurt. There's no good reason why you should feel extra care for me." And before I can protest, she adds, "Sleeping together is not a good enough reason."

"Damn, that's cold." As if "sleeping together" can adequately describe this. We're both liars.

Is it a lie if we're so upfront about it?

"Please don't wrap me up in cotton wool while I'm trying to do my job. I need to learn. I need to prove I can do this."

Because of her father. And he's the last person I need on my ass, especially after our ill-fated first meeting.

Still, I want to push the boundaries. I want her to draw the lines, lay it out there clearly. "You think your father wouldn't understand you getting involved with a fellow firefighter? It happened to him."

It's happening to me. I am involved to a worrying degree.

"Yeah, and sometimes I think he wished it never did."

"I can't believe that. You're the result of that union. And they were happy, weren't they?"

She looks torn. "I thought so. But he encouraged her to give up her job, her career, and that had to have created a lot of tension. Relationships between two first responders are going to be stressful." Her words and expression are a warning: We're not in a relationship so don't make this into something that impacts her job.

I get it. Easier said than done, though. Whether she's my crew, my lover, or both, I'm going to worry about her.

"Roman, I mean it."

"I know you do. What I'm hearing is don't fall for you because you don't want the hassle of worrying about me. Or me worrying about you. When I'm gonna do that anyway."

She throws up her hands. "Why are you pushing on this?"

Point taken. Why am I even trying to logic my way into a relationship with this woman? Maybe because I see the potential. I saw it that first night we met at the diner and the peculiarity of our situation has thrown a wrench in the works. We're fooling ourselves that sex alone can be enough.

"Because I like you. And I think you like me."

She growls and it's so damn cute I laugh my head off.

"Not funny, Rossi. I will be using your body and occasionally, asking that you cook those killer meatballs. The only uses I have for you."

"Got it."

She pushes at my shoulder. "Do you? Because I'm feeling waves of condescension from your corner."

"From this corner? No way. I'm determined to not fall in love with you, either. Shouldn't be difficult as you're a pain in the ass."

She flops back on the pillow, mutters "asshole," and orders me to return to my family so she can get some sleep.

Thirty-two

Abby

My phone buzzes with a message from Lena. Since the night I had dinner with the Rossis, she's been texting me with fun tweets from Evil Dick, a former Big Brother housemate who's made a career out of snarky show commentary. She's also talked a little about her mom's wedding, and this morning, she's sent me a photo.

This is what my mom wants the bridesmaids to wear.

It looks like a cupcake explosion and I'm guessing Lena wouldn't be sharing it if she liked it. She's waiting for me to weigh in.

I go for neutrality. ***That's interesting.***

Yeah. I hate it but I can't tell my mom or she might get mad. I can't tell Dad, either, because they'll get into a fight.

Hmm. Not sure how to respond here. I don't want to give the wrong advice but I think her mom should hear the truth.

Maybe tell her you'd like to wear something more

your style. You could check the website for the dresses to see if there's anything in the same color. Lots of weddings have different outfits in the party, just the same color to keep the theme.

Okay, I'll look at the site. Thanks, Abby!

Feeling like I've done some holy work, I close my locker door, kiss my mom's Claddagh pendant and head to the lounge. Gage is cooking up French toast this morning and the scent of vanilla, cinnamon, and nutmeg wafts through the air like a sweet-smelling holiday breeze. But before I make it to the corridor I run into Wozniak.

Tension has existed since he walked in on Roman and me on the last shift. He hasn't said anything to me directly, so I'm waiting for an anvil to drop on my head. Maybe today's the day.

"Sullivan, got a minute?"

"Sure, what's up?"

"Listen, there's no easy way to say this ..." He scrubs a hand through his hair. "You're not doing yourself any favors gettin' involved with Rossi. Only one direction that can go and it won't be good for you."

I could deny but what would be the point? Besides, I'm semi-curious about how this might play out with an audience. "It's just casual."

"No such thing as casual in the firehouse. Too much at stake and too many ways it can go wrong. In the heat of the moment, people make bad calls for good reasons." He shakes his head, all pity I don't believe for a second. "Look, you don't have to listen to me, maybe talk to your friends about the wisdom of hooking up with your CO."

"Thanks for the advice." Deciding I don't like where this conversation is going, I make to move past him.

"But then I'm guessing you don't want anyone to know, which should tell you everything about why you shouldn't be doing this. Venti wouldn't like it, but maybe he'll give a pass to the golden boy. The Italian thing and all. Your father? Now that's another story."

Sneaky agenda, come on down. "Are you threatening me?"

"'Course not! You've got it all wrong." He moves in closer. "Remember I told you about that LT position going at 70? Well, I need a favor."

"From me?"

"Yeah, I need you to ... uh, recalibrate that warehouse incident. Make me look a bit more ..."

"Heroic?"

He grins. "Yeah, no reason why my equipment failure should be such a big deal."

"Except that it is. It was. You didn't check it and you ran out of air. And I ended up on the mop for a week because of your dumb mistake."

"Abby, Abby, Abby, you're going about this all wrong. You need to be thinking of how much trouble Rossi will be in for taking advantage of the boss's daughter and not reporting it. He's running out of bridge."

"No one's going to care about that," I say, though my bluster is obvious.

"You want to take that chance? Be a good girl and tell Venti and your pops that I pushed you out of the way of that crashing ceiling. That you wouldn't be here without me. It's more true than not."

He leaves it at that, walking by me into the locker room. Rage ripples through me, a veritable storm in my chest. My first instinct is to run to Roman and let him handle it, but I know what he'll do.

Punch Woz in the snoz. Get himself fired. Tell the world that we're sleeping together.

Not necessarily in that order.

Now this fling is negatively impacting crew dynamics.

Either I keep Woz quiet with a "recalibration" of that warehouse run or I report his mustache-twirling ass and get my CO in trouble.

I brought this on myself. I should have let Roman do the right thing from the start: report our relationship to the brass and deal with the shift changes that would make it right.

Now I can't reveal this shoddy attempt at blackmail because if I do, Roman will go berserk. Heads will roll, and one of them might be the man I'm starting to care about against my better interest.

🔥

"Sammy!" Jude stands and hugs our friend as if it's been years since they last saw each other instead of a week ago at the Dempseys' cookout. "Been on any good runs lately?"

Sam catches my eye. "Is that what this brunch is about? Let me get out the tape measure."

I stand to give him a hug. "No, it's about Bloody Marys, chocolate banana chip pancakes, and waffles. No dick comparisons, please."

He grins, activating those cute dimples, and takes a seat opposite. "There *is* no comparison. We all know I'm the flat-out winner there."

A scoffing Jude settles into our booth at Fern's. "They must love you and your big ... *mouth* at 70."

We spend the next few minutes catching up and trying to —yep—one-up each other on the coolest situations we've encountered so far. I thought I'd have a head start with Betsey the Boar, but by the time Sam has regaled us with a tale about a guy covered in molasses and handcuffed to a radiator, we know we have our winner.

"Alright, enough of this work stuff," Sam says after our

orders are in. "Time for the true gossip. Jude, baby, who ya bangin'?"

Suddenly on edge, I pick up an empty sugar packet and start to fold it into little squares. It's one thing to omit details of your dating life, it's quite another to deliberately lie about it to your friends. I can hardly tell the truth: that my brain's been full of Roman for the last few weeks. That I'm living and breathing him.

I can't even tell them about Wozniak and his sneaky blackmail attempt. They'd probably have good advice but it would involve coming clean about my dirty affair.

Jude grins. "Well, there's this bartender at the Manhole—"

"Subtle," I murmur.

"—and he's called a few times since our wild night."

"Have you picked up?"

Jude looks horrified. "Why would I want to do that? One and done, friends. Too much man candy for me to be wasting this goodness on the same dick and balls for more than a night. It's not fair to the rest of my public."

We give him a hard time about that but it doesn't matter —he's unmoved by our teasing. When we rotate to Sam, he's unusually coy.

"What do you mean you've got your eye on someone?" I throw a confused glance at Jude who shrugs his ignorance. "Why aren't you telling us more?"

"Because it's at a delicate point in the proceedings."

Jude grabs Sam's arm. "Are you saying there's some woman not dying to let Sammy the Whammy into her panties? Who is this paragon?"

"I'm over here," I kid, though we all know I wouldn't go there.

Sam rolls his eyes, but also looks a little uncomfortable. "She's not coming around as quickly as I'd like. But I'm up to the challenge."

I wonder if it's Madison Maitland, the first Mrs. Cooper. He was chatting her up at the cookout and couldn't take his eyes off her at Dempseys'.

The food arrives and we dig into French toast and amazing omelets, letting Sam off the hook while we chat about TV shows we're watching (my current girl crush is Rebecca in *Ted Lasso*) and how the Cubbies are doing (not great, but it's only June).

"So Alex Dempsey was looking for you at the party to introduce you to Bastian Durand," Sam says to me around his chewing. "But you'd already left."

"Yeah, right. Can you see me with a pro-hockey player? I don't even like hockey!"

Sam gives me a weird look. Maybe I protested too much.

Jude shakes tabasco on his eggs. "Who cares if you like hockey or not? You can't make time for a quality piece like Bastian Durand?"

Sam chuckles. "You know Jude would if Hudson Grey came calling."

"Who?"

"Hudson Grey, the new Rebels player they traded in from Jersey," Sam says.

"Wait, is Hudson Whatshisface the hockey player you have that huge crush on?"

Jude's face is the color of the red leather banquette we're sitting in. "It's not a crush. I just think he's ... hot. I think lots of guys are hot."

"Yeah," Sam starts, "but you don't tell me to shut my piehole whenever Cal Foreman or Theo Kershaw are on the ice. You've got a major thing for Mr.-Grey-Will-See-You-Now. I think it's cute."

"He came out this year, didn't he?" I recall it being a big deal, though why we're still at the point where any pro-athlete's announcement about whichever way his dick points continues to make news is beyond my comprehension.

Jude nods. "Yeah, it's more common now but the NJ team org wasn't as cool about it as they could have been. Rebels will be a better fit. More progressive."

"Is he dating anyone?" Not that I care but I'm curious to see Jude's reaction. He's usually so devil-may-care about this kind of thing.

Sam chimes in. "Well, he's missed his shot with Cade Burnett as that guy's all loved up." I don't follow hockey closely but even I know about Rebels defenseman Cade Burnett, the first out player in the NHL, a situation made even more newsworthy because he was, and still is, in a serious relationship with the then Chicago Rebels general manager. "Plenty more fish that swim his direction these days," Sam goes on. "Maybe if you're nice to our girl here, she can get you an in with Hudson Grey. She's *almost* dating Bastian Durand and his brother plays for the Rebels."

"I'll talk to Alex about getting you a coffee date with him," I offer, stirring the pot and anxious to deflect from my own never-dating-Bastian situation.

"Don't even think about it!" Jude snaps, much to our surprise. We're only kidding around, but he looks like the prospect of meeting his crush is the worst possible outcome.

"Just joshin', man." Sam cocks his head, curious about Jude's overreaction, but soon tilts his attention toward me. "What's happening with Film School Dickhead?"

"Nothing much. It's kind of fizzled."

I'm pretty proud of how smooth I am. I can do this. I can handle a down and dirty double-secret-probation affair with my boss. Jude and I are not on the same shift and I'll never run into Sammy on the job, so my secret's safe from the guys who know me best.

And then because the universe thinks I'm a smug cow, the

door opens and in swaggers Roman Rossi, the hottest guy on the planet, headed to the counter to grab a coffee. His golden skin is sheened with sweat, the damp patch on his shirt further testament to his expended energy and the heat of the day. In a long list of things that affect me on a deep, cellular level, Roman's legs are at the top. Absolute rock-solid pillars I can't take my eyes off of.

Jude lets out a low whistle, back to his usual flirtatious self after that uncharacteristic outburst about that hockey player. "Wow, the LT sure does dirty up well."

Roman looks up, meets my gaze, and it's as if no one else is in the room. Or at least that's why I think his gorgeous mouth cracks in a smile upon seeing me out with other people.

I don't smile back.

His grin falters, but he regroups quickly when he realizes I'm not alone. By the time he's walked over, his expression has evened out to neutral.

"The probies are plotting, I see."

"Hey, Lieutenant, how's it going?" Jude asks cheerfully. "You live around here?"

"A few blocks over."

Roman's not looking at me. In fact, he's doing a bang-up job of ignoring me. But you know who isn't?

Sam.

Jude's still chatting to Roman about running along the lake path or his favorite Frappuccino flavor or the best places to find men. Actually I've no idea what they're saying because my ears are filled with a rushing sound brought on by the knowledge I'm keeping a secret from my friends and that one of them has rumbled me.

"Enjoy your day," Roman says finally, and we all wave as he heads back to the counter to pick up his coffee to go.

Jude is still checking out Roman because the man checks

out anything with a pulse and a penis. "Didn't know he lived around here, did you?"

"Yeah, he's on Greenview," I say, "with his sister and kid."

"Cool, cool. Okay, let me get the check."

"No, don't," Sam and I say half-heartedly while Jude mumbles, "not buying it, fuckers," and goes to the cashier.

Knowing he only has a couple of minutes before Jude returns, Sam doesn't waste a second. "You've got to be fucking with me."

I meet his hard-nosed gaze, very aware that Roman is still in the diner and that I'm trapped on all sides. "What?"

Head shake of disgust at my miserable efforts at evasion. "Tell me it's just flirting and no one has had an orgasm in the other person's presence yet."

"It's just flirting." It emerges from my mouth with a certain indignation.

Sam, usually such a cool cat about everything, almost has a breakdown. After a couple of tense seconds where I think his head might spin a full 360 degrees, he manages to get his emotions under control.

"How do you think this is going to go? Because it can't end well. One of you will be forced to move, assuming you don't fuck up first while getting distracted on the job."

"No one's going anywhere. It just needs time to burn out." That's what I've been telling myself. Insisting.

"Who else knows? Does ..." He jerks his chin at Jude.

"No, and no one else will." I don't mention Wozniak because it's yet another reason why I should be quitting Roman. Sam and I are hissing at each other now, testy little felines. For a brief second, I consider telling him that this is Diner Dude, he of the cherry pie rom-com moment, that it's not my fault and practically fated but Sam's acting like such a diva that I don't think he deserves that context. "It's not going to last. And then I—we'll forget it ever happened."

Sam looks more concerned now than angry. "He shouldn't be doing this. He's your superior officer and—"

"This isn't all him. I made it very clear I was interested, made it hard for him to say no. It's just sex!"

The couple at the next table are now all ears.

This seems to cheer Sam. "Sullivan the Seductress. You and your wiles are going to be the death of you."

Out of the corner of my eye, I'm aware that Roman has left. I should be happy he's no longer in my orbit and I can act like a normal person, but instead I feel oddly abandoned. Not his fault, just that I wouldn't mind if he could acknowledge me—us—in public.

It can never happen. Never mind all the other drama, I have strict rules about dating firefighters, so why am I feeling off-kilter about it?

"Me and my wiles are overrated."

Sam stares at me hard. "You really like him, don't you?" His tone is gentle, a direct counterpoint to his censure of before. The relief that he's no longer mad at me lulls me into dropping my guard.

"God, I do. But I can't."

He frowns, thinking it through. "Not just because of the optics or the rules."

I grimace. I don't see Sam as much as Jude but he's always been more perceptive.

His next words throw me. "I've already told you a million reasons why you shouldn't be banging, but I'm never going to say you shouldn't because it stops you from falling for someone you might lose."

"That's not—okay, that's some of it." Am I so transparent? The death of my mother on duty means I'm very aware of the potential for pain if I were to lose someone else I love. Not that I love Roman. That's not—is it? *No.* Yet I could easily fall for a man who cares so deeply about his family, his crew, and his job. Roman is the whole package and any woman would be blessed to have him in her life.

Sam covers my hand with his. "Find yourself a stock broker or an accountant. Nice and safe."

"Sure," I respond morosely.

I've dug myself a whopping great hole here.

I've been holding Roman at arm's length, insisting that making it official is potentially detrimental to our careers. But that's an easy fix. I could switch to another platoon at 6 and solve my Woz problem in one fell swoop. I'd get some ribbing from co-workers but after a while no one will care. My father would give me hell, maybe make trouble for Roman, but we'd get over that hump. Roman's already said he wants to date.

Because I like you. And I think you like me.

If I keep heading down this road, it could develop into something that could break me and my doing-just-fine-right-now heart. The boss-candidate excuse has been keeping me safe from going all in. I might be an adrenaline junkie but when it comes to the heart, definitely not.

And certainly not when it comes to Roman.

Thirty-three

Roman

That was a close call, I text.

Yep! Don't worry. No one noticed your drooling over me.

That makes me laugh, but then Abby knows exactly how to cheer me. Not that I need cheering. In fact, I'd say everything is going well. So Chiara is down because Devi's not around, but at least my daughter seems to be in good form.

The only turd in my punchbowl is Woz. He thinks he knows something, and while he might be acting all concerned for Abby, I know he's thinking about how to use that information to his advantage.

My phone rings. *Abby*. Damn, my heart sure does enjoy the skip as I pick up.

"Really, Sullivan. I saw you five minutes ago."

"Hmm, too desperate?"

"I'll allow it. You make it out of the diner alive?"

"Just." She chuckles nervously. "Sorry if I acted weird. I'm not sure how to be cool around you."

That she might be a bit flustered thrills me. Sure I want her to be rock solid on a run but when we're off the job, I want her all aflutter.

Aflutter? Jesus, I am acting like a giddy kid with this woman.

Her honesty makes me brave. "I liked seeing you, too."

There's a pause while we both absorb those mini-confessions. Maybe keeping it on the down low with the friends is wearing on her. The energy between us has the capacity to be so much more, but I'll play her game a little longer.

"So is this a booty call, Cherry Pie?"

"At 1 p.m. on the Lord's Day? You bet it is. Unless ... well, unless you're busy."

Not a chance. "Open up."

"What? You mean—"

"I'm downstairs."

Two seconds later she buzzes me in and ten seconds later —I scaled those stairs like fire was nipping at my ass—I have her wrapped in my arms. She tastes so sweet and feels so good. I'm losing my mind, kiss by kiss, one heartbeat at a time.

I draw back, conscious that I'm still sweaty from my run. "I need a shower, sweetheart."

"I like how you smell." She nuzzles against my neck, inhales deep. "So. Good."

"Let me clean up before I get down and dirty with you."

Smiling, she takes my hand and leads me to the bathroom. While she turns on the shower, I strip, grab a condom from my wallet, remove her clothes—leggings and a T-shirt—and finally drag her under the spray.

"Turn around," I gruff out.

With her back to my chest, I soap her up, enjoying the feel of her as I drag my hands across every curve. Her tits are the perfect weight in my palms, their tight points like sweet buds against my callused fingertips. My cock slips between the inviting cleft of her ass, and I can't help dragging through and creating friction that drives me wild.

"Put your foot on the ledge, Cherry Pie. Gimme a little space to work with."

My good girl does as she's told and I clamp my hand on her mound, pushing my fingers between her thighs to make my claim.

Her moan bounces off the tile. "That's—God, that's good."

Everything about this is. Fucking everything.

Her skin gleams like satin, wet and slick, and her body feels like a dream against mine. But it's not enough. With Abby, it's never enough.

"Give me your mouth." I sound rough and animalistic, and every cell in my body stands to attention when she obeys, offering her lips for me to devour. I move my fingers, glancing against her clit. She starts to shake as her orgasm takes hold, and I wring it out of her one breathy moan at a time.

I'm not finished.

I turn her around and fall to my knees.

A kiss between her legs starts her up again, then I add a long lick of my tongue. This isn't the first time I've treated her to my oral skills, but today, it seems more purposeful, like every lick and suck can convince her of my intent. Hungrily I feast on that pretty pink flesh, spearing inside her with my tongue until she's writhing against my mouth.

Just before she reaches that peak again, I stand, slip on a condom, and slip inside her.

"Good?" I ask as I fill her up hard and deep. Staying still, I watch her expressions dance and waver. She turns her head away but I cup her chin to face me. "Tell me."

"You know it is," she gasps as I repeat the thrust, this time angling to stroke her clit, so sensitive after I sucked it to readiness.

Sure I know, but I know something else.

We could be incredible together, a real force to be reckoned with.

A tear escapes, slipping like a liquid gem from the corner of her eye. The shower's spray could be the cause but I know the difference.

"Abby, what is it?"

"Nothing," she says. "Just so good."

She's hiding something, and maybe I need her to tap into that current of feeling because it'll bring her closer to the truth. The truth of us.

"It is. So good." I close my eyes, then open them because I don't want to miss a thing. "It could be like this all the time."

"Roman," she whispers, a plea for me to stop or continue, I don't know. But I have to get under her skin.

I move inside her, marveling at how wet and tight and perfect she feels. She clutches at my shoulders, then my back and my ass. Pulls me closer, sealing the connection, telling me with her hands what she can't say with her words.

I fuck her deep, rocking into her with unmistakable intent.

Finally, she gasps, "Please, don't stop. Stay right here."

Words in the passion of the moment, but as close to Abby's truth as I've ever come.

"Not going anywhere. Staying right here with you."

Her eyes meet mine, those blue oceans I would happily dive into. She recognizes the moment and Christ, does it scare her.

She's not the only one. I've fallen for this woman in the worst possible way. I shouldn't even be receptive to it—I just got out of a multi-year hellscape and never thought I'd be looking for someone to share the load. Because that's what it feels like: a heaviness in my heart that's numbed me for years.

But with this woman, I feel lighter, like a true meeting of minds, bodies, and souls is possible. With her, I feel free.

She looks away, but I won't let her. "I'm right here, ciliegina. Nowhere I'd rather be."

Maybe that's the assurance she needs because something in her lets go of the fear. She softens, in body and spirit, and holds my gaze. It's a little defiant, as if she thinks doing that will harden her against me.

Nice try, Cherry Pie.

I keep everything connected: the erotic tie that binds us together, the locked gazes that force us to reckon with what's possible, the heartbeats syncing with every thrust. I interlink our hands and squeeze, and she arches up into me like she can't get close enough.

I push deeper to let her know she can.

I can give her close. I can give her the world.

She just has to take it.

Thirty-four

Abby

We're en route to a structure fire in Humboldt Park and I'm in my usual spot, sitting across from Roman. Both of us are quiet, the playful banter of our co-workers swirling around us. As Gage takes the truck in a wide turn, my foot shoots out to steady myself and accidentally touches his boot.

"Sorry."

"No problem," he murmurs.

I'm ultra conscious of Wozniak watching for any crumbs he can use against us. If it was just a sexy affair, I might not care so much. Roman's a big boy and he knew what he was getting into. But I'm beginning to wonder if it ever was casual. If we've been fooling ourselves all this time.

That night he walked me home after dinner with his family, he said: *How about we pretend that's all it is?*

We agreed to lie about our intentions in hooking up. We both knew it felt like more, that saying it means nothing would be merely paying lip service to the notion of a fling. Like we're so clever and above all that emotional nonsense.

But we're not—or at least, I'm not.

He agreed to my rules, but I wonder if he knew it was only a matter of time before I fell headlong into him.

Maybe he knew already. Recognized the connection for what it was.

The truck pulls up outside a three-flat and everyone jumps out, all eyes drawn to the gray smoke billowing like a steam engine's output from a window on the second floor. Two trucks from different stations are already in play, so any rescues are likely done and dusted and we're probably here to help with venting and fire suppression.

Roman talks to the officer in charge and returns to us.

"They've already pulled a grandmother and two kids out. Looks like we're here to make the pretty flames go bye. Brooks, Simpson, work on the aerial and assess for venting the roof. Acosta, Sullivan, you get us connected to the water. Woz, do a recce around the back. I'll head in and see where we're at."

With affirmations of "yes, LT," we set off to do our jobs. After opening the hydrant and hooking up, we head inside where Roman meets us.

"No fire on the first floor, but the second is smoky and hot. Let's advance the line up the stairs and find it." He eyes me, his gaze all steel but with something different there. I worry it's already changed between us, that our relationship is placing a weight where none should exist. "You good to go, Sullivan?"

"Yes, Lieutenant."

Danny and I haul the hose up the stairs while Woz and Roman scout ahead. The hose is heavy as hell, but this is why I work out—to make sure I'm ready when I'm needed. No visible signs of fire greet us, just heavy smoke and sweltering heat. It's weird not to see any flames but feel like it's all around us, waiting to announce its arrival.

Roman raises a hand, calling for quiet. "Listen."

I strain my ears, trying to hear whatever Roman does.

"Don't hear anything," Danny says, just as it hits me. An odd, keening sound, low and almost unearthly.

"It's a whimper, like a pet, maybe? No one said anything about animals." I can't hear it now and neither am I sure which direction it came from.

Roman nods at me. "Just wanted verification my ancient ears are still working. Keep looking for the fire, Wozniak. I'll check on the noise." He heads off through the smoke, shouting for anyone who might be here to call out.

We follow Woz's lead. The visibility is becoming worse, the air thicker and hotter.

"Where the fuck is this fire?" Danny asks.

I sniff the air, detecting something else beyond the smoke. Something fishy.

Plastic insulation for burnt wiring often gives off a briny smell. Not so strange, except it reminds me of something I read about during training.

"Maybe it's in the walls?"

Woz turns to me, putting the clues together quickly and coming to the same conclusion. "You might be onto something, Sullivan. Let's open her up."

He means taking a hook to the walls. A slither runs down my spine. "Maybe we should wait for the LT?"

It's the wrong thing to say. Woz gives me a look that says I shouldn't have challenged him.

"Don't think we need to wait for your boyfriend."

I don't look at Danny, who had to have heard that crack. Of course, it could be just a typical workplace jibe, given that I'm the only woman on the crew.

But there's more to it than that. Woz won't be waiting for Roman. He's making the call and to hell with it.

Just then Roman comes out of a room near the end of the corridor, and goddamn it if he isn't carrying Spider Man. Or a little kid dressed like your friendly neighborhood Spider Man.

Could I love this man any more?

Oh.

I really thought that.

Three long, ground-eating strides, and he's with us.

"Where did he come from?" My voice sounds weird, and while I want to think it's my mask, I know it's because of the terrifying knowledge I now possess.

I'm crazy-stupid in love with this amazing man.

"Asleep in the closet. He woke up a second ago but he's suffering from smoke inhalation." His tone is angry because the responding crew should have found him, but he's trying to rein it in so the kid stays calm. It's not clear why no one reported a missing kid but I expect we'll get the details of who fucked up and in how many ways later.

That's when Roman notices Woz poised with the Halligan.

He's barely asked, "What are you doing?" when Woz takes the all-purpose tool to the wall.

Rip! The blow back is immense and it's just as I suspected.

Hidden fires look like they're out or non-working but often in older houses with voids, knee walls, and attics, they are secret killers ready to strike. I didn't notice any dormers in the roof but that doesn't mean there isn't some attic space with deadly flames racing through the rafters.

And this is exactly what's happening. As soon as Woz vents, the entire hallway erupts. Fire and flame are pouring out of the walls and the ceiling.

Hello, disaster, welcome to the party.

The blast of heat has knocked Woz back, Halligan in hand,

and he falls heavily against me, sending me crashing. As I regroup, my first instinct is to check Woz as the person nearest to me.

He's unconscious.

Worse, a slew of burning debris has crashed from the ceiling separating our crew, me, Woz, and Danny from Roman and the kid. Thankfully, Roman was able to turn and shield himself and the little superhero from the force of that blast.

He shouts through the flames. "Situation assessment!"

I poke at Woz who's starting to come to. How many times do I need to save this guy's ass? "Woz, you awake?" I look around for Danny.

"Right here, Abby. Come on!" Danny pulls on Woz and shoulders him under his arm. The guy is heavy, so even though Danny could probably carry him, two people would definitely be better.

But I can't leave Roman.

A side table in the hallway is now on fire, as is a gallery of framed photos. I stand and knock them off the wall with my Halligan, hoping that'll help to slow the fire's progress.

"Danny, get Woz out!" I shout over my shoulder, though he's already dragging him toward the top of the stair. "Roman, can you get through?"

Still protecting his charge, he's inching back as the flames in the hallway start to consume everything in its path.

He assesses the space, up-down, side-to-side. "Can you clear the floor?"

The debris is lighter there and starting to burn out. Using my hook, I knock fire-ravaged plaster out of the way, creating a narrow pocket. Roman places the kid on the floor and pushes him across, far enough that I can grab his hands and pull him to my side. The kid moans, which I take as a good sign. Moaning children are live children.

"Got him?"

"Yes!"

"Take him to the medics now."

"But—"

"Now, Abby!"

In this moment, the kid is the prime directive. I turn and race down the stairs—also on fire, by the way—and meet Gage at the entrance.

"Gage, get him to the EMTs!"

"On it." When I turn back, he shouts after me, "What the hell, Abby?"

"Roman's still up there!"

His response is lost to the air because I'm already hauling ass back up, the smoke now so thick I can't see one foot in front of the other. Climbing blind is no fun, but we've practiced this in the smoke box at the academy. Sure, Sam had to save me one of the three times I entered it, but two successes are better than none.

"Rossi, call out!"

Nothing but the crackle of burning paint. I fall to my knees where the smoke is thinner, and a couple feet in, I encounter an immovable object.

Roman.

Somehow he got past the bottleneck in the hallway but collapsed about six feet from the top of the stair. I yank at his shoulder.

"Roman, wake up!"

He lifts his head. Blood is oozing from a wound on his temple. He must have hit his noggin along the way.

"Abby, what the—?"

"Can you get up? Or do I have to drag your ass out of here?"

By sheer Roman Rossi will, he shakes himself awake. "I'm right behind you." He sounds groggy but at least he's speaking.

"Age before beauty," I yell. "Get moving."

He does, going ahead of me, though I imagine it kills him to do it. He's the one who's compromised in this situation, potentially concussed and dizzy, so I have to take the rear. We're crawling along the landing to the top of the stair and reach a pocket of space that's not filled with smoke and flame. He stands, dragging me upright with him.

"I told you to leave." He coughs the words out.

"So you can claim all the glory? No chance."

He grimaces. Blood trickles from that cut on his forehead; he blinks it away behind his mask.

In sync, we both assess the stairs. They're practically engulfed and there's a good chance we'll break our ankles if we try to descend.

"I'm really pissed that you came back for me," he says, his voice scratchy, "but then you're such a pain in the ass that I suppose it's to be expected. Christ, I love you, Abby Sullivan."

Did I hear that right? Did he say he loved me? No, it has to be the head injury. He loves that I'm here saving his hot Italian ass, that's all.

Only my heart appears to have gone with the original interpretation. It's soaring, and it's not just the adrenaline of being slap bang in the middle of a working fire.

Roman is still talking, like he didn't just tell me that he loves me.

"But now you're going to follow orders, okay? We're going to have to make a run for it down the stairs. If we wait any longer—"

"Yeah, I hear you."

I take a step; the next rung collapses and Roman hauls me back by my jacket with my foot in the air like a Looney Tunes cartoon.

"I'm Indiana Jones in this scenario, Abby."

Meaning he's going first like Indy in *The Last Crusade*,

stepping on those stones to avoid the Grail Chamber's death traps. It's about twelve steps, but one of them is gone and Lord knows the condition of the rest. Roman takes the first step past the collapsed rung, treading carefully, testing his weight. If it can hold him, I should be good.

One more step ... *He loves me.*

Another one down ... *And I love him.*

Step number three ... *He fucking loves me!*

He's made it halfway down with me following in his wake when I hear it: a creaking sound. Not good. Ceiling tiles rain down on us, burning plaster bombs, and the stairway's bannister shakes, a fiery tremor that portends an earthquake.

The stair starts to give, like it's had enough of our pussyfooting nonsense and has lost all respect for anyone with such a careful tread.

I grab onto Roman's arm just as the bannister falls away, my lieutenant with it.

And I fall with him ...

Thirty-Five

Abby

Hospital waiting rooms are the saddest places on the planet.

Hospital waiting rooms filled with smoke-stinking, dirt-streaked firefighters are even worse. All the members of B Platoon are standing around, scrolling through their phones, like it's completely normal to have two of our own receiving medical care after being pulled from an inferno that destroyed a three-story building.

"How can you be so calm?" I say to Gage.

He looks up, his clear blue eyes troubled. "This isn't the first time and it won't be the last."

Of course. He was sixteen when he lost his dad and brother, and I've no doubt he's punctuated other runs with visits to the hospital.

Perhaps realizing that his last statement isn't all that helpful, he turns his phone over. "Okay, let's get your mind off the obvious, Candidate. Would you rather accidentally like an old photo of your ex on Instagram or accidentally send a sext to your dad or mom?"

Tyler points at Gage. "That's evil, man!"

Gage grins. "I know. As for me, sexting all the way. If my dad was still here, he'd understand completely."

Danny shudders theatrically. "Nope, nope, nope. Option number one, all my exes love me."

Gage mutters, "Typical. What about you, Abs?"

"Ex, for sure." My father would have a coronary. I reach for the soothing vibes of my mom's pendant.

It's gone.

No no no!

Maybe it's stuck in my clothes but a quick pat down assures me of the worst—I've lost my most precious memento. This day continues on its relentless quest for premium suckage.

Tyler notices my unease. "You okay?"

"My necklace. It must have slipped off."

I'm searching the ground in case it fell off when I arrived when Captain Ventimiglia blows in and takes a seat beside me.

"How are you holding up, Sullivan?"

"Okay. Have you heard anything?"

He shakes his head. "They're tough guys, so let's assume the best. You want to tell me what happened?"

I'd rather not but the captain probably wants to take my mind off our injured colleagues. "Roman—Lieutenant Rossi—and I got caught at the top of the stairs. It became involved pretty quickly, the steps no longer safe. Roman went first and as we neared the end of the second flight, the bannister collapsed. I grabbed him but he had too much momentum."

I landed right on top of him, probably broke his ribs, maybe even punctured a lung. The next minutes were a haze of action as Gage and Tyler dragged us out. Throughout it all,

Roman was unconscious, as he was strapped to a gurney and whisked away to Northwestern Memorial.

"Why did you go back in? I heard you handed off the kid to Simpson."

"Someone had to!"

And that someone had to be you? The least experienced person on the crew?

He doesn't say it but I can tell he's thinking it. They all are. Maybe it should have been Gage but I was the last person to see Roman on that landing. "He was out cold when I found him. Flat-out on the floor. Concussed. Groggy when I woke him up. He wasn't making it out on his own."

Venti nods. "And what about how it started?"

A shadow falls across the entrance to the waiting area. It's Woz, a bandage on his head, his face smoke-streaked and blotchy. On shaky legs, I walk over to him.

"Hey, Woz, you okay?"

"Yeah, Sullivan. I'll live."

Pity. He has maybe two inches on me but it's not enough to keep his nose out of the trajectory of my fist. I probably should have gone for his jaw, but I've always found a nose punch much more satisfying.

His squeal is reminiscent of Betsey the Boar. "What the hell, Abby?"

I don't stop there, picking up the thread of rage with a push against his chest as he clutches his nose. My knuckles sting but my righteous anger is the perfect salve. Blood drips over his lips but it only makes me angrier, recalling that Roman was injured with a wound on his forehead, a wound sustained after this guy fucked up—and that was before the man I love crashed over that bannister and broke my fall.

"You fucking asshole! You and your macho pissing contest." *Push.* "You had to mark that wall and prove to everyone that you're the man." *Shove.* "The minute I mentioned Roman's name, you saw red and ripped a hole that almost killed us!" I add another hard shove that lands him against the wall.

He's still holding his nose. Someone grabs my arm and pulls me back. "Abby, leave it," Gage says.

"Why? So he can weasel his way out of this like he did before?" I gesture angrily at Woz. "We don't even know how Roman is and you're here, you blackmailing little turd, right as rain with barely a scratch."

Woz wipes the back of his hand across his nose, smearing the blood I raised over his stubbled cheek like war paint. "Don't worry, your boyfriend will be fine, Sullivan, and you can go back to screwing in his office."

So maybe I shouldn't have reminded him that he has the goods on me, but at this point I don't care. I lunge for him again, only this time he defends himself with a hand on my shoulder. I can take it. I am Captain Fucking America. I can do this all day.

"Get your hands off her."

We all turn at the sound of that voice. *Roman.*

He's standing at the nurses' station, steri-strips on his forehead, arm in a sling, wearing a hospital gown with little ponies on it.

He looks amazing.

And though it has to hurt him like a mother to move, he does so anyway, right to my side.

"You okay?" he asks me.

"Am *I* okay? Roman, how are you even walking?"

But thank God he is, and then because I'm so relieved, I promptly burst into tears.

Some tough girl I am.

"Hey, sweetheart, it's okay." He pulls me into his arms and he doesn't even flinch though I know it has to hurt him. I've cracked ribs before; it's not pleasant.

"I thought—I thought the worst."

I was holding it in like a ticking bomb while we waited to hear the news. Seeing Wozniak emerge first looking like he was going to skate clear, and with no sign of a safe, healthy Roman, turned me into a rage monster at the unfairness of it all. Not pretty thoughts, I know, but I can't help it.

Roman is murmuring soothing words against my temple, assuring me I'm safe, he's safe, and the world is right again. This man's arms are the best place to be. Awareness comes at me in fits as I become conscious of how quiet it is.

Everyone is staring at me. At us.

Because there's no doubt that we are an "us."

I take a step back, then another. Roman levels me with an expression that reads as hurt, though that might be the pain he's in from his numerous injuries.

"Abby, it's okay."

No, it's not. I don't say that but my head is shaking, my heart is thundering, my skin is itching with panic. Feeling so exposed makes me want to crawl into a hole beneath my feet, the grave I've dug for myself by getting involved with (a) my commanding officer and (b) someone who could die at any minute.

It's hypocritical, sure. The same thing could happen to me. Anyone I'm with romantically would have to suffer, wait on a scalpel's edge, knowing I could be hurt on a run. But I don't want to be the one feeling that way.

I don't want to hear that the man I love died in the line of duty.

And because it's not enough that my entire crew knows I've been sleeping with my boss, the last person I want to see— even more than Wozniak—is standing not ten feet away from me, blocking all the sun.

Commissioner Chuck Sullivan.

"I can't do this," I say, finally putting my panic into words.

The rest of the crew are gaping. Roman's eyes have never left my face, his expression unreadable. My father's stormy presence is rolling toward me, a wave of disapproval, though he hasn't moved an inch.

Roman reaches for me, but I pull away. One more second under this heated scrutiny—from all of them—will lay me out flat. I push past him, bypass my father without a word, and leave what I can't face behind.

Times like this I wished I smoked. Though I suppose I could just inhale my turnout gear and get the same carcinogenic effects. Or walk to where the smokers are huddled like Biblical lepers twenty feet from the hospital entrance.

"Abigail," I hear after a few minutes pacing and trying to calm down.

My father looks concerned, though I know that won't last. I brace for the Chuck Sullivan onslaught of censure.

"Are you okay?" he asks, and my heart thaws a fraction at his apprehensive tone.

"I've been better."

"You want to tell me what I just walked in on?"

Where to start? The part where I lost it on a fellow firefighter or the part where I burst into tears on realizing my lieutenant, the man I love, was going to be okay?

I figure he saw the latter so I may as well start at the beginning. "I punched one of my co-workers because he's an ass who almost got us killed."

His eyes widen, no doubt surprised at my candor. *Thought I'd try to sugarcoat it, Dad?*

"You're not the judge and jury here, Abigail. There are procedures to follow. An investigation to open. You don't get to decide how a fellow firefighter should be punished." He inhales deeply. "How long have you and Rossi been seeing each other?"

I swallow my discomfort. "I don't see how that's relevant."

"Oh, you don't, do you? You're disobeying orders, getting into physical altercations, engaging in inappropriate relationships with your superior officer, and you've been on the job for little more than a month. You're just like your mother. Reckless, emotional, not suited for this kind of work at all."

Finally, we're getting to the heart of the matter. "I know you hated that she was a firefighter, Dad. That she didn't fit inside the cage you made for her."

His eyes flash. "All I wanted was for her to be safe. For you both to be safe. But she always thought she knew best. She had a rash streak a mile wide, and you have it, too. You like to push back against authority which I assume is related to your attitude to me. When someone tells you no, you see my face and give them the bird."

Is he blaming Mom for what happened to her? Did she make a mistake the night she died? So today I disobeyed an order, went back up that stairway. Perhaps I should have left it to someone more experienced on the team, who could have helped Roman instead of hindering him. Maybe a more seasoned firefighter could have hauled them both down the stairs before the bannister gave way.

"It's not always about you, Dad." But even as I say it, I see it through his eyes. Not just the pain of knowing someone you love is in danger, but also the risks I'm willing to take to prove my father wrong.

And taking that risk might have seriously injured Roman.

He ordered me off those stairs, and while I believe my return to that spot saved him, it might also have forced him to second-guess his decisions going forward.

He had already told me he'd worry about sending me into a dangerous situation.

On the stairs, he scouted ahead, checking that every step could hold our weight.

The man said he loved me, for God's sake!

Those weren't merely the actions of a commanding officer. His feelings for me dictated his choices in the field and who's to say they didn't break differently than they would have with another crew-mate? When we crashed over that rail, he went first and twisted his body to break my fall.

I close my eyes and pinch the spot between them where a headache is starting to form. When I look up, I meet frost in my father's gaze.

"Maybe I screwed up. I don't know anymore."

"You're suspended pending an investigation into this incident and what just occurred in that waiting room when you assaulted a fellow officer. Your behavior with Rossi will also be addressed."

No, Roman can't be hurt because of my actions.

"This isn't Roman's fault. He wanted to report it but I asked him not to."

"So it's not serious."

"I didn't think so ..." Until today.

Until I thought I might have lost him.

Until I went ape shit on a fellow officer.

Until I exposed my underbelly for all to see.

"Roman can't be in trouble for this, Dad. He didn't do anything wrong."

"Except cross a line with you, a direct report. He knows better than that."

He did but he did it anyway. And I knew better but I let it go too far, caught up in the craziness of my attraction for him. My love.

Because that's what it is. A love that hurts more than heals.

"It doesn't feel good, does it?"

"What?"

"Waiting to hear if someone you care about is going to be okay."

No, it doesn't.

"He'll be okay," my father continues. "This time. But do you want to experience that 24/7? While you're on suspension you'll have time to think about whether this is truly the right career choice for you."

Thirty-Six

Roman

Fifteen minutes ago, I opened my eyes to the room spinning, a pounding headache, and a body that felt like it had been through a meatgrinder.

But I'm alive. Which is not what I was thinking when I took a header off that second floor landing with Abby wrapped around me.

I tried to push her back as I fell but she was holding on too tight, tying her fate to mine. I had just enough time to twist as I fell ... and that was the last thing I remembered.

On waking and learning I wasn't in imminent danger of dying, I went looking for her. Seeing her going toe to toe with Wozniak—and that prick laying a hand on her—had me moving faster than the docs would probably recommend given my battered body.

I hated to see her upset, but I figure it's a good thing for her to let it out. More than that, it tells me what I need to know: this woman cares about me.

So much so that she freaked out and took a walk. While I

wanted to follow her, it's probably best she takes a moment to breathe. It's a lot to take in.

We're both alive and now we have to deal with the consequences.

"Don't know what you have to be so smug about." Venti stands by my bed like the Grim Fucking Reaper. "The doc says you have a concussion, a broken wrist, and two cracked ribs from Sullivan using you as a gym mat."

None of that matters. "She's okay?"

"You saw her. Physically, she's fine." He raises an eyebrow. "Don't know how much you witnessed out there, but she punched Wozniak."

"Bet no one rushed to stop her." God, I'm so proud of her.

"And there's that smug expression again, Rossi. Give me the broad strokes on what happened in there."

I do. Abby took it upon herself to come back when I told her to book it out of there, but she also saved my ass. I'm not sure I would have made it across that landing if she hadn't been there to haul me back up.

"So Sullivan disobeyed an order. Again."

"She should be written up," I say, which is pretty much my stock speech where Abby is concerned, "but in the circumstances she went with her instincts and it played out for the best. She saved my life, Cap."

Venti doesn't look like he agrees or is even glad I made it out relatively unscathed, but it's my report that will go on the record. I'll defend her to the last no matter what anyone else tries to make of it.

"I need you to answer a question and don't bullshit me."

"Okay."

"Are you in a relationship with Sullivan?"

Ah, so any hopes of keeping that under wraps are dead in the water. I'm not going to lie, not even hedge. "I am. We are."

"And you didn't think to report this?"

"She wanted to stay on my crew and we weren't sure where it was going."

Well, I was sure. But Abby needed time.

"That's supposed to make it right? There are rules for a reason." He holds up a hand. "And the reason is not that they should be broken, asshole. Now all I'm going to hear from Chuck Sullivan is that I have no control over my firehouse."

He grumbles some more but I barely pay attention. I'm anxious to see Abby and soothe her after her freak out. Let her know it'll be okay. All of it.

A nurse comes in and makes some adjustments to a pillow, then Simpson, Brooks, and Acosta put their heads around the door to check up on me. No sign of Woz, probably because he's not in the mood for his second fist of the day. Soon the nurse is shooing them all out, and all I can think is: where is she?

While waiting, I call Chiara and tell her what happened and that she should stay home with Lena. (My sister freaked out for about sixty seconds, but calmed down enough to call me "a fucking asshat." Twin dynamic restored.)

Ten minutes that feel like ten hours later, Abby appears. Worry rules her pretty features but I try a smile to put her at ease even though it hurts my head to stretch my lips.

"Damn, ciliegina, you're a sight for sore eyes. You okay?"

"Am I okay? Roman, you were unconscious!"

"And now I'm not." She has a cut over her eyebrow but otherwise looks amazing. And safe. Most important of all, safe. "Wish I could have seen you take a swing at Wozniak."

"It was something, all right. Suspension pending investigation, courtesy of the mighty Commissioner."

"What? That's ridiculous! I haven't even had a chance to file a report."

She swipes at a tear, and it pisses me off that she's not

coming close enough for me to touch her. "Did I screw up, Roman? Tell me the truth."

"You probably should have gotten that kid to the medics yourself and sent someone else back in. On the other hand, I might be dead now if you hadn't stuck around."

"Or if you weren't so concerned about getting me down the stairs safely you might have gotten out of there more quickly. Wouldn't have had to worry about breaking my fall *and* saving my ass."

We could argue about this all day, but I don't care. We're both here, gloriously alive, and I'm absolutely certain about what that means for the future.

I plan to use this gift wisely. No more sneaking around, pretending it's just s-e-x. Something will have to change with the shifts at Engine 6 but we'll work it out.

I reach for her, and she takes my hand, allowing me to pull her closer to the bed.

"I'll take care of it. Talk to Venti, sort out this suspension bullshit. Right now, we need to talk."

"I know." She sounds miserable about it. "Roman, this can't go on."

"Yeah, something has to give," I agree.

A flash of hurt in her eyes ratchets up my pulse. I have a bad feeling about this.

"We have to end this," she says. "Before someone gets hurt. More than they already have."

I sit up straighter. Pain ricochets a pinball path off my sore ribs. "Abby."

"I almost got you killed because I disobeyed an order. I'm not good for you, Roman. My presence on your shift puts you and the whole crew in danger because the dynamic is off. I'm too willing to push back against you because I think I can get away with shit and you're second-guessing your calls because you're worried about me."

She's not wrong. But we can fix this.

"Which is why you should be on another crew. And then we can be together outside of the firehouse."

She pulls away from me. "I finally understand what my dad's been feeling all this time. My mom leaving him, knowing I'm in danger. I don't want anyone else to feel like that. And neither do I want to be with someone who walks that fine line between heroism and death."

Like her? This makes no sense.

"Abby, let's talk about this."

"It's best to stop and draw a line under it, before we get too involved."

Too involved? Too fucking late. I'm already in so deep here, I'm drowning in her.

Try to see it from her side. She was spooked about the call, how close we came to taking a dirt nap. The first time you make it out of a life-or-death situation, it can mess with your mind. Some people retreat to prudence, others achieve a certain clarity or feel invincible. Add to that her meltdown over Wozniak and the suspension, she's bound to be on edge. She needs to be guided through this.

"You're not thinking straight. I can fix all this. Let's take a breath and figure it out."

She shakes her head. "For the first time since I walked into Engine 6, I'm finally clear-headed, Roman. I've let my attraction to you override everything, and now I need to focus in a way I can't when I'm near you. You've listened, been there for me when I needed a shoulder. We had a good time, but it muddled everything at work."

My skin breaks out in a clammy sweat. *A good time?*

That's all I was to her: a rash of bad decisions, a steamy roll in the sheets, and the guy to bounce her problems off of?

I already did this, tried to make it work with a woman who

got bored less than an hour after the "I do's." Today, I told Abby I love her and this is what she comes back with?

Man, did I get that wrong.

When I speak, I barely recognize my own voice. "So the adrenaline junkie only gets her kicks when it's dangerous, huh?"

Shock at being called out sparks in her eyes. "No, that's not it."

"Isn't it? Maybe you liked it better when we were screwing under the radar. You liked the sneaking around, the thrill of it. But now everyone knows and you decide this is where you get off the ride."

Her mouth wobbles. "You almost died and I can't help thinking I contributed to that somehow. And if I were to lose you..."

"Sure, Abby, you keep thinking that. Whatever fits the story you want to tell yourself. You screwed up, you're not good enough, we don't work well together, lives are on the line. All that sounds great. But what it boils down to is that you have the heart of a lioness in a fire, but you're a fucking coward in life."

Her eyes go wide and hurt. Yeah, no one likes to hear the truth.

Delivering it doesn't feel so good, either.

"I-I'm sorry. I'll let you rest now." She walks to the door. Once there, she turns. Those blue eyes blaze with emotion and something that reads as regret. Sorry she let this go as far as it did, I suppose.

"Thanks for saving me, Roman. Thanks for everything."

I barely hear the door close over the waterfall of fire and blood in my ears.

Thirty-seven

Abby

It's been two days since the fire—since I told Roman I couldn't face another day like that—and I need to figure out my next steps. I'm still on suspension but I'm hopeful I'll be back after the investigation, which is why I'm at the firehouse trying to future-proof my career. I really want to stay at 6, and if I can't be on B shift, I have to shoot for A or C. If no one at the firehouse will have me, I'll put in for a transfer. I pray it won't come to that.

It'll be tough seeing Roman when we're both back at work. I let things get out of hand there, and while it'll take a while for my heart to recover, at least now I know the danger of getting too close to a man who could destroy everything I'm trying to build.

If that isn't progress, I don't know what is.

Approaching Lt. Almeida's office, I run into Danny.

"Hey, Abby, you okay? I heard about your suspension. That shouldn't have happened at all." He looks more upset than the situation warrants, and abruptly it hits me.

"Have you been talking to my father? All this time?"

He makes a face but thankfully doesn't try to gaslight me. "He just wanted to know how you were doing. Make sure you were safe."

The Engine 6 spy revealed at last. I get it now. Danny is one of those toxic nice guys, the kind of man who thinks if he's sweet, he'll eventually get what he feels is owed to him with little to no investment at all. "And what was in it for you?"

"Nothing, Abby. If my sister was working at this job, I'd want to know she was doing okay. We have to look out for each other."

"I don't need that paternalistic bullshit from you or anyone on this crew, Acosta. Take your 'someone to watch over me' attitude and shove it."

"Abby!"

I push past him and practically burst into Luke's office before I realize he's not alone. Captain Wyatt Fox, Luke's foster brother and my academy instructor, is also present.

"Captain." I nod at Wyatt, who nods back with a graveled, "Sullivan."

"I can come back," I say to Luke. "When you're not busy."

"No problem. How's your speech coming along?"

The memorial service honoring my mother and the other fallen firefighters is in a few days. I'm supposed to be working on my speech but it's hard to represent the future of women in CFD when I'm screwing up so spectacularly.

"It's slow going. You guys going to say something?"

"Leaving it to Wyatt."

Wyatt's biological brother, Logan Keyes, also died in that high-rise fire with his foster father Sean. Alex and Eli named both their boys after their lost loved ones, which is so sweet it forms a lump in my throat.

Wyatt sniffs. "Heard you're savin' firefighters who should know better."

"You taught me well."

His lips twitch. "Wozniak has the worst luck with his equipment. Good thing you were there."

"Or is it?" Luke comments with a chuckle.

The most recent incident, and Woz's role in it, is currently under investigation. As I'm not on duty I haven't had to face him.

No one has told me I shouldn't have landed that punch, though.

"You here to ask about transferring to my crew?" Luke grins. "When you're back from your suspension?"

I divide a look between the two of them, figuring that Luke has broached the topic and it's okay to discuss it in front of his brother.

"I don't want to assume anything, and it would mean you'd have to switch Jude to Lieutenant Rossi's platoon. I understand it if you feel there's already a bond there."

Luke strums his fingers on his desk. "We're already having to rethink some assignments. If Woz makes it out of the investigation intact, he'll probably be on C-shift because Rossi won't stand to have him on his team. And as much as we'd like to be shot of him, we're not in the business of exporting our problems to another engine. We prefer to deal with it in house."

Okay. Time to grovel.

"I know it might seem like I'm a troublemaker. I'm not, really. Sure, I disobeyed an order and ended up on light duty. And I disobeyed another one from Rom—Lieutenant Rossi, but I truly thought it was for the best because I knew exactly where he was on that landing. And I punched Woz, but it was more of a reflex—"

"We've all had those," Wyatt deadpans.

"Yeah, you actually hit the mayor at City Hall. Though less of a reflex and more premeditated." Luke grins at his brother, then shares that grin with me. "Then the asshole married into the family so we can't hit him anymore. My sister would beat me to a pulp if I harm a hair on Pretty Boy Cooper's head."

Speaking of harming hairs, Alex has already been in touch to congratulate me on my excellent problem-solving skills regarding Woz.

Wyatt raises an eyebrow. "At least when I punch someone I'm not stupid enough to let someone record it."

Luke tips an imaginary hat at that observation, clearly amused by the memory. A few years ago, a YouTube-covered dust-up between Luke and a CPD officer in Dempseys' bar resulted in notorious headlines, a firefighters-with-kittens calendar, and at least three marriages.

"So, Sullivan," Luke says, "what we're saying is that punching someone who probably deserves it is pretty much a rite of passage at this house."

Wyatt adds, "And is generally not a reason for excluding someone from a crew."

"Though I have to wonder what you meant when you called Wozniak a 'blackmailing little turd,'" Luke says casually.

Gage must have blabbed. "It doesn't matter."

"Oh, I think it does. You want on my crew, you need to spill."

Reluctantly, I relay the conversation I had with Wozniak a week ago. By the time I'm finished, Luke's entire demeanor has changed from jocular to stiff-as-a-board.

"How is it possible that dick has sunk lower in my already rock-bottom opinion? And you didn't tell Rossi?"

"He would have gone nuts, and with the thin ice he's on with my father, it seemed best to handle it myself."

"With a right hook." Wyatt stares at me. "Might be a spot for you in the Battle of the Badges, Sullivan."

My laugh is joyless. "What I just told you about Woz, any chance we can keep that from Roman?"

Luke and Wyatt look at each other, a whole conversation happening before my eyes. Having witnessed this kind of silent dialogue between Jude and Sam, I recognize that the answer is a big fat negative.

Luke locks his hands behind his head. "So you and Rossi? Can you still work in the same house, now that you two are no longer a couple?"

"I can be professional. And he's been nothing but."

"Except for sleeping with his candidate," Wyatt comments drily.

I feel a blush coming on. "Except for that."

Both of them look sympathetic. "Sorry, we're just teasing," Luke says. "Abby, you're welcome on my crew anytime. As long as you square it with Torres."

🔥

"Yeah, I'll leave the best crew in CFD so you can avoid your bae at work." Jude and I are in my aunt Kathleen's kitchen, having both arrived at the same time for Sunday lunch.

"You know I wouldn't ask if it wasn't important."

He gives me a fond look. "Abs, I'm kidding. Of course I'll switch. Probably better to spread the bitch badassery around anyway."

So I would miss the opportunity to work with Alex when she returned from maternity leave, but them's the breaks. "I owe you big time."

"Yeah ya do. So are we not going to even talk about it?"

"What?"

"You and Rossi. We're gonna pretend that never

happened? Or that you actually kept this a secret from me but somehow Sam knows?"

The big doofus blabbermouth walks into the kitchen at that very moment.

"You had to squeal, Killian."

"You and your LT?" Sam picks up one of my aunt's rosemary rolls and takes a bite. "Thought it was common knowledge now that it's pistols at dawn over at Northwestern Memorial."

I face Jude again. "Big Mouth here guessed that day we ran into Roman at the diner. I didn't tell you because the fewer people who know about that kind of thing, the better. And now everyone knows and it's finished. Donezo."

Jude and Sam exchange a glance.

"Don't do that."

"What?" they both say in unison.

"Act like I'm a problem to be solved. I'm not." I acknowledge Jude's eyebrow lift and relieve Sam of his half-eaten bread roll. "Okay, so this shift switch thing is a problem and you've helped me solve it, but that's it. The rest, is just ..." I lower my voice. "S-e-x."

"You think I'm deaf or stupid, Abigail Josephine Sullivan!"

"Christ on a hunk of soda bread," I mutter as my aunt blows into the kitchen like an Atlantic wave crashing against the Cliffs of Moher.

"Oh, you'll have to whisper lower than that to get away with that kind of language." My aunt opens the oven, eyes the roast, and closes it again. The boys inhale happily. I pour another glass of wine, suspecting I'm going to need it.

"So you met someone. Finally. And he's a firefighter like your father."

Like my mother. That's the problem, isn't it?

I take a bite of Sam's roll and chew while I think of a

response. "He's my shift lieutenant, or he was. And I'm not in the market for dating firefighters."

"That's what your mother said. Look what happened there." In case I don't cotton on, she points. "You! That's what happened."

"I heard Rossi's pretty cranky while he's home on medical leave," Jude says, apropos of nothing.

"How do you know?"

Jude takes a long swig of his beer before answering. I want to kill him.

"Chiara said. That's his sister," he explains for the others.

"Since when have you been talking to Roman's sister?"

"She asked me to be involved with this program for the LGBTQ teens she works with. And when we met at the diner the other day to chat about it, she mentioned her brother's mood. 'Emo grunting' was the term she used, which sounds kind of hot, actually."

It does sound hot. "He's recovering from his injuries. Of course he's going to be in a mood."

Another look between the boys, another urge to murder. "Stop talking about me when I'm right here!"

"She likes him," Sam says to Jude.

"I think it's more than like. I think she lurves him! Abby and Roman sitting in a tree, hiding from a boar named Beh-het-sey ..."

I throw half a bread roll at him. "That doesn't even rhyme right, you idiot."

"No throwing of my bread!" My aunt is back on the CFD intranet using Johno's login and the iPad I gave her at Christmas for evil. "Abigail, are you telling me you had this fine young man in your sights and you let him get away?"

"It's not as simple as that. It was just a fling. That's all! Lots of great sex." I make a face at Jude and Sam. "Are you happy now that you've made me talk about sex in front of my poor innocent aunt?"

"More like scandalized," Sam says. "Kat, did you hear she dumped him while he was lying in a hospital bed with cracked ribs, a broken wrist, and a brain injury, all of which she caused?"

"Practically in a coma," Jude adds. "Talk about kicking a guy when he's down."

Tears well, and I turn away, opening the fridge to cover for my emotion. I know they're kidding, the big brothers I never had, but it's a little too close to the bone.

Someone squeezes my arm and lays a chin on my shoulder. It's Sam.

"Sorry, Abs. We're jerks."

Jude circles me from the other side. "Yeah, Sam's a total dick. Want me to punch him for you?"

"Yep." I sniff. "No."

"Out of my kitchen, all of you!" As we turn to troop out, my aunt points at me. "You stay."

Jude and Sam send me faux-apologetic glances before leaving me alone with Kathleen.

"So what happened and how much is your father to blame?"

"He's not—it's not his fault." Sure, he makes me doubt my abilities every day but I can't blame him for Roman. That's all on me. "I just made a clean break with the guy I shouldn't have been with in the first place."

"Because he's your boss?"

"Sort of."

She folds her arms and leans against the counter. "Explain it to me like I'm a child."

"We can't be on the same shift, so I'm switching with Jude. When Roman—Lieutenant Rossi—comes back from leave—" and when my suspension is lifted "—I'll be in a different platoon. It'll make things easier."

"So what's the problem? Now you can see him, right?"

I open up the flatware drawer and remove knives and forks for dinner. "I lost my necklace, the one that belonged to Mom. I think I must have dropped it at the fire." I'm not usually superstitious, but it seems like a sign, telling me I edged too close to the sun with Roman.

She studies me for a long beat. "I worried about her every day she was on duty. Every day she wasn't. She was always getting into trouble, accidents, even arguments with strangers in parking lots. If she saw something she didn't think was fair or right, she let you know about it."

He told me he loved me. Then he called me a coward.

He was right.

"I'm technically following in her footsteps, but I'm not as brave as she was. I don't know how to be."

She pulls me into a hug, patting me on the back, and sending me back to those early days after my mom died when I was a mess. I inhale her comforting scent and try to draw some strength from it.

"Yes, you do. You're Jo Sullivan's girl, and that means you have her blood pumping in your veins and her heart beating in your chest. She would be so proud of you. Just ask yourself what she would do, and you'll have your answer."

Thirty-eight

Roman

It's been a week and I'm still on medical leave, which suits me fine because I don't think I could face the rest of my crew and their sad-eyes over the whole Abby fiasco.

I'm still not sure what happened.

I understood the words coming out of her mouth, but it was like they were arranged in a puzzle I couldn't solve. Or maybe I don't want to dwell too long on what she was really trying to tell me.

I'm not the kind of guy you commit to for the long haul.

I can see that. My ex never bought into the whole notion of a deep connection with me. Forced into marriage by an unplanned pregnancy, she resented having to see me in any other light than her first impression of me: a guy who could show her the goods between the sheets. Seems Abby saw nothing more than that, either.

At least my sweet Cherry Pie added the gloss of potential —if she let what we have bloom into more, she'd only end up getting hurt if something happened to me. Covered all her bases there.

You're not worth getting serious over, but if you were—and that's a big if*—my heart might not survive.*

Fuck that.

My phone buzzes with a call from Luke. I answer and put it on speaker because I'm cooking Chicken Marsala one-handed.

"Hey."

"Rossi, how goes it?"

We chat for a few about my injury, the firehouse, and how much of an asshole Woz is.

"So, Sullivan came to see me about a transfer to A-shift."

My heart squeezes at the mention of her name. It shouldn't surprise me that she wants off my crew but it still hurts to hear it.

"Figured that was on the cards," I mutter. "You okay with that?"

"Sure, if you are. Torres is a good guy. Should fit right in with your team."

"Yeah." I don't want to talk about this anymore, but Luke's still yammering. It takes me a second to realize what he said. "Wait, did you say Kinsey is pregnant?"

"Sure did. She's just gone three months, so ..."

"She's been in the family way for the whole time your idiot co-workers were placing bets."

"Ah, better to let the kids have their fun."

I let loose a chuckle. "Congrats, Almeida." We chit-chat about families some more, and just as we're winding down, I find the words I need. "Could you do me a favor?"

"Sure."

"Could you watch out for Abby? I know I don't have to ask but I'm asking anyway." Redundant as it might sound, it's important that he knows my feelings in this area and that

I have an interest that needs to be acknowledged. It might be the only way I can say she's mine without speaking the words.

Because, despite everything that's happened and knowing that she doesn't want me, I am still all in with this woman.

Abby Sullivan is mine in every way that matters.

"She's safe with me, Roman. I promise."

We close it out and I return to dinner, desperate to get my mind off Abby, who will no longer be on my crew. Or in my life, at this rate. I'm trying and failing to view it as a blessing when Chiara crashes into the kitchen like a bull and yells at me. "What the hell are you doing?"

I raise the spatula in my free hand. "What does it look like? Smashing the fucking patriarchy."

She takes the tool from me and examines my handiwork, chicken breasts flash-frying in the skillet. "You're supposed to be resting, though I appreciate you pushing through in order to keep me free from chains. Isn't this why we have the next generation?"

"She's on her computer, looking at wedding stuff." Of course, I told Tori that Lena should be allowed to wear pants but my daughter is being more mature than me and taking it on the chin.

Chiara makes a face. "Sit down, I'll do this."

I do as she says and wait.

Ten seconds.

Twenty.

Finally, she asks, "So, what am I doing?" She prods one chicken breast with the spatula, as if she's never used one. This would not surprise me.

"Turn them over in about a minute."

She screws up her mouth. "Are we having visitors tonight?"

"Not that I know of."

"Well, all your crew have dropped by in the last week. Everyone but Abby. She okay?"

"Fine, as far as I know." Moving on, figuring it out. Good for her. "Turn them now."

She does, splashing oil all over the stovetop. Deliberate, of course, so I'll never seek her help again.

"Uh, don't flatten them. Let them sit for a bit."

She puts the spatula down on the counter, though there's a spoon rest right fucking there. Jesus, I am grouchy tonight.

She turns to face me. "What happened with Abby?"

"Nothing. Literally nothing."

"Ro-Ro, come on, this is me. You think I don't know when your heart is broken?"

She hasn't called me Ro-Ro since we were kids. I rub my mouth as if it can change the words about to leave my lips and shape them into something that won't feel like broken glass in my throat.

"She called it quits. Said it would be too stressful worrying about me, so best not to let us go any further. And y'know, she's right. I don't want to worry about her, either."

A very playground response. Like I'm going to *stop* worrying about her because we're no longer ... whatever we were to each other.

"She saved your ass, then told that same ass to take a hike?"

"I think it scared her. She lost her mom on the job and what happened to me brought it all back. I suppose I should be flattered she's worried about the prospect of losing me ..."

"But you're not."

Needing action, I stand and pick up the spatula. "I don't believe it's her reason, or her only reason. I think she's trying to let me down gently. She said it was just a fling for her. Which is fine."

"Roman, as usual, you are 100% wrong. I saw how she looked at you and your spicy meatballs."

That earns a snort from me.

"Do I need to hurt her?"

"Thanks for being my personal pit bull, but you can stand down."

"Need to hurt who?" Lena has just walked in.

"Abby," Chiara says at the same time I say, "Nobody."

Lena looks concerned. "Why would you want to hurt Abby?"

I shake my head imperceptibly at my sister.

She ignores me because she thinks children should never be shielded from the truth. "She told your dad she doesn't want to see him anymore. As a boyfriend."

Lena blinks. "Oh. Is it okay if I talk to her?"

"You want to talk to Abby?"

"We've been texting about Big Brother. And I sent her some photos of the dresses Mom wants at the wedding. She gave me her opinion and I told Mom I wanted to wear something else. Like this." She shows me a picture on her iPad. It looks like a satin two-piece pantsuit in the same color as Tori's wedding theme. Unfortunately I'm acutely aware of this theme and other details like the size of the centerpieces and the composition of the various floral arrangements because my daughter has talked of nothing else for the last two weeks.

Meanwhile, Abby's been lending an ear to my girl? I'm so confused. My heart aches at the notion that my daughter is getting all this love and support from someone I care about deeply but who doesn't feel the same way.

"What did your mom say?"

"She said yes!" Her joy evaporates. "But if you don't want me to talk to Abby anymore ..."

"No, that's fine," I answer quickly. "Fragolina, you can talk to who you want. As long as I know who they are."

"So does Abby ask about your dad?" Chiara winks at me.

"She asked if his injuries were healing. I said not fast

enough because he's always here." She assesses me for a moment. "Dad, do you need a hug?"

A lump the size of a meatball forms in my throat. "Yeah, I do."

She wraps herself around me and gives me the best hug I've ever received. I kiss the top of her head and let myself be healed a fraction by the warmth of my daughter's love.

I draw back to face her. "Thanks, sweetheart."

She smiles, fully aware of her power over me. Her phone buzzes in her hand, and she wanders into the other room to respond.

When I catch Chiara's eye, I find her looking a little softer than her usual.

Using the spatula, I set the flash-fried chicken breasts to one side. A few knobs of butter in the pan, then some Marsala, thyme, and mushrooms. It's harder than you'd think to do this one-handed.

Ever helpful, Chiara pours more wine for herself. "Why did you stay married to Tori for so long?"

"What's that got to do with anything?"

"Just tell me."

I blow out a breath. "Because we had Lena. Because I'm not a quitter. So I knew it was a mistake from day one, but I wanted to try for my little girl."

"You're stubborn and you hate being wrong."

"Everyone hates being wrong."

"True." She grins. "But I think there's another reason why you stayed. You're not built for casual relationships. You can say you're having a fling or you're going to hook up with someone for a one-night stand, but that's not you."

So she knows me well. "Where is this going?"

"I think you knew that with Abby. I think you wouldn't risk your job or what you're building in Chicago if you didn't think this thing with Abby had a future from the get-go. And

I also don't think you'd take a risk like that with someone who wouldn't reciprocate. You have good instincts, Roman. You knew exactly what you were getting into with Tori, but you made that choice for Lena. You wouldn't make that mistake again. Abby is not Tori, and you recognized that. She's afraid of what she feels for you because of her parents. Her mom left her, her dad's emotionally checked out and not supportive of her career choice. That's abandonment 101 right there."

I growl. "I'm not one of your teens."

"I know." She pats my arm condescendingly. "Abby's nuts about you, but she needs to do some healing before she's ready. Don't give up on her just yet."

Thirty-nine

Abby

I straighten the jacket of my uniform for what feels like the fiftieth time. My reflection in the mirror is a funhouse facsimile, like my *Us* doppelganger who's been living in the bowels of the earth and now wants to usurp my life.

Same hair, eyes, nose, lips. But there's something sunken and dark about what I see. Hollowed out. She feels like an impostor.

Outside the restroom, it's quiet as everyone is in the bay for the memorial service. At the Wall of the Fallen, I pause, needing a moment with Joanne Sullivan.

"Hey, Mom," I whisper, but I can't get out anything more. My shoulders heave with the emotion jamming my chest. I have to get it together because everyone's expecting the best speech ever in about five minutes.

"Hey," I try again. "I wish I could talk to you properly about what's going on. I feel like I'm screwing things up at every turn and I'm just one big fat disappointment."

"You could never disappoint anyone, Abby."

He's here. I'd alternately hoped and dreaded. When I pivot, my heart turns over several times at the sight of him in his dress uniform. His wrist is in a cast, but not a sling.

"You're going to make mistakes," he continues. "But your mom's proud that you're still here, forging ahead. And so am I."

He always knows the right thing to say. I'll miss him as my mentor.

As so many things.

I swallow my pain. "How's the wrist?"

"Achy. But that's to be expected."

"And how's Lena doing? Wait, is this the weekend of the wedding?" I am full of questions!

"It is. She's in New York with Chiara."

I blink. "They're *both* at the wedding of your ex?"

His smile is wry. "I wouldn't let her go alone and I didn't trust Tori or my former sisters-in-law to keep an eye on her. It's a wedding, so they're going to be a bit overboard, drunk off their asses. But Chiara can do what I can't."

"For Lena. And for you. She's a good sister."

"She is. I'm lucky to have her, which she reminds me of every day. And Lena's lucky to have you. I heard you've been giving her advice."

"Yeah, I hope you don't mind. She reached out."

"Of course not. I'm thankful you've been there for her. For all of us." He eyes me with a darker gaze. "I also heard you're leaving my crew."

"Yeah, I thought it was for the best. I hope you're okay with signing off on that." It's only now occurring to me that he might not do that, that he might not like being told how to manage his crew.

He moves in, his solidity a force I'm no match for. "I think we were a good team, but this is probably the right call."

A good team. *We were.*

"Looks like you'll be losing Wozniak as well." Apparently he's been moved to the C-shift while the investigation into the incident is ongoing. There's talk that he'll be forced to go through academy training again.

"You should have told me about the blackmail."

"So you could beat him to a pulp?"

He scoffs. "I wouldn't—okay, I would have. But hell, Abby, you don't have to protect me."

"I know how hard you've worked to make a new life here. I didn't want anything to get in the way of that—the captain, my father." *Me.* It seems I've done nothing but threaten Roman's self-control and career since I arrived.

"Well, I'll get a reprimand in my record, unless your father decides to take it further."

I don't think he will. I'll make sure of it.

"You'll be okay, Roman."

"In my job, yeah." He grasps my hand and places it over his heart. "Not in here, though. Not for a long time, maybe never."

His eyes bore into me, filled with all the pain I caused. I try to calm myself, only I can't shake the force of my feelings. The proximity of him turns me into a gloopy mess and I'm left with trying to convince myself—inadequately—that this is why I can't be with him.

I'm too emotional. Losing him like this hurts. To lose him on the job would kill me.

"Abby, about what I said at the hospital, about you being a coward. That was wrong, completely out of order. You're not, you're the bravest woman I know."

"No, you don't have to apologize." He was right but if I admit it, we'll end up in a place I don't think I can go. "We both said things in the heat of the moment." I don't explain any further because if I do, I'm opening a door to a world I can't have.

Understanding my reticence, he nods and takes my hand.

"Listen, I have something for you." He presses a small metal object into my palm.

I look down and gasp.

"My mom's pendant!" Only half of the chain remains, but the Claddagh symbol is there, its golden heart tarnished yet still intact. "Where did you find it?"

"In the ashes of the fire, Abby. The chain must have broken when we fell and this slipped through your turnout gear onto the ground."

"And you went to look for it?" My eyes are wet with gratitude and love for this man.

"Brooks told me you lost it. I know it means a lot to you."

You mean more. You mean everything.

"Abby, we're about to start." Maria Fernandez from Media Affairs is standing over at the corner leading to the bay corridor. She grimaces in apology at having walked into the middle of something intense.

"On my way. Thank you, Roman. For everything."

I pull myself from his grasp and walk away, placing my mom's pendant inside the breast pocket of my uniform.

Over the heart that beats for him.

Forty

Roman

Captain Wyatt Fox, having just finished a heartfelt speech about the brother and father he lost fourteen years ago, steps off the dais into the arms of his wife, Oscar-winning actress Molly Cade. The Dempseys and their extended clan are here, supporting each other as family does. As Abby ascends the steps to the lectern, I can't help thinking of how alone she looks up there.

Her father is here, but it's not for her. It's so he can look good for the press.

Her friends are here—Torres and that Killian guy from 70—and I've no doubt they'll take care of her, but not the way I could.

I want to be the one she turns to when she breaks down later, because I know she will. She came close to it inside the firehouse as she spoke to her mom.

Sure, she'll keep it together up there. It's the future I worry about—and selfish prick that I am, my future without her in it.

"Hello, everyone. Brothers and sisters in fire, families of the fallen ..." She looks over to her father. "Dad."

CFD Media Affairs *loves* that. A camera happily clicks away.

"I was six when I lost my mother, Jo Sullivan, the first female firefighter in the Chicago Fire Department. I knew what she did for a living and I especially knew it when she came home smelling of smoke and perfume. I used to think she wore that scent on the job, to assert her womanhood in some way. But later I realized that she did it for me. Spritzed it on her before she came home, so it would comfort me somehow and make her job less scary. It didn't. I was always terrified.

"I never worried about my dad, not until later, which probably taps into some unconscious bias I carry about women in the fire department. Men don't need our concern because they're doing the job they're expected to do. The one they're meant to do." Her eyes flicker to the area of the crowd where I'm standing, and I feel a burst of emotion so strong I almost keel over.

"But a woman? We should worry about her. And in return, she should make her kid feel better with a dash of Elizabeth Arden Sunflowers."

The paper in her hand shakes. I would do anything to jump up there and hold it for her. But Abby's strong. She will survive this.

"My mom didn't want me to worry about her. She didn't want anyone to do that. She just wanted to do her job and be respected for it, because she was good at that job. She had people watching her back but I like to think it wasn't overbearing or patriarchal or any different than one guy on a crew watching out for another. She saved lives, even the night she lost her own." She takes a sharp inhale. "Because she was trained to do this. She was born to be a firefighter."

On that word—*firefighter*—Abby meets my gaze square on.

"Someone once told me that I'm a good firefighter with the potential to be great. I'm not sure I believed him. That lack of belief—that impostor syndrome—wriggles inside our heads and makes us question everything. Whether we should be here doing this job we love. Whether we put other people at risk because we're not good enough. Whether we're just a distraction or a token or a number to make up a quota. Whether we deserve the things we want more than anything. When I get those doubts I remember what Jo Sullivan achieved in the face of so many obstacles. Opposition from co-workers, the public, even her own family. I remember the lives she saved. The hearts she touched.

"I remember that I can have all the training in the world but if I don't have the support, both inside and outside my family of fire, I won't succeed. Jo Sullivan sits on my shoulder, telling me I can do this. Telling me this is important. Telling me that I'm born to do it.

"It's been twenty years but you're not forgotten, Mom. I carry you inside here"—she touches her chest, the pocket where she stashed her pendant—"every day." Her gaze seeks me again and I'm filled with such love for her that I want to rush that dais and carry her off it.

"Thanks, Mom. Thanks for inspiring me and thousands of firefighters to take up this baton and run with it into the next burning building."

A tear escapes her shiny eyes and runs down her cheek. A round of applause erupts and she walks away, stopping only to kiss her father on the cheek. He says something to her, then she's in the arms of her friends, Torres and Killian.

They'll do for the moment, but I need to fix this—and I suspect I know how.

I head into the firehouse, thinking about my next move. But I don't have long to ponder because the man I want to see is walking toward me, Venti at his side.

"Commissioner, could I have a word?"

Venti stares at me. I try to convey that this is okay, even if it isn't, and refocus on Chuck Sullivan. "It won't take long."

"Sure, Lieutenant. Matt, could we use your office?"

"Go ahead."

I nod at Venti, who gifts me a look that's very familiar, one that says "do not blow up your career right now, idiot." Once in Matt's office, the Commissioner and I stand opposite each other like gunfighters at high noon.

"How's the wrist?" he asks after an extra-charged beat.

"Healing."

"I never got a chance to thank you for what you did, looking out for my daughter."

"It was a mutual thing." We saved each other, in more ways than one. "That was a good speech she gave out there. Pity it means nothing to you."

Sullivan frowns. "Is that what you think?"

"You want her out of the service, you've never supported her, and sure she's here but she's been alone for a long time."

The man looks torn between acknowledgment I'm right and sheer annoyance that I am.

"I've never doubted her ability, her commitment, her desire. I just don't think she *should* be doing it. She's my only child, all I have left of Joanne. I don't want to lose her. Is that so hard to understand?"

"No. I'm a father myself. I wouldn't want my kid in this business, and with the loss you've already suffered, you're doubly careful. I get it. But she's here, straddling the line between all in and craving your approval. She's internalized that fear of yours and it's made *her* careful. Not on the job, but in here." I strike my chest, over the heart that beats for Abby Sullivan. "She's already lost her mother, she may as well have lost you—"

"She hasn't lost me. I'm right here."

"Yeah, in the flesh. But you're not here in the way she needs. Showing pride in her accomplishments, mentoring her in her career, giving her the unconditional love she deserves. She needs someone to believe in her."

Sullivan's gaze is hard and flinty. "Someone like you?"

"Yeah, someone like me." I believe in her, but it's clearly not enough. Because if it were she would be in my arms right now.

"You were supposed to take care of her, Rossi, not seduce her. I could have your badge."

He's right. But we all make bad decisions, especially where the heart is in play. And I've no doubt that I only crossed the line once my emotions were thoroughly engaged. Chiara's right. I was crazy about Abby Sullivan from the jump.

"You could, but I don't think you will. Because I think you and I have more in common than you'd care to admit. You met your wife on the job, right?"

"I don't see how that's relevant."

"Come on, Chuck, fess up now."

He walks over to the window and looks out. A long silence ticks over before he speaks.

"I didn't want her to come back to work after Abby was born. She'd been off the job for a couple of years and there was no need, not really. But she loved it so much. And I couldn't deny her the chance to do something she loved. If I'd put my foot down, she'd be here today."

He says all this to the window, giving voice to something he's probably buried deep for years. Laying out his guilt because he didn't employ whatever fucked-up marital privilege he thinks he enjoyed twenty years ago.

"You think raining your disapproval on Abby is going to make her give up? Keep her safe?"

He turns sharply. "Eventually."

"And if you got what you wanted, if she upped and quit today, you'd be happy?" I don't wait for him to respond. "How long will that happiness last, Chuck? Because you'll lose her in every other way that matters. It will always be between you, this wall you constructed to keep her safe. To stop her from living."

From loving. Because that's what he's done. Placed her in a glass box where she can keep her heart safe from assholes like me.

Well, this asshole isn't content to let Abby Sullivan remain cut off from her heart. That thriving, pumping lump of love belongs to me, like mine belongs to her. If I have to be a dick to make it happen, then so be it.

"If you're willing to play hard ball like this, Chuck, then you don't deserve her. And I think you know that."

Forty-one

Abby

"Are you sure you don't want to come with us?" Jude searches my face, his concern evident. We're standing at the door to my apartment, after hanging for a while eating Thai take-out after the memorial service. "We can watch Killian getting hit on and make fun of his moves."

"Hey!" Sam punches Jude's shoulder. "The only fun you can make is of my *dance* moves. I freely admit I dorkify on purpose to even out the hotness factor."

Jude looks at Sam fondly. "Your strategies are surprisingly well thought out."

I pin on my smile until my cheeks ache. "Nah, I'm just wiped after today."

Sam squeezes my arm. "You did great, Abs. Your mom would be so proud of you."

Please leave before I start crying.

"I hope so!" If I raise the inflection at the end of every sentence, maybe I can fake my way through this.

Steps sound on the stair, and behind the boys, a burly figure comes into view. My father. He's still wearing his dress uniform, but looks like he's just come from a callout that zapped him of all his energy.

"Abigail, am I interrupting?"

"No, the guys were just heading out."

I hug them both, holding on for a beat or two longer than usual. Jude whispers, "Should we stay?" and I shake my head.

"Thanks, guys. I'll text later though I won't expect immediate answers. Because dancing."

"And sex," Jude says, then grimaces when he recalls my father's presence. "Sir."

My father nods at them and I stand back to let him in.

"Can I get you something?"

"A beer?"

"I have Sam Adams, if that's okay." I grab it from the fridge, and try to work out why my father is here. He was softer with me at the service, probably because of the day that's in it. Likely, normal hostilities are about to be resumed.

I know my father opposes my candidacy because he loved Mom. Still loves her. I saw his emotion when I spoke about her today and I can't fault him for trying his best to drive me out of the service. If I had a kid, I like to think I'd be all fly-free-little-bird, but probably not.

He's seated on the sofa, his top shirt button open, his elbows on his knees. Weirdly, just like Roman when he sat on my sofa that first time. I think they'd like each other if they gave it a chance.

I hand him the beer. "You look tired, Dad."

"Long day. For you, too. You did great up there." He holds up his beer bottle and clinks against mine. "To Jo."

"To Mom."

We sip, then sip again, both all up in our heads. Neither of us is ready to start, and I'm determined to wait for him to make the first move.

"When I met your mother, she had just graduated from the academy. I was her lieutenant and I fell for her the moment I saw her. All that gorgeous red hair, those bright blue eyes, and the way she could rip a man's ego—well, she had a temper and could slice ribbons off you. But I couldn't do anything about it so I suffered in silence until one day I had a bad callout. Got burned. We didn't have the Nomex hoods back then and the gear wasn't quite as fire resistant." He carries the scars of that time on his neck. I used to run my fingers over them when he held me in his lap as a girl. "Your mother came to see me in the hospital and brought me a six pack of beer, just snuck it into my room."

I chuckle. "That's pretty badass."

"That was your mom." He studies me for a moment. "We met at Engine 6."

My heart thumps hard. "I thought it was a different firehouse. I thought she went there after I was born."

"That's where we met. I heard later someone calling it Chicago's most romantic firehouse because the Dempseys' love lives kept making news, but before that lot, there was Chuck and Jo Sullivan. The original CFD supercouple." His smile is fond. "Things were different then, the rules about relationships between crew members not quite as clear-cut. When we got engaged, I transferred out to a different station, but 6 is where it all began, and where she came back to after you were born. When you asked to be assigned there, it seemed like you were trying to follow in her footsteps a little too closely."

"You thought I was headed down the same road as Mom."

He raises his gaze to mine, his pain evident. I want to hug away his hurt but I can't let him off the hook. Not yet.

"I know you don't trust me, Abigail. When your mother died, I worked a lot, extra shifts even, to block out the pain. If I was too tired, I wouldn't have to think about her. About losing her. I know I wasn't around much and I came off as ... distant. Maybe I was trying to prepare you if something happened to me. But all my life I've wanted nothing more than to protect you. I hoped you'd grow out of this desire to become a firefighter, that something else would be the outlet for your passion. I know you're good. Everyone I've talked to —Fox, Venti, Rossi—have all told me how good you are."

"You spoke to Roman about me?"

He snorts. "He spoke to me about you. Came to talk to me after the memorial. Has it all figured out."

My heart flips over and thuds into my stomach. "All what?"

"How I've hurt you and why it makes you reluctant to trust people. To give your heart."

"I understand," I manage to choke out. "You don't want to lose me."

"But I may already have."

I don't deny it. This Dad-knows-best business is all well and good when you're a little girl, but not a grown woman.

He takes my hand and clasps it tightly. "You are more precious to me than life itself, Abigail. You're all I have and if I lost you ..." He swipes at a tear. Suddenly he looks much older than his fifty-seven years. "I'm not sure I could survive that."

"Dad, I—I get it. I do. But I could be hit by a bus or get a weird disease or I don't know, trip down the stairs out there! I know you think I'm reckless but not where my job is concerned. Not where the lives of my crew and the people I serve are concerned."

He nods slowly. "If this is what you want, it's your choice."

"And if I choose it, will you respect that choice? Respect me?"

He kisses my forehead. "Yes, mo chroí, my heart of hearts. I will respect that choice. And speaking of choices ... what about Rossi?"

I remain silent, unsure where to start. The look on my father's face says he's about to give me one of his famous arguments.

"I suspect you have an opinion."

"Your captain says that Rossi wanted to report the relationship sooner, but you refused. Sure, it would have been frowned upon but if you really wanted to be with him, you could have dealt with that. Gone on the record. So why didn't you?"

I blow out a breath, reaching for the stock justification I've played over and over in my head. "I was sure it would just burn out. A flashover that would scorch everything in its path and leave nothing but ash. It seemed like a lot to risk for something that might potentially go nowhere."

He stares at me. "Rossi seemed pretty sure of the potential for the two of you from the beginning."

"He said that?"

"Not in so many words. But I could tell from talking to him that he's crazy about you. I remember what that felt like with your mother."

To hear my father speak in such candid terms unlocks something inside me.

"I—I might have felt the possibilities from the beginning but I wanted to keep it to the—uh, physical ..." I grimace at putting thoughts of his daughter having sex into my father's head. I rush forward. "It seemed safer. I wouldn't become emotionally invested in someone who I need to have my back and vice versa. And if something happened to him, I'd be sad for a while because I once knew of and laughed with and slept with Roman Rossi, but my heart would remain intact because I hadn't done something foolish like fallen in love with him. I hadn't made a life with him, a life that would have this great big void in the middle of it if he was gone. Like our lives when Mom died."

His eyes are wet, and so are mine. It's weird to be sharing this with my father, and even weirder to realize that if anyone could understand this, it's him.

We should have talked long ago.

"Abby, do you think I'd trade those years with your mom so I could escape the pain of losing her?"

"I don't know! Would you?"

He shakes his head. "Not a damn second."

"So you're saying I should just make my peace with the fact anything could happen and my heart could break if I lost him?"

He raises an eyebrow. "Did you not just tell me that you could fall under a bus or get a disease that would take you from me so I shouldn't be worried about you on the job? You could marry a guy with the safest job in the world and still get your heart broken, but think of what you might have missed. There are no guarantees in life. Every moment I spent with your mother was precious. And every moment I spend with my brave, fearless, beautiful daughter is also precious. Life is full of risk and benefit. When it comes to loving someone, I would think any daughter of mine would go all in."

The tears stinging my eyelids fight to break free. I swipe at the first escapee.

I recall Roman's words, that grief is a kind of unexpressed love, stuck inside you with no place to go. He had said one outlet for it was to honor my mother by being the best at my job. Here's another: talking about her with the people who knew her and ensuring she's never forgotten.

"Oh, Dad, I'm sorry we didn't do this sooner."

"I didn't make it easy for you. But no more keeping it in. The channels are open." He squeezes my hand. "Sometimes it's easier to say you don't care than to explain all the reasons why you do. If you think Rossi is worth it, you need to give him a shot as well."

Forty-two

Roman

My heart is a galloping mustang in my chest as I push through the doors of Fern's Diner and look around. That cute old couple is in one of the booths, some teens are making out in another, and the counter is disappointingly empty.

Except for a slice of cherry pie.

The text came in ten minutes ago.

Meet me at Fern's.

That was it—and that was all it took. I threw on a shirt and jeans and raced over here like they might run out of damn pie.

Which, history says, is a distinct possibility.

Tessa the server, now with a name badge that says "Flo," appears and places a menu on the counter to the right of the pie. I don't need it.

I know exactly what I want.

One step toward my future and she appears from around the corner, her eyes glossy, her cheekbones glowing with heat.

The woman I love in the flesh.

"Hi, there," she says, a shyness in her tone I've not heard before.

"Hey, Sullivan, it's been a day, right?"

She laughs. "That it has. But pie is in my future, so it's looking up."

Tessa/Flo puts a couple of forks on either side of the pie with a wink and a smile. I take Abby's hand and lead her to the same seat as last time, only now I take the one directly to her left. No buffer or barrier like before.

I pick up a fork.

She picks up the other.

We clink our flatware.

And we eat our pie, casting sly looks at each other like either of us might vanish at any moment. It seems we've determined that the important words can't be spoken without full stomachs. The last bite is a piece of crust with a gob of cherry pie filling. I nudge the plate toward her. "All yours."

She swallows. "You'd give me your last bite?"

"I'd give you my last anything." Tears fill her eyes. "Abby, sweetheart. Please." I cup her jaw and catch a tear, then hold on because touching her is everything. I never want to let go.

"I'm sorry I hurt you, Roman. That I pushed you away."

"It's okay. I get it, or I think I do." We need to get to the bottom of this. I haul a breath but can't seem to fill my lungs. "You said we had a good time but we should stop before it got too far. Did you mean that?"

"Yes ... and no. I had a good time. More than a good time." She half smiles at the innuendo but my nerves are too shredded to appreciate it. "The part about stopping before it got too far wasn't entirely accurate. 'Too far' had already happened. I was crazy about you. I *am* crazy about you. It seemed easier to make the break even though it really hurt."

"Tell me about it. You certainly picked your moment, Abby." Concussed, bruised, battered, and high on painkillers.

"I know." Her cheeks are flushed, every freckle glowing. I love seeing her so emotional, her heart on display. "The thought of losing you in the line of duty brought some stuff to the surface. Whether I'm too reckless, my mom's death, how my dad feels about potentially losing me. He's terrified and I didn't respect that enough. Seeing it from his side when I was smack bang in the middle of being mad at him was pretty confusing."

I can see that, but best of all, she seems to be making peace with the messiness of it all. "You're still scared about losing me on the job?"

"Of course. But that's life, isn't it? Abject terror that we'll lose the people we care about. I've been through it and it sucks. But I can't let that fear rule and stop me from opening my heart." She lets out a gentle sigh. "I know you went through a rough time with your ex and here I am, jerking you around. I didn't mean to do that, Roman. To make you in any way doubt how special and amazing you are. That you're the best man I've ever known."

My heart catches. Now we're getting to the good stuff. "You could have talked to me instead of taking one for the team. Because that's what we are, y'know. A team."

She blinks those beautiful blues. "Like the crew at Engine 6?"

"No, like you and me. You in my life and the lives of my kid and my sister. And me in your life and the lives of your friends and your family, and probably, your father. If he's still talking to us."

She's looking a touch dazed, probably whiplashed at how I've laid out our future. I won't tell her just yet about how she needs to move in with me now and how Lena will likely be attending another wedding in the family before the year is out.

One scary step at a time.

Instead I take a half shuffle back. "How did it go with your dad?"

"You knew he was coming over to talk to me?"

"I suspected he might. Hoped he would." I swipe a little filling from the corner of her mouth and suck my thumb. "He and I had a good talk about you, your mom, the hotbed of passion that is Engine 6." I waggle my eyebrows before turning serious. "I told him that he can't keep you in a glass box, with your heart and emotions locked up. That a woman as amazing as you, with all that passion and desire, has to be able to fly free."

Abby needed to resolve this with her dad before she could come to terms with what loving freely means. Going all in with no reservations. Of course, there was no guarantee that a stubborn dickhead like Chuck Sullivan would listen to a word I said, but it was worth a shot.

She smiles wide, that soul-stirring grin I adore. "I want that. I don't want to be afraid anymore." Her tone is soft though the words are strong.

That's my girl. "Today when you were talking about your mom at the service, I realized something else. Not only are you born to be a firefighter, sweetheart, you're also born to be mine. We are stronger as one, so that's what you need to remember. Inside the firehouse, in bed, in the diner—all of it. Together, we make everything better."

Her lips curve. "What about the kitchen?"

"Sure, you're *really* good at opening the wine."

She gasps a laugh, releasing all that nervous energy. Swiping at a tear, and somewhere in between laughing and crying, she says, "I love you, Roman. So much. And I'm sorry I didn't say it back during the fire. It took me by surprise and we were—well, in danger of dying."

"Best way to do it, when you've got a captive audience relying on you to get them to safety."

She sniffs. "Sneaky."

"I love you, too." Because you can never say it enough, right? And then we're kissing, soaking up the rays of each other. It's so good to claim her in public.

Someone clears a throat. Tessa again. "More pie?"

"I think we've got all the dessert we need," Abby says, licking her lips. "But I'm not sure what happens next. With us and Engine 6."

"The crews are already being realigned but we'll report our relationship through official channels. We'll fuck on the fire truck one night while everyone is sleeping. We'll eat pie. We'll live happily ever after."

Tessa looks impressed. "Fire truck sex, huh?"

"It's not as hot as it sounds," Abby says drily.

I lean in close. "Then you haven't been doing it right."

She laughs, that dirty-sexy sound that ignites every part of me. "Now if there was some sudsy water, a fire hose, and a shirtless lieutenant, I might be able to get on board."

I brush my lips over hers, a preview to a future I've only dreamed of and can't wait to start.

"You can climb aboard me anytime, Firefighter Sullivan."

Epilogue
Three Months Later

Abby

A firehouse at 2 a.m. is a strange and magical place, alive with the spirit of past adventure and potential for future action. Most of the crew are catching some Z's, half-in and out of slumber, their bodies on alert for a call. No one sleeps well here (except Gage who can sleep anywhere and through anything). I prefer to wander the corridors in between power naps and check in with my mom at the Wall of the Fallen.

"Hey, Mom, you're not going to believe the call I went on today." In deference to our regular ritual, I fill her in on one more escapade in the annals of CFD, involving a puppy who got his silly head stuck in a sewer grate. Never a dull moment at Engine 6.

Outside it, too. "Dad and Kat came to ours for dinner last Sunday. Well, I mean, Roman's." I lower my voice. "It feels like ours because I spend all my free time there."

Dinner was great. Roman made this amazing osso buco and creamy polenta, and even my aunt was impressed though she kept trying to help him in the kitchen because she can't not be a domestic goddess. My father was in hard-ass dad mode around Roman, but I saw signs of softening toward the end of the night as they united in smack-talking Woz. Not exactly professional, but whatever makes my boys happy.

"And things are going well with Dad. Better than ever. I don't think I realized how much he missed you. How lonely he's been, and how he was clinging onto anything that would stop that loneliness from getting worse."

In the investigation into the incident that hospitalized Roman, I was found to be "overzealous," which Roman says is not official reprimand terminology but more likely inspired by one Chuck Sullivan. My wrist was lightly tapped, and on my return I was assigned to Luke's platoon, where I've remained ever since.

But I have the best of both worlds: two great mentors in Luke and Roman, and less likelihood of running into a situation where Roman would feel compromised about making a call. Luke has no problem telling me what needs to be done on the job. And now that we're talking again, Dad's *very* free with his advice, making sure all that experience is passed on to the next generation. Basically I have more mentors than I can shake a Halligan at.

I'm a lucky woman to have landed here. The house of my mom, the house of my heart.

A shuffling sound followed by the whisper of a door opening and closing somewhere else in the building interrupts the silence. A love note from Jo Sullivan, perhaps? I've become more superstitious since I started at Engine 6. It's hard not to feel blessed and protected by her presence.

A text comes in on my phone, ***My office now, Sullivan.***

Ah, I knew there was a reason for my restlessness.

Less than a minute later, I find the door to Lieutenant

Rossi's office open, the dimmed light raised by half, and the most amazing gift awaiting me.

Cookies.

On a plate, chocolate with powdered sugar, and enough to make my mouth water.

Or maybe it's the cookie courier, who's sitting in his chair, looking as delicious as the baked goods on the desk.

"Close the door, Abby, and come get your treat."

I push the door flush with my butt and lock it (with my fingers because my butt's not that talented). With a touch of insolence, I pick up a cookie.

My man cocks his gorgeous, dark head. "Really?"

"Oh, you thought ..." My waved hand is the epitome of mock-casual. "Uh, no. Sugar always wins. Tell Lena I said thanks."

The last cheeky word is barely out of my mouth before I'm positioned on the desk with the hard body of Roman Rossi slotted in between my thighs.

"The cookies are for after, *ciliegina*."

I take a bite ... of his fleshy, lower lip and let myself fall into sweet and spice and the innate knowledge that Roman will always protect me in every way possible. It feels wonderful to be loved with such assurance and clarity.

"How's your mom doing?" he murmurs against my lips.

"How did you know—How did you even know I was awake?"

"I know you talk to her and I know you don't sleep well here. Probably because you sleep like the dead when you're in my arms."

I chuckle. "Your body is like one of those weighted blankets."

"And right now, you're only getting it—and the perks of sleeping in my bed—for two nights a week. It's not enough, Abby."

This is the downside of being on different shifts at the same house. Every third night, I can be with him and his family. But those other nights, two shifts of mine and two of his, are tough.

"I miss you, too," I say quietly.

"What if I told you it could be more?"

"That would mean one of us—"

"Me, Abby. I want to put in for a transfer for the LT spot at Engine 70. It's on the same shift as A platoon here, so—"

"We'd work the same 24 hours." My throat feels tight. "You'd do that for me?"

"For us. I want as much time as possible with all my girls. I want to prioritize us and our family and I think this is the best way to do it. Maybe that'll change when we have kids—and I'm not rushing you into that—but I do want to give Lena a little brother or sister one day. When that happens, we'll figure out what works for us. But I won't apply for the job if you'd rather I didn't."

He's not trying to end run me or force me into a corner. His generosity floors me. It always does.

"I was going to say that I can't believe you'd do this for me. For us. But that's not true. I completely believe it because you are as solid and dependable as the walls of this firehouse, Roman Rossi. Chicago is so lucky to have you on the front lines and I'm so lucky to have once mistaken your pie for mine."

I kiss him with all the emotion in my heart, all the love that's his.

"Baby, my pie is yours," he whispers, his voice rusty. "All of it, my body and my soul, everything belongs to you."

He goes on to prove it. His hands on my ass pull me into a seal against the part of him I need pretty badly right now. Urgency dictates our movements as we break all the rules about getting busy on city property. Not the first time for either of us, but then I've been pushing the envelope since day one and it seems I'm not quite ready to become a rule follower.

Where this man is concerned, I'll do what it takes to ensure he's 100% mine.

He buries his face in my neck as I take him in hand and absorb the hard, pulsing heat of him alongside his yeah-that's-it groan. Joined as one and hurtling toward release, we murmur words of love and appreciation as we christen another surface at Engine 6.

The man of my dreams, the house of my heart.

With Roman Rossi, I am home.

About the Author

Originally from Ireland, *USA Today* bestselling author Kate Meader cut her romance reader teeth on Maeve Binchy and Jilly Cooper novels, with some Harlequins thrown in for variety. Give her tales about brooding mill owners, oversexed equestrians, and men who can rock an apron, a fire hose, or a hockey stick, and she's there. Now based in Chicago, she writes sexy contemporary featuring strong heroes and amazing women and men who can match their guys quip for quip.

Also by Kate Meader

Hot in Chicago
REKINDLE THE FLAME
FLIRTING WITH FIRE
MELTING POINT
PLAYING WITH FIRE
SPARKING THE FIRE
FOREVER IN FIRE
COMING IN HOT

Rookie Rebels
GOOD GUY
INSTACRUSH
MAN DOWN
FOREPLAYER
DEAR ROOMIE
REBEL YULE
JOCK WANTED

Chicago Rebels
IN SKATES TROUBLE
IRRESISTIBLE YOU
SO OVER YOU
UNDONE BY YOU
HOOKED ON YOU

WRAPPED UP IN YOU

Laws of Attraction
DOWN WITH LOVE
ILLEGALLY YOURS
THEN CAME YOU

Tall, Dark, and Texan
EVEN THE SCORE
TAKING THE SCORE
ONE WEEK TO SCORE

Hot in the Kitchen
FEEL THE HEAT
ALL FIRED UP
HOT AND BOTHERED

For updates, giveaways, bonus scenes, and new release information, sign up at katemeader.com/newsletter

Milton Keynes UK
Ingram Content Group UK Ltd.
UKHW011336030823
426276UK00001B/12

9 781954 107120